Books in the D BRANCH Series
Razor Sharp
Too Sharp To Hold
A Sharp Edge

Books in the TALBOT Series
Talbot
Fortuna
Return
Conflict

Books in the AGENCY Series
Eve of War
The Favor
The Cure
Marque
Reprisal

Books in the PANTHEON Series
Hecate
Tridyma

Books in the COLONY Series
QUANT
ARCADIA
GALACTIC SURVEY
SILK ROAD
LOST COLONY
EARTH

Books in the EMPIRE Series

by Richard F. Weyand:
EMPIRE: Reformer
EMPIRE: Usurper
EMPIRE: Tyrant
EMPIRE: Commander
EMPIRE: Warlord
EMPIRE: Conqueror

by Stephanie Osborn:
EMPIRE: Imperial Police
EMPIRE: Imperial Detective
EMPIRE: Imperial Inspector
EMPIRE: Section Six

by Richard F. Weyand:
EMPIRE: Intervention
EMPIRE: Investigation
EMPIRE: Succession
EMPIRE: Renewal
EMPIRE: Resistance
EMPIRE: Resurgence

Books in the Childers Universe

by Richard F. Weyand:
Childers
Childers: Absurd Proposals
Galactic Mail: Revolution
A Charter For The Commonwealth
Campbell: The Problem With Bliss

by Stephanie Osborn:
Campbell: The Sigurdsen Incident

A Gent
Of Vega

by

RICHARD F. WEYAND

RICHARD F. WEYAND

ISBN 978-1-954903-25-8
Printed in the United States of America

Cover Credits
Cover Art: Luca Oleastri and Paola Giari,
www.rotwangstudio.com
Back Cover Photo: Oleg Volk

Published by Weyand Associates, Inc.
Bloomington, Indiana, USA
June, 2025

A GENT OF VEGA

CONTENTS

RICHARD F. WEYAND

First Contact

Steven Bach took one last look around the living room and shrugged. Bachelor pad. No getting around it.

The single common room of the apartment was cluttered, as had been the case for the several years he had lived here. His bicycle – the best way to get around campus, given the expense of a parking space – leaned against the wall. His desk, with the clutter of a college student in residence, against another wall. Backpack. Extra cases of beverages, both alcoholic and not, stacked in the kitchen.

At least the kitchen was cleaned up, without a pile of dishes in the sink, and the sitting area was clear. A couch and an armchair, with the low table between them. The kitchen table, too, was clear.

He didn't ever have many guests.

Well, none, really.

Bach was a loner. A dweeb. Between work and studies, he had been too busy to make many friends. Not particularly good at it, either.

He had decided to put the effort into it, though, and tonight he was having a friend over. Well, not a friend, really. A social media contact. Someone he had met and conversed with numerous times over the past several months on the net.

Arthur Vegan was a fellow who seemed to share many of his interests. Science. Science fiction. Not really much interested in politics, or religion, or social events.

Bach had worried that Vegan meant he might be a vegetarian or something, but it was just his last name. Like Bach was his last name. That didn't mean he was into classical

1

music. He tended more toward rock and pop, to the extent he had any interest at all.

So it was with Vegan. It was just his last name, and, he was assured, did not indicate anything about Vegan's dietary preferences.

Both being loners, and both being of a mind to change that, at least a little, they had decided on an evening together. Just talking and getting some human interaction outside of classes and work.

There was a knock at the door.

Bach went over to the door.

"Hi, Arthur," he said as he opened the door.

"Hello, Steven," his visitor said.

He was just under six feet tall, and he was not human.

Bach's eyes rolled up into his head and he fainted dead away.

"Oh, my," Vegan said.

The Visitor

Steven Bach came back to consciousness slowly.

The last thing he had seen – the alien at his door – was the first thing that sprung to mind as he fought his way back to awareness.

Orange, it had been. Orange and brown. Multifaceted eyes gleamed green above a proboscis. It wouldn't be fair to call it a mere nose. Below that, mandibles bracketed a mouth. Above, antennae rose from its head.

It had six appendages, though it stood upright on the rear two, and had four arms ending in hands of four fingers each, including an opposable thumb.

"Steven, are you all right?"

The concerned voice called him back to the here and now. Bach opened his eyes to see the insectoid nightmare leaning over him. He was lying on his couch, in his apartment, and he scrambled futilely to get away from the creature that looked down at him.

"I'll tell you what. I'll sit over here while you come to terms with my appearance."

The creature moved over to the armchair and sat, looking at Bach.

"Who— Who are you? What are you?" Bach asked.

"I'm Arthur Vegan. The fellow who made the appointment to get together with you tonight. As for what am I, I am a Vegan. I did give my name on social media as A. Vegan, after all."

"Yes, but, but, but, …"

"Yes, yes, I know. A million questions. Should we start our

little get-together now? And yes, I would love a beer. Thank you."

Bach sat up on the sofa, then got up and went to the fridge. He got a couple of beers. The normalcy of the activity served to calm him, but he put Vegan's beer down on the very corner of the table and sidled to a seat on the sofa while maintaining the maximum distance possible between them.

Vegan shook his head and chuckled.

"You know, Steven, were I to wish to harm you, I had no better opportunity than when you fainted in your doorway. Instead, I carried you into your apartment and lay you on your sofa until you recovered."

He popped the top on his beer and inserted his proboscis into the can, drinking as though through a straw.

"Oh, that's good," he said. "It's very strange. Long-term or in large amounts, it is poisonous, but in small amounts once in a while, truly delicious and relaxing."

Bach opened his own beer and took a healthy swig.

Oh, that helped.

"So why are you here? Why haven't I heard anything about you guys? How many of you are there?"

"All worthwhile questions," Vegan answered. "Perhaps I should tell the story first, and then see what questions remain. Does that work for you, Steven?"

"Yeah. Sure."

"I am, as I say, a Vegan. Our species colonized a planet that orbits the star you call Vega. Or near enough, anyway. Astrography isn't my field. It's roughly that way."

Vegan waved his hand vaguely northward and up.

"Obviously, Vega isn't what we call our star or homeworld, but I think that's what you call it."

"How did your species evolve to be so large, Arthur? I

thought insects were limited in size because they had no respiration. Oxygen had to enter through the skin."

"Well, yes, that was the original limit. But our original planet, like yours, went through a period when the oxygen content of the atmosphere was much larger than now, and very large insects were possible. When the oxygen decreased on your planet, insects became much smaller. On our planet, the oxygen decrease triggered the development of respiration and circulation."

"Why the difference?"

"I don't know. It could have been that there were other mutations about."

"OK, Arthur. I guess that works. What are you doing here on Earth, though?"

"I am what you might call a grad student, doing research in my specialty."

"What's your specialty?"

"Well, Steven, this is rather embarrassing. There's not a direct translation for my field. Something like primatology and anthropology. That is, the study of inferior, extraterrestrial life forms. In this case, humans."

"Inferior?"

"Well, yes. Of course. You are not yet capable of interstellar travel."

"Ah. Not sure how I feel about that inferior bit, Arthur."

"Yes. As I say, somewhat embarrassing. In any case, I have been studying humans for some years now using your social media platforms. It is of great benefit to me, because I need not worry about exposing my appearance."

"On the internet, anybody can be a dog."

"Or a Vegan. Yes. Exactly. As for how many of us there are, I'm not sure how to answer that. On our home planet and the planets we have colonized, well, there are billions of us. Tens of billions. On Earth, at the moment, I don't know."

"You don't know, Steven?"

"No. How would I? They don't tell me every time someone leaves from or arrives on Earth. I assume there are others doing studies like my own, but I don't know how many. Perhaps a dozen or so, total?"

Vegan shrugged.

"It's not a major push, Steven."

"It's not?"

"No. Why would it be? You have your own little planet here. OK, fine. Leave the primitives alone. Who cares?"

"Wait. So you're a low-level academic who has spent years on a backwater planet studying a race of primitives none of your people cares about."

"Well, yes. Basically."

"Wow. Now I know why there aren't a bunch of you. Who would want to do that?"

"Exactly."

"I'm still surprised I never heard of you, though, Arthur."

"Oh, you're the first person I've contacted directly. I doubt any of the others have ever contacted a human being."

"You mean, this is a first-contact scenario?"

"Oh, yes. You see, we're not supposed to let our study targets know we exist. It may change their behavior."

"Like how?"

"If you knew interstellar travel really was possible, for instance, and not just a pipe dream, then you would probably figure it out."

"So?"

"So if you figure it out too early, Steven, before you get out of your primitive stage, you could cause real trouble for us.

You might come out with all guns blazing, for example. Not unknown in human history."

Bach nodded. He could see it.

"But if you're not supposed to be seen by your study targets, haven't you just broken the rules by coming to see me?"

"Oh, yes, but there is only so much I can do by pure observation. I think some interaction is necessary if my research is to make further progress."

"What would your people do if they knew you broke the rules, Arthur?"

"Well, they probably wouldn't kill us."

"*Probably* wouldn't?"

"I wouldn't expect them to, Steven. They might just evacuate us from Earth and isolate us. To prevent contagion."

"How about we not let them know you broke the rules, then?"

"Yes, that would be very good. That's one of the reasons I picked you. Loner. Not a lot of friends. Someone who can keep a secret, mostly because he has no one to tell it to."

Bach nodded. Yeah, that was him, all right.

"Another factor, Steven, is that your apartment is not off an interior hallway in a building. The standalone triplex format, with exterior doors in alcoves on the apartments, allows me to sneak to your door in the dark, when no one is looking. Being the end unit is even better. Above all, I have to stay out of sight."

"Which is going to be a problem soon, Arthur. As the days get longer, it'll stay daylight much later. Soon you won't be able to come here before ten o'clock, and I need my sleep. I have both work and classes, you know."

"Yes, I know. I had hoped to make you an offer."

"An offer?"

"Yes. How about if I stay here with you, and pay you rent?"

"There's only one bed, Arthur."

"I don't sleep in a bed. I sleep standing up. Here in the living room, for instance."

"That would make it hard for me to study. We would be talking all the time. Together with work, I don't think I can spare the time."

"Ah, but I can pay a large rent, Steven. Larger than your rent. Larger than you make working."

"How can you do that?"

"I have a large amount of gold-pressed latinum."

"Of *what*?"

"Sorry, Steven. Science fiction joke. I have a large amount of gold bars. Gold is basically a waste material of the process of asteroid mining. I have a large quantity of them to support myself on Earth. You can actually help me cash them, then I can pay you a large rent."

"How have you been cashing them until now?"

"I usually leave some of them lying around. Someone finds them and cashes them in, then I steal most of the money from him."

"Most of the money, Arthur?"

"Of course. I leave him a commission."

"How do you steal it from him?"

"Oh, humans are not hard to render unconscious, Steven. I have a device that works pretty well for that."

Bach shook his head. Living with the alien? Somebody he had just met, after all, the alien thing aside. How could that even work? Then again, there was the money issue.

"How much rent are we talking about, Arthur."

"Shall we say, four times whatever your rent is?"

That was more than half again what he made right now. He

8

wouldn't need to work at all.

"Deal."

This was insane. Bach had second thoughts about it almost immediately and added a caveat.

"At least, we'll see how it goes."

"That's fine, Steven. As long as we keep it just between us."

The Roommate

Vegan went off to gather his things from wherever he was hiding out and returned two hours later, in the middle of the night. He came in wearing a backpack, one of those big jobs that mountain hikers wore. He set it down just inside the door.

Bach thought to move it out of the way, but he couldn't budge it. It must weigh well over a hundred pounds.

"Let me get that, Steven. Where do you want it?"

"In this little storage area here," Bach said, motioning to the walk-in closet off the kitchen.

"Got it."

Vegan moved the backpack, then came back out of the closet.

"You'll have to cash in some gold tomorrow, then I can pay you for the first month."

"OK, Arthur. But right now I need to get to sleep. I still have work in the morning. Even if I give notice tomorrow, that's usually two weeks."

"I understand, Steven. Good night. Sleep well."

Bach didn't sleep well that night. His thoughts kept coming back to the alien in his living room.

He got up once during the night, and looked in on Vegan. The alien was standing to one side of the door, completely motionless. Asleep, perhaps.

Bach shrugged and went back to bed.

He had nightmares of being eaten by the alien.

The next morning, Vegan joined him at the kitchen table as

A GENT OF VEGA

Bach had his first cup of coffee.

"Arthur, I had a thought last night. Your kind don't actually eat humans, do you?"

"Hardly ever, Steven."

"That's not a No."

"No, it's not. I did eat a human once, years ago. When I was first getting set up. I was starving, and, well, he surprised me. He saw me, so I killed him. You know, don't let humans know about us or that we're here. That rule. Since I was starving, and he was already dead, well, it solved that problem for a while."

"And now, Arthur?"

"Once I got set up, it wasn't an issue. And I've since learned you humans have quite a taboo about it. So I haven't eaten any since. Not sure about any of my fellows here on Earth, though. We don't really have any contact with each other."

"So there could be Vegans on Earth eating humans?"

"Oh, sure. But not me. That's your real issue, isn't it, Steven?"

"Yes. I suppose. Anyway, I have to get going. See you later."

Bach took his bicycle and headed off.

Bach was back within half an hour. Vegan looked up from some device he was using while sitting on the couch.

"That was quick."

"Yeah," Bach answered. "I gave my notice. I said I had come into a small inheritance and I didn't need the money anymore. And I needed to spend more time on my coursework. He said, 'Yeah, and you need to be getting more sleep.' He said I didn't have to serve two weeks' notice, that they would get along without me, and told me to concentrate on school."

"He sounds like a nice guy, Steven."

"Yeah, he is, actually."

Bach sat on the armchair.

"So now what, Arthur?"

"We can cash in some gold, so I can pay you for the first month."

Vegan set the device aside and went into the walk-in closet, returning with two small shiny yellow bars. He held them out to Bach, who took them.

"Heavy."

"Yes, Steven. That's why my backpack is so heavy."

"Wait. That backpack must weigh a hundred or more pounds."

"Yes. I have about a thousand of those with me at the moment. Sixty pounds or so. As I say, they're a waste material where I come from."

"And how much are these worth?"

Vegan produced the equivalent of a shrug.

"Three or four thousand dollars apiece. Depends on what the market is doing on any given day."

"Wait. Arthur. You have three or four *million* dollars of gold bullion in your backpack?"

"And several thousand more stashed in various places. Yes, of course, Steven. I could have had as much as I wanted when I came here. The only expense was casting it in these little one-ounce bars. I brought several hundred pounds of it."

"Several *hundred* pounds...."

Bach gaped at him, then his gaze sharpened.

"What's to keep me from killing you and taking it, Arthur?"

"But you wouldn't, Steven. First, unlike humans, we are pretty hard to kill. I doubt you could manage it. Second, based on your social media posts, I judge you to be an honorable man. If you were to overpower me somehow, and steal the backpack, it would bother you a great deal. Until you tracked me down to repay it. Lastly, it would do little to frustrate me, as I have several hundred more pounds of the stuff stashed in places you don't know about. The real point is that we do not need to worry about funds."

"I'll say. We could live like kings."

"Yes and no, Steven. There are practical limits to how fast we can sell these. If you were to show up at a gold dealer with sixty pounds of the stuff, they wouldn't be able to cash it out for you. There's a limit to the funds they have on hand. You would also attract a lot of attention, and the lack of provenance would become an issue."

Bach nodded.

"OK. I can see that. But a couple bars now and again?"

"That is not a problem. Has not been, in any case."

"All right, Arthur. So how do I go about this?"

"There are three coin dealers in town. They also trade in precious metals. Try to get two percent below the spot price."

"The spot price?"

"That's the market price, Steven. Dealers sell above the spot price, and buy below it. They make their money off that spread. You can generally get them to agree to two percent below spot, especially if you are going to be a repeat seller."

"OK. And then they give me cash?"

"No, Steven. For that amount of money, usually it is a bank transfer. From a rare metals dealer, you can trust the bank transfer. Let me give you my bank routing and account numbers."

"You have a bank account?"

"Yes, though it was difficult to set it up. There are a lot of checks and such. But I managed to get it set up."

"How did you do that, Arthur?"

"All the checks are implemented by the clerks, then they

create the account. So I broke into the bank's systems and set up the account myself."

"That was easier?"

"Yes, Steven. Your computer systems are not secure against even modest efforts by an advanced species."

Bach raised an eyebrow, and Vegan shrugged.

"It's true, Steven. And much easier than appearing before a human and answering questions about myself."

Vegan wrote a pair of numbers on a slip of paper from memory and handed it to Bach.

"Those are the routing and account numbers for the transfer. Give me your phone and I'll set it up so you can see that the transfer took place."

"May I help you?" the fellow behind the counter asked.

He looked to be the owner, not a counter clerk. That was expected, as coin and rare metals dealers normally ran their own stores.

"Yes. I was looking to sell some gold. One ounce bars."

The store owner nodded.

"That's fine. We usually offer three percent below spot."

"Hmm. I was hoping for two percent below spot. You see, I'm getting a small inheritance. From my uncle. He was one of those prepper types, and it's all in gold bars. It's in trust, and I get a couple gold bars every month or so. So I'm looking for a dealer I can do business with over the medium term."

"For a repeat seller, I can do two percent below spot. You have two bars today?"

"Yes. That's right."

Bach took the two gold bars out of his pocket and set them on the counter. The store owner set them, one at a time, on a precision scale on the counter, then nodded.

"Very well. Spot price today is thirty-five forty-seven."

He punched at a calculator.

"That will be seventy ninety-four at spot, giving you sixty-nine fifty-two at two percent below spot."

"That's fine."

"How do you want payment? Bank transfer, internet account, or cash?"

"Bank transfer," Bach said, and put Vegan's slip of paper on the counter.

The store owner nodded, and went to his laptop computer, off to one side of the counter. He took the gold bars with him, and, after a few minutes, came back without them.

"Done. No problem."

"Pardon me while I check."

"Of course."

Bach took out his phone and checked Vegan's account. There it was, sixty-nine fifty-two.

"Excellent. Thank you so much."

"Thank you."

Bach turned toward the door.

"See you next month."

"It'll be my pleasure. Have a good day."

"Well, that was simple," Bach reported to Vegan when he got back to the apartment.

"And you got two percent below spot?"

"Yes, once I explained I would be back every month or so."

"Excellent. Now I can get something to eat. What do you think of Cattle Baron?"

"Sure. It's a great restaurant. But how are you going to do that? You can't exactly waltz into the restaurant and order whatever you want."

"No, no, no. We get a delivery service to bring it to us. They have a twenty-four-ounce steak I love."

The alien bent to his phone and started setting up the order.

"What do you want, Steven? My treat."

Bach pulled out his own phone and looked up the menu.

"How about the eight-ounce filet? Medium. Mac and cheese and a garden salad for the sides."

"All right. What do you want my sides to be? You can have them, since I don't eat them."

"You don't eat them?"

"No. I'm a pure carnivore, Steven."

Bach chuckled. The thought of the Vegan being a pure carnivore tickled him.

"More of the same, Arthur. Mac and cheese and a garden salad. Oh, and honey mustard for the salad dressing for both."

"Got it."

Vegan finished the ordering, then sat back with a sigh.

"It's nice to have a regular flow of funds again, where I can order whatever I want."

"What were you doing, Arthur?"

"It was hit or miss. Getting someone to find a gold bar and sell it, then I rob them. Or getting someone from the net to do the old invalid a favor. One of my net aliases is of an elderly invalid."

"Wow. So it really was hit or miss."

"Yes. I managed an apartment, by overpaying a landlord who was willing not to meet me in return for the overpayment. But everything was hit or miss. Even simple things were hard, like the bank account. Oh, speaking of which, I owe you a month's rent. What's your monthly rent here?"

"A thousand a month."

"All right. Give me your routing and account numbers, and

I'll send the bank transfer."

Bach gave Vegan the routing number and account number off a check, and the next thing he knew, there was four thousand dollars more in his checking account. More than he made in a month of working – by a lot – and no withholdings for taxes or Social Security or Medicare. It was just money.

"That's astonishing, Arthur."

"No, it's well worth it, Steven. To finally have things set up reasonably? It's well worth it."

Dinner showed up then, and it was wonderful. Bach's was, anyway.

Vegan took his steak rare, holding the whole pound and a half of bloody meat up in front of his face and gnashing at it with his mandibles.

Bach tried not to watch.

After dinner, it was just early afternoon.

"I have some homework I need to do before classes tomorrow, Arthur. So I need to be left alone for several hours."

"Of course, Steven. Not a problem. I'll entertain myself until you're done."

Vegan was as good as his word and spent the afternoon quietly on the net as Bach studied. It was just like any other roommate situation in college.

Well, other than that one of them was an alien.

Spare Time

It was six o'clock when Bach broke from studying.

"How about dinner?" he asked Vegan.

"Oh, I'm good. I only eat once a day. If I eat like that, anyway. How about you?"

"I still have that extra mac and cheese and garden salad from lunch. I can do that. Then I think we should do some grocery shopping. We need extra food on hand. Some big raw steaks for you, I would think."

"That would be nice. I order rare from the restaurants, but raw is even better."

Bach heated up the second mac and cheese from lunch in the microwave, then sat down to the table with that and the extra garden salad for a light supper. Vegan joined him to keep him company.

"How did studying go?" Vegan asked.

"Good. I have everything done, and the whole evening to myself. I actually have spare time."

"Nice," Vegan said. "What are you going to do with it?"

"I don't know. It's been so long since I had any spare time, I'm not sure what I want to do."

"You know, without having to work, it may become a common occurrence. You should spend the time on something worthwhile."

"Like what?"

"I don't know, Steven. What have you always wanted to do, but never had time for?"

"Well, I always wanted to be a science-fiction author. Never thought I would have the time, though. It takes a long time to write a book."

"Not necessarily. You're just telling a story, aren't you?"

"Yes, but how do you do that while typing? And there's all that other stuff. Outlining and plotting and everything. I don't know that I can do that, Arthur."

"Do you need to do all that other stuff?"

"The creative writing people say you do. You know, people who teach creative writing."

"But a lot of published authors say you don't, Steven."

"Really?"

"Oh, yes. I looked into it at one point. They just tell the story, and make it up as they go along."

"Huh. Well, I guess I could try it, Arthur. I still have to type it in as I go, though.

"Maybe not. You could just dictate it to the machine. I can correct the punctuation and stuff as you go."

"You'd do that for me?"

"Sure, Steven. Why not? It sounds like fun to me."

"OK. Let's get some groceries ordered, and then we can give it a go."

At one point, Vegan interrupted.

"You know, Steven, that's not the way the interstellar drive actually works."

"Do you want to educate our science people into where they should be looking, Arthur?"

"Ah. Good point. That would be bad. Carry on."

The groceries arrived just after nine-thirty, as the local grocery had professional shoppers who worked until ten. Vegan went into the bedroom as Bach answered the door.

The shopper handed Bach a box full of groceries.

"There's a second box. I'll go get it."

Bach put the first box on the table, then went back to the door to get the second box.

"All right. That's it."

"Great. Thanks."

He slipped the shopper an extra five.

"Thank you."

Bach put the second box on the table with the first, then went back and closed the outside door.

"All right, Arthur. The coast is clear."

Vegan came in from the bedroom.

"Did we get all our stuff?" he asked.

Bach looked down the shopper's list.

"Looks like. Everything except the raisins. They must be out of them at the moment."

"But we got all the steaks?"

"Oh, yes."

"Excellent."

"We need to decide how to split groceries, Arthur. I appreciate you paying this time – those steaks are pricey – but we have to decide on the split for the future."

"How about you buy the groceries, and I'll buy dinner when we have it delivered, and we'll switch off between delivery and cooking at home?"

"That's OK with me, but I think you'll be picking up the bigger share."

"That's all right, Steven. Money's not an issue. Shall we get back to writing?"

"No, it's late now, and I have classes tomorrow. We'll pick it up tomorrow. How many words did I get, anyway?"

"A little over three thousand."

"Three thousand words?"

"Yes, Steven. Do that every day for, oh, five weeks or so, and you've got a novel."

"Wow. That's great. Well, tomorrow, then."

"All right. Good night."

They fell into something of a routine, the nerd and the alien. They ate one big meal together every day, one day getting something delivered, the next cooking at home. That last amounted to Bach cooking for himself while Vegan ate a large, raw steak, or a whole chicken, or a whole rack of pork ribs.

Bach continued his studies and going to classes regularly, while Vegan continued his internet-based research into human sociology and culture. As Bach was only a part-time student, however, this left him a lot of free time. In that free time, they often worked on Bach's novel together, with Bach dictating to Vegan, who used voice-recognition software and manual corrections on the fly to polish the text.

It was a comfortable existence for both of the two loners. Much of their time was spent doing things by themselves, but they had company for meals. They also had the project of the book together, but even that, the way they had structured it, featured the two operating somewhat separately from each other.

For Vegan, the arrangement sidestepped all the problems he had had arranging an apartment and getting meals and cashing gold bars without revealing himself. For Bach, the arrangement solved his money issues and relieved him of the need to work.

A month went by. Bach cashed in another couple of gold bars. Vegan transferred another four thousand dollars to Bach's account. He wasn't halfway through the last four thousand, but he had another tuition payment coming up. This one was for summer school, so it would be about half as much as the big fall and spring ones.

The next week, he finished his first novel.

"Finished," he announced to Vegan. "What do you think of it, Arthur?"

"Honestly?"

"Yes. Please."

"It's complete crap, Steven."

"Really?"

"Oh, yes. You have a kidnapping, a gun fight, a car chase, an airplane chase, another gun fight, aliens, an interstellar human civilization, a prehistoric human civilization, four different alien cultures, three space battles, all between different belligerents, a self-aware artificial intelligence, and lots more. Any of those things could be a complete novel.

"Your characters have no inner life, so the reader has no inkling what moves them to do what they do. There is no love interest. And your main character is always right, is always adept at whatever particular skill he needs, and never makes a wrong move. Like I said, complete crap."

"Is there any good part, Arthur?"

"Oh, yes. Your prose is clear and easy to understand. You don't go in for long run-on sentences. You got much better by the end than you were in the beginning. And you have a sense for story."

"So now what do I do?"

"Write another novel."

"But I'm no good at it. You said so yourself."

"Steven. Writing is a skill. Do you think Eric Clapton was born knowing how to play guitar?"

"Who?"

"Never mind. The point is no one who is good at anything

started out being good at it. They practiced. Oh, sure, they had some inclination or ability or sense for it that made it easier for them to learn than it might be for someone else, but they still had to learn it. They had to practice.

"Look. Steven. Read the first three chapters. I'll wait."

Bach read the first three chapters and sighed.

"I see what you mean. It's flat. Lifeless. Sort of 'he did this, he did that.' There's no pizzazz."

"Now read the last three."

Bach read the last three chapters.

"Well, that's better, at least."

"Much better, in fact. You had no experience when you started, but you had a hundred thousand words of experience when you finished. You're getting into your characters. What they think. What moves them. There's more emotion. More involvement for the reader."

"So write the next one?"

"Absolutely."

"Not rewrite this one?"

"No. Waste of time. Start a new novel. New characters. New situation. New plot. And limit what you include. I mean, it's good you got all that stuff out of your head, so you can work with a clean slate. It's also good that you got experience writing them, so if you need a space battle or an AI in a novel, you're not starting from scratch, but you need to pare down what you include. By a lot. And get some love interest in there."

"That last is gonna be hard for me, Arthur. I don't have any experience with a love interest."

"You don't have any experience with gun fights, or interstellar space battles, or airplane chases, either, Steven, but that didn't stop you from including them. Get some romance in there. That's something every reader can identify with, so it's a freebie, from a writer's point of view, in getting readers' interest."

"What do I do with this novel?"

"Shelve it. Put it in the trunk. Everybody took practice to learn their craft, so every decent writer has a trunk novel. The first novel they never published."

"Really?"

"Sure. Sometimes they get published posthumously by the family, and I think the writer spins in his grave over it."

Bach chuckled.

"Speaking of which, Steven, why do you not have any experience with a love interest? Are you not interested in women?"

"No, it's not that. I just, I don't know, I just never know what to say. It's hard enough for me to talk to men. And I guess I'm afraid of being turned down."

"Which would result in your being alone, so you don't take the chance, and are therefore alone anyway? That sounds self-fulfilling."

"I guess. There's not a lot of women around anyway."

Vegan made a show of looking around the room.

"You mean, not in this room? Well, that's certainly true. But this is a college campus, Steven. Half the students on campus are women."

"More, actually."

"You see. It seems to me you're spoiled for choices."

"I suppose."

"That's something else we're going to have to work on, Steven. Seriously. More experience will make you a better writer."

"But how do we do that?"

"Let me think about it. Do some research on it."

A GENT OF VEGA

"You're going to research how to date women?"

"Of course. Why not? How hard can it be?"

The Research

They started on Bach's second novel. A couple of weeks passed, and it was going pretty well. Bach, though, was curious about Vegan's work on the dating problem.

"How is your research on dating women going?"

"Not well."

"How so?"

"Steven, you people are completely crazy."

"Did you not find any materials?"

"Oh, I found plenty of materials. All of which are completely contradictory."

"They are?"

"Oh, yes. 'You should ask out the plainer-looking women because they'll be grateful' and 'You should ask out the most beautiful women because most men won't and therefore they sit at home.'

"'What's most important is a sense of humor' and 'What's most important is to be in good shape.'

"'You should be sensitive and vulnerable' and 'You should be manly and strong.'

"And what about this one? 'Authenticity is the key. Once you can fake that, you have it made.'"

"That last one is a joke, Arthur."

"Ah. I wondered. But it's all over the map, Steven. 'Women secretly want to be treated like princesses' and 'Women secretly want to be treated like sluts.'"

"These are all written by men, Arthur?"

"Yes, but the ones written by women are worse, if anything. 'You want a guy who takes care of himself and is in good shape' and 'Stay away from the guys in good shape, they spend all their time at the gym and have no time for you. They're probably gay anyway.'

"Or 'You want someone who's in touch with their feelings' and 'The strong man you want doesn't spend any time thinking about his feelings.'

"How is someone supposed to make any sense of this?"

"You don't have any of this at home, Arthur?"

"No. We're all workers except for the queens and their drones. They have all the babies. We don't have any part in all that."

"They have all the babies?"

"Oh, yes. In big batches, not this one-at-a-time stuff that humans do. I have two thousand, three hundred and forty-seven brothers."

"Wow."

"Yes, but we're not close the way human siblings are. We're more like all second cousins or something. And a queen only does that every ten years or so. It depends on the population needs. It's very organized. Not like this chaos you humans have. This is insane."

"So what do we do now, Arthur?"

"Oh, I'm still working on it. I think a lot of it is that all the writers have limited experience. They're drawing conclusions from their personal experiences, which involves a small sample of a very large population."

"That sort of makes sense."

"Yes, but it means a lot more work to see if some general principles apply. They may not, Steven. People may be so different, one to the next, that no general principles apply."

"What do I do then?"

"There are a couple strategies that might apply. One is to

read social cues to classify the woman you're talking to into one of several large categories to know how to proceed."

"That sounds iffy, Arthur."

"Yes. Reading social cues is not one of your strengths. The other is to decide what sort of woman you want – pick from one of the major categories – and treat them all in the best way for that category."

"And if they're not in that category?"

"Then it won't go well. But that isn't the woman you want anyway, right? Because you picked the category you wanted."

"I don't know, Arthur. This all sounds wrong somehow. Too clinical, maybe."

"We'll just have to see what I come up with, Steven, but the early signs are not promising."

It was a little over a week later when the subject came up again. Bach had just cashed in another two gold bars, and Vegan had paid him another four thousand dollars. The money was really starting to pile up in Bach's account now.

Of course, he needed money for summer tuition, but that wasn't that bad at the state university. Room and board was always the big expense.

Once business was done, Vegan took up the subject.

"Steven, I have more input for you on the subject of dating women."

"Really?"

"Yes. Although, oddly, this has more to do with you than with women. All of my citations are agreed, however."

"OK, what is it, Arthur?"

"All of them mention the concept of being well-kempt. Based on both the text and the pictures accompanying the articles, you fail in this regard."

"I'm OK that way."

"No, Steven, you're not. For example, the articles all mention showering every day, when you get up."

"Mostly I just have my coffee and split."

"Yes. That will not avail if you wish to date women. They put it like this. When you ask a woman out, she decides if she wants to go out with the fellow standing in front of her. That answer is likely to be No if you are not up to dating standard at the time you pose the question."

"Huh. OK, Arthur. I get that, I guess."

"The shower is just one part. Shower, body wash, shave, aftershave, deodorant, shampoo, brush teeth, mouthwash. It's a whole litany of things."

"All of that? Every day?"

"Every day, Steven. Or, rather, any day in which you are likely to meet a woman."

"But I meet women every day. At classes. At the food store. Wherever."

"Then every day is surely the correct answer."

"I don't even have some of that stuff, Arthur."

"Then you should purchase it. I have suggestions from the articles."

"All right, all right. I'll give it a try. What else have you got?"

"With regard to clothing, Steven, you need a style."

"I have a style."

"A style other than 'functional.'"

"Like what, Arthur?"

"There are many choices. Casual. Urban. Athletic. Rugged. Retro. Biker. Rural. Cowboy. Hipster. Ivy League. You probably couldn't pull off Biker, though. You don't have a bike."

"I have a bike."

"A motorbike, Steven."

"Oh."

"So which do you think?"

"Can you send me the list, Arthur, so I can look at them?"

"Of course. Just let me know."

"Then what?"

"Then you go out and buy new clothes, Steven."

"You're talking serious money, you know."

"But you have money now, do you not?"

"Point. OK. I'll look."

"And the toiletries, Steven? One thing everyone is agreed on is that you want to avoid B.O. Whatever that is."

"Body Odor."

"Ah. Yes, that makes sense from the context. You need to avoid that."

"I'll order them, Arthur. You have a list for me?"

"Of course."

"Great. Thanks."

"No problem, Steven. And then we need to talk about a haircut and a manicure."

"A haircut I understand. That'll depend on which style I adopt, won't it?"

"Yes, certainly."

"But a manicure, Arthur?"

"Yes. You want to take care of any appearance items that someone might find objectionable in a dating prospect. A manicure is much preferred to your rather utilitarian habits in that regard. Plus it has another advantage."

"What's that?"

"It makes it look like you have money, Steven. One thing a woman is going to be looking for is someone that can support himself. Not be dependent on another. Not be a deadbeat."

"But I'm dependent on you."

"Not officially. That's what matters."

Vegan shrugged with all four shoulders.

"Our arrangement is off the record, after all."

Classes and homework intervened. It was two days later that they brought it up again.

"On the style thing, Arthur, I think I could pull off Casual, Urban, Retro, or Rugged. I'm not in shape enough for Athletic. Biker I don't think would work. And I probably don't have the speech pattern or vocabulary for Rural, Cowboy, Hipster, or Ivy League."

"That's fair. You want something you can be comfortable with."

"What's Rugged, anyway?"

"Oh, you know, Steven. Lumberjack stuff. Plaid flannel shirt. Work jeans. Heavy hiking boots. Knit stocking cap. Denim jacket. All that sort of thing."

Vegan looked Bach up and down in such a way it made Bach uncomfortable.

"Personally, I think Rugged or Casual would be best for you, Steven. They're a little more upscale than Urban or Retro. If you try one of those and you don't pull it off, you just end up looking shabby. And of Rugged and Casual, Rugged is more distinctive."

"You're really getting into this stuff, aren't you, Arthur?"

"I've been reading up on it. I find it fascinating. We have no equivalent."

"No style equivalent?"

"No, Steven. We don't wear clothes – workers have no sex organs, so there's no issue from that point of view, and we're not as sensitive to the weather – so clothing styles are completely alien to me. Pardon the expression."

"You seem to be adapting well to it."

"Oh, it's fun. I never understood it, and now I'm starting to."

"So we're decided, Arthur? Rugged?"

"Yes, I think so. You know, there's one more thing about the Rugged style. You can grow out your beard, and your hair can be a little longer."

"No shaving every day?"

"Oh, no. You still have to shave every day. To keep it mostly off the neck. But you can grow it out. That means you also need a beard trimmer."

"I'll add it to my toiletries order. And when do we start all of this?"

"You can start now, by not shaving for a while. We'll worry about trimming the beard later."

"OK. Done."

"Good. And now, back to the book?"

"Sure. Let me get settled."

Vegan sat at the desk with the laptop, while Bach took the microphone and his drink over to the big armchair.

"Now let's see. Where were we, Arthur?"

"The big, furry alien just started a fight with the crocodile alien."

"Oh, yes. That's right. You ready?"

"All set."

Bach started to dictate.

The Transformation

A couple more weeks passed. Bach's beard was starting to grow in. He was assessing it in the mirror that morning, then went out into the living room to talk to Vegan.

"My beard's coming in, so I think we're getting close. What's the next step, Arthur?"

"Clothes, I think."

"Ah. We finally get to the style thing."

"Yes. Now, I think you want to go to one of the farm stores."

"Farm stores?"

"Yes. You know, Steven. Farm King or Rural Supply or something like that."

"Why?"

"They'll have the right things. You don't want froufrou stuff."

"Froufrou?"

"Yes. It's a new word I learned. Do you like it?"

"I don't know yet, Arthur. What does it mean?"

"Fussy, or garish, or showy. You want plain clothes. Stylish, in terms of your style, but not fancy. They're more likely to have what you want."

"I suppose. Do you have a specific list?"

"Yes, Steven. Jeans, a denim jacket, tee-shirts, plaid shirts, real hiking boots."

"You can get all that most anywhere, Arthur."

"No. Not the ones you want. You want Levi's 501 jeans. Nothing else. Nothing froufrou. Nothing stonewashed, or pre-torn, or any of that nonsense. Same with the other things. Solid, basic stuff."

"OK. You trust me to buy the right things?"

"No, Steven. You can keep me updated by phone."

"Really? You're going to ride herd on me?"

"Yes. This is the critical element, and you have to get it right. I've been studying all this while you've been doing your class work, remember."

"All right, all right. And I get what? Like half a dozen of each, maybe?"

"Of the shirts, yes. Of the pants, one pair."

"One pair?"

"For now. They'll shrink, and we need to make sure they fit right after laundry. That's hard to gauge, and you don't want them too tight. Not for Rugged style. Should be two to three inches of slop at the waist for now."

"OK. So I get them now?"

Vegan looked up at him, faceted green eyes gleaming.

"Now would be good. And don't forget to check with me on the phone."

"All right, Arthur. I'll have to take my bike and the backpack to carry things home in. Rural Supply isn't on campus."

"That's fine. Just be sure to call in."

"I can't believe I'm taking style advice from an alien who doesn't even wear clothes."

"That makes it simpler for me, Steven. I don't have anything to unlearn."

Bach sized himself up in the mirror.

"These feel right, Arthur."

"Then they're too small, Steven," Vegan's voice came from the phone. "Go two inches bigger on the waist and the inseam both."

"*Two* inches?"

"Two inches. On both. Those aren't prewashed. They're going to shrink."

Bach did as he was told, and sized himself up again.

"I'm gonna need a belt to hold these up, Arthur."

"They'll shrink, and you need a belt anyway. Let's look at belts."

Bach twirled the belt display in the phone view.

"There, Steven. That one with the double prongs."

"Isn't that kind of heavy, Arthur?"

"That's just what you want. Trust me. Try it on."

Bach found one in his size and tried it one.

"That actually looks pretty good, Arthur."

"You see. What about jackets?"

"They have what they call a denim trucker jacket. It looks like a match to the 501s."

"Try it."

Bach tried on a jacket in a large. It seemed too big on him, but he knew what Vegan would say.

"Yes, Steven, that will shrink, too. Now for tee-shirts."

Bach went back into the changing room and changed back into his own clothes. He came out with his purchases so far ready to go. Bach went over to the tee-shirts.

"They have colored tees here, Arthur."

"No. White only. Get the name brand."

"They're twice as expensive."

"That's fine. Do it."

"All right. Six, you said?"

"Make it eight."

"OK. What else?"

"Plaid shirts."

Bach went over to the plaid shirt rack and started flipping through the shirts, with a running commentary from Vegan.

"No. No. No. Yes. No. Yes. No. No…."

When he had six shirts picked out, Bach tried one on.

"That's perfect, Steven."

"But it's not too big."

"Yes, but those won't shrink. Really, Steven, I'm surprised you don't know all this."

"I never paid attention before, Arthur."

"Very well. Boots now. Get a clerk to help. Remember, not farmer boots. Heavy hiking boots. Like a lumberjack. And then let me see."

When Bach finished with the sales clerk, he checked with Vegan again.

"Yes. That's it, Steven. They're perfect. But now I see we need to do socks."

"I have socks, Arthur."

"White socks."

"White socks?"

"Steven, if you wear black socks with that outfit, you'll look like an idiot."

"All right, Arthur."

"Brand name, Steven. Get the best."

When Bach got back to the apartment, he laid out his purchases. Vegan looked on approvingly.

"There's one thing you forgot, Arthur. Underpants. You think I should go combat? Or stick with my tighty whities?"

"Combat?"

"Without."

"Oh. No, Steven. I wasn't sure Rural Supply would have what I recommend. You can get them mail order."

Vegan sent Bach a listing on his phone.

"Pouch briefs, Arthur?"

"Yes. They are supposed to be very comfortable, and have the added benefit of accentuating things a bit."

"In black?"

"Black doesn't show anything, Steven. Some artifacts of human gastrointestinal processes are apparently considered objectionable."

"Ah. OK."

Bach messed with his phone.

"Done. Now what?"

"Next, I think, is hair and beard."

"Barber shop?"

"Stylist. And wear the new clothes."

"They haven't shrunk yet, Arthur."

"Hmm. Good point. All right. First is laundry, then stylist."

The apartment actually had a stacked laundry pair in the storage closet. Bach put the jeans and denim jacket in the washer.

"What water temperature, Arthur?"

"For optimum results, warm."

"You're sure?"

"So I have read, Steven. And normal cycle."

When it came time for the dryer, it was the same conversation.

"Temperature, Arthur?"

"Warm, Steven."

"I have Hot, Medium, and Cool."

"Medium."

In the meantime, they worked on the book. Bach's second novel was coming up on the ending now. He couldn't believe it was apparently as easy as it was. No plotting, no outline, no nonsense. Just tell the story.

"I had always thought of a novel as a year's project, Arthur. But this one is winding up already."

"Everybody does it differently, Steven. At least, that's what I read. But I think just telling the story is the superior method."

"And what do you think of this one?"

"Much better. You may be able to publish this one."

"I may be able to? Not use a traditional publisher?"

"That's pretty old-school these days, Steven. I wouldn't think that'd be the way to go."

"So what's the next step once I finish it?"

"Let it sit for several days. Recede from memory a bit. Then read it through yourself. See if there's anything you trip over, and correct it."

"And then?"

Vegan shrugged with both sets of shoulders.

"Publish it."

"No rewrite or anything?"

"No. Write the next book."

When his clothes were dry, Bach tried them on.

"There you go," Vegan said.

"You think? They're maybe still a bit large."

"Yes, but not much. You got ninety percent of the shrinkage out of the way. You'll get a bit more with the next couple washings."

"How do you know all this, Arthur? You're an alien."

"But I read."

"Didn't help much with the woman thing."

"That's different, Steven. Too many variables, and they're not all the same."

"Hmph. But you think these look OK?"

A GENT OF VEGA

"Yes. You should go back to Rural Supply and get another five pair or so. In the same size."

"What about the hair stylist?"

"Let that wait until Monday. You want to go on a weekday when they're not rushed."

"All right. But I have classes Monday morning."

"Monday afternoon is fine."

"OK, Arthur. I'm off to the stylist. Any last words?"

"Yes."

Vegan handed him two pieces of paper. There were two men's head shots with haircuts on each.

"Can you tell the difference between these, Steven?"

Bach looked at the two sheets.

"Yes. These two—" He riffled one sheet. "—look too, I don't know, too something. Too soft. Or too slick. Too something."

"Yes. They're over-styled. You want the slightly rougher look of the other two."

"Got it. Can I have these? To show the stylist?"

"Of course. I printed them off on your machine. And change into your new clothes so she gets the idea."

"This late in the semester, it's too warm for three layers, Arthur."

"Oh, just the denim jacket over the tee-shirt is fine, Steven. It's perfect, actually."

"Really?"

For answer, Vegan called up a web search on Bach's machine. He searched 'denim jacket' and got dozens of pictures of men in denim jackets with just a white tee under.

"OK," Bach said.

"Hi. What can we do for you?"

"Oh, hi. I need a haircut that fits my new clothes."

"Change of style, huh? Are you gay or straight?"

"Uh, straight. I want something like these, not like these."

He showed her the pictures.

"OK. Got it. Come along this way. Wash first."

That was a new one on Bach. The barber shop didn't wash your hair.

She led him to a sink with a chair backed up against it.

"Umm...?"

"Just sit here and lay back. I'll do everything."

"OK."

Bach lay back in the chair, and the stylist leaned his head back on a cushion. She tested the water.

"How's the temperature? Is that OK?"

"Yes. Uh-huh. Feels good."

"OK."

She then lathered and rinsed his hair thoroughly, and took her time with it. During this, she kept up a patter of questions and talking.

Bach, for his part, couldn't see anything except her considerable cleavage. She was maybe a couple of years older than he, perhaps twenty-six, and in the flower of womanhood. Her right breast brushed his face repeatedly, to the extent that he limited his responses to uh-huhs and unh-uhs, afraid if he opened his mouth to speak he would get a mouthful.

"A change of style, huh?"

"Uh-huh."

"Good. Most men think 'unkempt' is a style. Grunge is OK, I guess, but you get tired of it. You know what I mean?"

"Uh-huh."

"I can understand, you know, with the university and all, that people are so busy with classes, they just don't take the time on their appearance. But it doesn't take that long, does it?"

"Unh-uh."

"That's what I say. And once they're out of university, with more time on their hands, they could clean up their act. Most don't, though, you know?"

"Uh-huh."

"I guess they just got bad habits. OK. Now let's move over to the styling chair."

"OK."

Bach moved to the chair indicated, and she put a barber cape on him, then started in on his hair. She was quiet now, as she concentrated on trimming his seven-inch-long hair back to the two to three inches of the photos he had showed her.

As she got close, she started using the blow dryer to aid her efforts in getting the curl just right.

Finally, she showed him the result.

"What do you think?"

"Oh, that's great. Thank you."

"I cut it just a bit shorter than the photos, so you have some time while it grows. With an eighth of an inch a week, you should be good for about two months before we should touch it up."

"OK. That sounds good."

"Do you want me to trim your beard, too, to match the photos?"

"Sure."

The stylist went after his beard with her clippers, touching up both sides, then scanning his face right and left to make sure she had a match. She cleaned off his neck with the clippers.

"There you go."

"Excellent. Thanks."

"Now, you need to shave the neck. I can't do that. I'm not

licensed for shaving. So you need to take care of that at home."

"All right."

She removed the barber cape. They went over to the register and he squared with her, giving her a twenty-percent tip.

"Thanks again," Bach said as he turned to go.

"OK, handsome. See you around."

On the way back to the apartment, Bach passed a woman from one of his classes.

"Hi!" she said.

"Oh. Uh. Hi."

She laughed and walked on.

Attention

Bach told Vegan about the encounter when he got back to the apartment.

"Well, that was a missed opportunity," the alien said.

"I know, but what should I have done?"

"Stopped. That's first. Then smile. That's second. Third, you want to say something that invites conversation. Something like, 'Well, hello there. How are you doing?'"

"Just that simple?"

"Just that simple. You stop, so she stops. You smile, so she smiles. Then you ask a question, which elicits an answer. The next thing you know, she's talking to you."

"But what do I say?"

"Look. Steven. I read this research study. They had a fellow go into a party and have conversations with people. He had interesting stories to tell about himself, and he did so. Then they had him go into a similar party and have conversations with people. This time, he offered no information about himself, but just kept asking questions. Eliciting information from other people. After the parties, they interviewed the people he spoke to. What do you think happened?"

"I don't know, Arthur."

"The people in the second party thought he was a much better conversationalist than the people in the first party."

"Really?"

"Absolutely. You don't have to say anything. Just keep asking questions. 'How did that make you feel?' 'Where are you heading off to?' 'What did you think of that last homework assignment?' Anything, really. Just keep asking questions."

"I find that hard to believe, Arthur."

"It's true, Steven. People don't want to hear about you. They want to talk about themselves. Do you find it surprising that people are so self-involved?"

"Not when you say it like that, I guess."

"There you go."

Vegan nodded his head sagely, casting glints off his faceted green eyes.

"So what do you think of my haircut?"

"Looks good, Steven. Maybe a bit short."

"Yes. She said it would grow out a bit going forward, and I should have it renewed every eight weeks or so."

"Makes sense. So tomorrow you do the whole thing, right? Including all the toiletry items?"

"Yes. I'll have to get up a little earlier to get it all done."

"It'll be worth it. You'll see."

"In the meantime, I'm going to get supper ready."

"Excellent. There's a two-pound chuck roast in there I'm dying to sink my mandibles into."

He rubbed all four of his hands together.

"Cows are really tasty," the Vegan said.

Bach got up forty-five minutes early the next morning. He showered with a men's scented body wash, and shampooed his hair, finishing up with a conditioner. He shaved the portion of his neck the stylist had cleaned off with the clippers, then used aftershave and deodorant.

Bach dressed in his new clothes, including the new briefs. He pirouetted for Vegan.

"Ta-da!"

"Teeth and mouth," Vegan said.

"Oh, yeah."

A GENT OF VEGA

Bach went back into the bathroom and flossed and brushed his teeth, then gargled with a mouthwash. He came back out to pose for the alien.

"Now?"

Vegan nodded.

"And you're done fifteen minutes early."

"I think I'm going to walk today. It's not that far, and it's a pretty day."

"OK. See you later."

Bach was an hour and a half late getting back to the apartment, given his normal Tuesday schedule.

"Oh, there you are," Vegan said when he arrived.

"Yes, sorry. I should have called you."

"I was getting ready to send out a search party."

Bach knew it was just a figure of speech, but he chuckled at the thought of Vegan going around looking for him. 'Excuse me. Have you seen a human around?'

Bach sat on the sofa and looked across at the alien.

"It was the strangest thing. It was like I had been invisible to women this whole time and all of a sudden they could see me. I got all kinds of smiles, and hellos, and little waves."

"Excellent. So it's working."

"Yes. And after my second class, I asked this woman where she was going next, and she said it was her last class of the day, so I asked her out for coffee, and she said yes."

"Wonderful. How did that go?"

"It was just like you said, Arthur. Whenever she would wind down, I would ask her another question, and she was off and running again. I heard all about her, and her roommates, and her family. It was kind of bizarre."

"What's she like?"

"She's beautiful, for one thing. Prettiest woman in the class. But she had smiled at me before class started, so I took a chance, and she said yes to coffee."

"Where did you leave it with her?"

"Well, after an hour, she said she had to go. Something with her roommate this afternoon. So we got up, then she took my hand, squeezed it for a moment, then let it go. A little wave, and she was gone."

"That was an invitation, Steven."

"I think so, too."

Bach sat, deep in thought, and Vegan was content to sit quietly. Then Bach stirred.

"It can't be this easy, can it, Arthur? New clothes and a haircut? That's it?"

"It's more than that, Steven. In your age group, something like seventy-five percent of people are overweight or obese. You're not, so that gives you a huge advantage right there. Given all the sugar and high-fructose corn syrup in your processed foods, that says something about a certain discipline.

"Of those who aren't overweight, what percentage of men take good care of themselves? Healthy, well-groomed, that sort of thing. You're in good shape, probably because of all the bicycle riding. That helps a lot.

"Add in well-groomed – getting rid of the lanky hair and the rummage-bin clothing – and it puts you in the top two or three percent of the male population your age.

"It's not rocket science. It's just numbers."

"I still find it hard to believe, Arthur."

"Steven. Look. The woman you took to coffee. Was she overweight?"

"No."

"Did she brush her hair this morning, or did it look like she just ran a hand through it after she got out of bed?"

"No, it was nicely brushed."

"Was she dressed just a little upscale, or was she dressed like a ragamuffin like all the other college kids?"

"No, she definitely stepped it up a bit from most."

"You see, Steven. You applied all the same criteria to her that you seem surprised by when they're applied to yourself."

Bach opened his mouth, then closed it, then tried again.

"You're right, Arthur. I didn't even realize it."

"She might not either, though I suspect she does. Women are more honest with themselves about that sort of thing."

"Huh. OK. So what's next?"

"Manicure and pedicure."

"I thought you were kidding about those."

"Nope. Do it."

Bach couldn't complain about Vegan's advice so far. For all he was an alien, he was a sociologist, and saw humans from outside themselves. Maybe that gave him perspective.

"All right. This afternoon. Lunch first."

"Call and make an appointment. Make sure they have someone available."

"Hello."

"Mr. Bach?"

"Yes?"

She smiled.

"We don't have many men come in. Come right this way."

Bach followed her back into the salon.

"Have you had a manicure or pedicure before?"

"No."

"Let me explain then. We're first going to soak your hands and feet in some solution to soften them. Then we'll work on your hands first, then your feet. All right?"

"Sure. Whatever you say."

"Let me take your jacket."

He handed her his jacket and she hung it on the wall nearby. She motioned him to be seated in the chair. Once seated, she removed his shoes and socks and rolled up his pants legs.

She then placed a small tub under his feet and filled it with a warm solution. Small bowls for his hands were also filled with solution and placed to the sides of his chair where his hands could hang in them.

"You relax there, and I'll be back in a few minutes to work on you."

"OK."

When she returned, she set a small table before him and worked on his hands. It felt weird to have someone manipulating his hands, but he just relaxed and let her work.

She scrubbed at his calluses and massaged a moisturizer into his hands, then went to work on his nails. She worked the cuticles and trimmed the nails, finishing up with a nail file.

"Polish or buff?"

"Buff."

She nodded, then buffed his nails.

That done, she worked on his feet. These took considerably longer, as there were more calluses on his feet and his nails were in worse shape.

If it had felt weird to have someone working on his hands, his feet felt even weirder.

Finishing up, she buffed his toenails.

"All right, Mr. Bach. You can put your socks and shoes back on now."

It was harder than usual to get his socks on, due to the

moisturizer making his feet stickier. But Bach got them back on, and his boots. She handed him his jacket, and led him to the counter to square up.

When he was paid up, he turned to go.

"Goodbye, Mr. Bach. See you next time."

When Bach got back to the apartment, he had been gone two hours.

"That took some time, or did you take the manicurist for coffee?" Vegan asked.

"No, it just took a long time."

"Let me see your hands."

Bach held out his hands to the alien, who examined them carefully.

"Excellent, Steven. I was worried it wouldn't be enough of a difference to be noticeable, but it certainly is. Obvious manicure."

"That won't be a turn-off to women?"

"What? A guy who takes care of himself? No. A turn-on more likely."

"So what's next, Arthur? Take out that woman I took for a cup of coffee this morning? Elaine?"

"No. Take some others out for coffee or a snack. Get their names and phone numbers. By the way. Did you get the name and number of the manicurist?

"A forty-year-old Chinese woman? No."

"You shouldn't disdain women because of age and ethnicity, Steven. The difference in experience and perspective could be educational. Anyway, how long to go in this semester?"

"Couple of weeks."

"Perfect. Get the names and phone numbers of any woman in your classes who interests you. Date them after the class is over."

"Why?"

"That way, if one of them decides you're a jerk, she doesn't poison all the others in the class against you. You will have all moved on to other classes. Besides, you need more experience just talking to women before you push further, I think."

"What will Elaine think?"

"That you're interested in other women, or that you didn't get her hint, or both, and she'll try harder."

"Where are you getting all this, Arthur? You're an alien."

"Yes, but I'm also a sociologist, and I've been studying this while you've been studying your class work."

"All right, Arthur. You've proved out so far. What do you say to ordering out tonight, then we can order some groceries while we wait?"

"Sounds good, Steven."

Over the next two weeks, Bach got the names and phone numbers of a total of eight women in his various spring semester classes.

He also finished his second novel. Vegan declared this one good enough to publish.

"So what's the next step in publishing the book, Arthur?"

"Wait a few days for memory to fade a bit, then read it through in one sitting looking for problems."

"OK."

With the book on hold and time on his hands between spring semester and summer session, Bach turned to the women problem.

Mixed Results

The first woman Bach asked out was Elaine, the woman he had first taken out for coffee. They went out for dinner and a movie, and everything went fine. For their second date, Bach offered to cook dinner for her. It had been Vegan's suggestion.

"It's a basic skill that many men don't have," Vegan had said. "Anything beyond heating a frozen pizza is beyond them."

"My father could cook, so I learned how. It seemed like the thing to do."

"And it was, Steven. Women love it when a guy can cook."

What to do about Vegan himself was another issue. The apartment simply wasn't that big. It would be next to impossible to hide the big alien.

Bach decided he wouldn't try to hide him. If Vegan stood motionless, without respiration, as he did when he slept at night, Bach could explain him as a statue of one of the aliens in Bach's new novel, due to be published soon.

He hoped for the best, but it didn't work out.

Spectacularly so.

"Hi, Elaine. Come on in."

"This your place? It's nice, being an independent unit with an outside door and all. Not some small apartment in a big block, with a door off a hallway."

"Yes. It's small, though."

Her eye fell on Vegan.

"My God, what's that thing?"

"Oh, it's a statue I made of one of the characters in my book.

An alien. So I would remember what he looked like as I wrote."

"How creepy."

"That's the name of the book. 'Hairy Scary, Deeply Creepy.'"

"Well, at least it's not in the bedroom. You wouldn't be able to sleep with that creepy thing looking at you."

They went on to the kitchen part of the unit. Bach got out a couple of beers. He had made Beef Stroganoff over egg noodles, with broccoli and fresh bread.

Dinner went well. They had ice cream for dessert. After dessert, they moved over to the sofa and started messing around.

Things were just starting to get interesting when Elaine excused herself to go to the bathroom. When she came back, she walked past Vegan. She stopped and looked at the alien.

"It's so weird. It almost looks like… *a costume.*"

She transferred her beer from her right to her left hand, then gathered up a fold of the alien's forearm between her right thumb and forefinger and pinched. Hard.

"Garak!" the alien said in Vegan. "That hurts!"

"I knew it. I *knew* it!"

She stomped on the alien's instep.

"Ow, ow, ow."

Vegan was now hopping on one foot, his two lower hands holding his other foot while his right upper hand was clamped over the pinch spot on his left upper arm.

She wheeled on Bach.

"And *you*! What an asshole. Were you getting your rocks off knowing your pervy boyfriend was watching you paw me? Oooooo!"

She threw the half-empty beer at him and stormed out, slamming the door behind her.

"Well, that didn't work," Vegan said once he had calmed down.

Bach rubbed at the spot where the can of beer had hit him. Good thing he hadn't served bottles.

"Clearly. She thought you were an accomplice in a costume."

"Better that than thinking I actually was an alien."

"We've gotta try something else to hide you somehow. Maybe I should move to a two-bedroom apartment."

"That's certainly one solution. Let me think about it."

"I'll check with the complex office tomorrow."

"Well, they have a two-bedroom available."

"Lucky," Vegan said.

Bach shrugged.

"It's a college town. Lots of moving around during the summer. Couple things, though."

"Like what?"

"It's more money. Fourteen hundred a month."

Vegan shrugged all four shoulders.

"A deal's a deal, Steven. Four times rent is four times rent."

"That means you'll get less money when I go in to sell gold."

"Some months, we'll do three bars, that's all. Steven, I have thousands of them. Money is not an issue."

"The other thing is it's not available for a week. They need to get in there and clean up. Paint and all that. And I have a second date with Barbara this weekend."

"I have an idea there, Steven. The best lie is the unbelievable truth."

"You're saying I should tell her…"

"That I'm actually an alien, yes. She won't believe it, but then she will come up with the book-related statue bit on her own. Once someone sees through a deception, they stop looking for a second one. So the best thing is to cover one deception with another."

"You ready to get pinched and stomped again, Arthur?"

"If I have to. I want to research the point. Cover a deception with a deception. I want to see if it works."

"All right. We'll give it a go. But I'm still serving beer in cans, not bottles."

"Oh. One more thing. I got this for you. It came mail-order yesterday."

It was a small basketball setup, with a six-inch hoop and a four-inch foam basketball.

"What do I do with this, Arthur?"

"It's an idea from a book I read. Here's what you do...."

The morning of their date, Bach called to check with Barbara.

"Hi, Barbara. Just checking to see if we're still on for tonight."

"Oh, yes. I'm looking forward to it."

"I am, too. Turns out my roommate Arthur is going to be around, but he's no trouble."

"Oh. Is he eating with us?"

"No. He's a Vegan."

"Ah. All right. See you at six."

"And you can find my place?"

"Oh, sure. Greenwood Apartments. I know it."

"See you then."

"Hi, Barbara. Come on in."

"Hi, Steven. Nice place."

"Thanks. It's not much, but it's home."

"Oh, my God. What's that?"

"That's my roommate Arthur. I told you he was a Vegan. As in, from Vega."

"Oh, you. That has to do with your book, doesn't it? You said it was science fiction."

She went over to the alien and looked him up and down.

"It's so perfect, it almost looks real. You did a nice job."

"It *is* real."

"Yes, a real statue. That must help a lot with your visualization."

"Yes, he's been a great help."

"So what's for dinner?"

"Spaghetti and garlic bread."

"Ooo. I love spaghetti."

"Well, I hope you like mine. I'm just about to start the pasta."

"Smells wonderful."

Bach put the pasta in the boiling water, then turned the heat down so it wouldn't boil over. He set a timer for thirty minutes.

"OK. Thirty minutes and we're good to eat."

"What do we do in the meantime?"

"Shoot a little hoops?"

Bach picked up the foam basketball from the kitchen counter.

Barbara looked around.

"Where's the court?"

"This way."

Bach led her into the bedroom, where the basket was mounted on the wall over the head of the bed.

"We lay on our backs on the bed, and play over our heads."

"Sounds like fun."

"It's not as easy as it looks."

They kicked off their shoes and both lay on the bed about a

foot apart. Bach took the first shot and missed. Barbara got the rebound and took the shot. She made it. Bach got the ball and shot again.

It got pretty competitive. Before long, going for rebounds was a full-contact sport, and they got their arms and legs all atangle going for the ball. The side effect was that any body shyness they had about touching each other was long gone.

At one point, Barbara got the rebound and held the ball out of his reach. Their faces were inches apart.

"My ball," she said.

She leaned in then, and kissed him tenderly.

At that point, the timer started beeping in the kitchen.

"Time for dinner," Bach said, and rolled off the bed.

"Ooo. Bad timing."

"Hey, it's half-time."

"OK."

Dinner went well. Bach really did have a good spaghetti sauce recipe, and Barbara seemed to enjoy it.

"That was wonderful, Steven."

"My father's recipe. So what do you say? Time for the second half?"

"Sure."

They went back into the bedroom and got back on the bed. Bach held the ball out to her.

"As I recall, it was your ball," he said.

She took the ball from him and threw it over her shoulder.

"We don't need the ball. Let's see. Where were we? Oh, yes."

She leaned in to kiss him.

They took their time undressing each other, appreciating each new discovery as it was exposed.

Bach was not a virgin. The summer between his senior year

of high school and freshman year of college, his older sister's college friend Deirdre had spent the summer with them. She had decided that it wasn't a good thing for Bach to go off to college a virgin.

They had made love three times that heady summer, when the family was all out of the house. His sister, too, was sometimes gone without her friend, as she interviewed for jobs on their campus. There were three days that summer when they had the house completely to themselves.

Dee had been gentle and had taken her time with him. They had never been in a hurry. It had been a wonderful introduction to the art of lovemaking.

Dee had been gentle at the end as well, leaving him not heartbroken, but grateful.

That had all been six years ago, but there were some things, after all, that one did not forget.

Bach woke in the morning all tangled up with Barbara. She was already awake and looking at him.

"Heavens. You're still here."

"Yes, I'm still here."

She snuggled into him further, and he appreciated the dappled sunlight coming in almost horizontally through the trees as it played across her body.

Her luscious body, he corrected. Barbara was one of the most beautiful women he had ever seen. Her body was flawless, like a perfect diamond.

"So how shall we start the day?" he asked her.

"Well, I know how I want to start the day."

She rolled onto her back and pulled him to her again.

For his part, he completely lost himself in the pure hedonistic joy of making love to her once more. He immersed himself in her sun-dappled beauty as he pleasured her.

"Oh, that was dreamy," she said. "A great way to start the day."

"And now what we need is breakfast. Pancakes coming up."

He rolled out of bed, pulling on the jeans he had worn last night, then headed out into the main room.

When she followed along, completely dressed as she had been last night, pancakes were just coming off the skillet.

"There we are," he said, putting a plate of pancakes before her.

"What about you?"

"Already cooking. The skillet is only so big."

"You should get one of those big two-burner griddles."

"Perhaps I will."

She waited for him to be seated before digging in.

"It's just so nice to meet a guy who isn't a jerk. Oh, God. Did I just say that out loud?"

Bach chuckled.

"That's OK. So what kind of behaviors would make me a jerk?"

She shook her head.

"No. I wouldn't want to give you any ideas. You just keep being you."

"Then how will I know what to avoid?"

"OK, I'll give you a big one. Most guys are just so into themselves, all they do is talk about themselves. It's like, 'Hey, don't let my presence interfere with your monologue about yourself.'"

"Not to defend every guy, but some of them are probably just nervous talking to you and they're just babbling."

"I suppose. But it is annoying when they're just going on about themselves continuously. When they aren't busy goggling at me, that is."

"You are very beautiful."

"Yeah, but that's not me. It's not something I did. It just happened. What about me? You seem to actually care about me. Who I actually am. Or at least you fake it very well, which amounts to the same thing."

Bach chuckled, but he was on the verge of some realization. He filed it for later consideration.

"It's not that I'm immune to your beauty, Barbara."

"No, I know. But it's not the same. It's different somehow. Do you know what I mean?"

"I think so. I'll think about it."

"Good. When you figure it out, maybe you can teach some other people. Other guys."

"Like how?"

"In your writing, perhaps. You're a writer, right?"

"Yes. With a single novel, not yet published."

"Are you stopping after one novel?"

"Well, no."

"There you go, then."

They had finished their pancakes. She looked at her watch.

"Oh, gosh. I've got to go. I have a million things to do today."

Bach got up and walked her to the door.

"Thank you for a lovely evening," she said.

Wait. *She* was thanking *him*?

"We should do it again sometime," she continued.

"I will give it every consideration," he said, pompously.

She laughed, then hugged him, her head against his bare chest.

"You take care, Barbara."

She pulled back and kissed him.

"You, too, Steven. See ya."

A wave over her shoulder then, and she was gone.

Bach went back into the apartment, to the fridge, and got a beer despite the hour. Then he went to sit on the sofa.

Vegan stirred, then moved to the armchair.

"That was truly remarkable."

"Did you have a good time, Steven?"

"Oh, you might say that, Arthur. You might say that. Making love – three times – with the most smoking hot woman I've ever seen? Yeah, that was what one might call enjoyable."

"Are you in love then?"

Bach opened his mouth, then closed it. He was reminded about what Barbara had said about her looks versus her inner self.

"No, Arthur, I'm not. Not yet, anyway. I don't know her that well. We're certainly friends."

"Yet you performed a mating ritual with her."

"No, a mating ritual is marriage. What we did was practice a fertility ritual."

"Ah. I see, Steven. So if she is fertile, and a larva results, do you then go through a mating ritual?"

"You mean a baby, not a larva. And it is unlikely that a baby will result. She is likely on birth control of some version or another."

"Did you check with her as to her status on birth control?"

"No, Arthur. It is traditionally a woman's responsibility to see to that before she makes herself available for sex. After the first time, it may be wiser to inquire."

"That first encounter seems iffy, then, Steven."

"It can be. Or so I've heard."

"What if a baby does result, Steven? Despite your expectations?"

"Then I might, in fact, marry her, Arthur. I could certainly do a lot worse."

"A roll of the dice, then."

Vegan shook his head.

"Humans are so weird. You think you have them figured out, and then they surprise the hell out of you."

Moving

As the time approached for moving, Bach had twenty banker's boxes delivered. That and borrowing the complex's hand cart were all he needed to pull off the move.

The beginning of summer session was fast approaching, and he needed to get the move pulled off before the more compressed summer classes started.

"So how are we going to do this, Steven?" Vegan asked.

"Well, we pack everything in boxes, and I cart the boxes over there. To the new apartment. Then we unpack all the boxes."

"How do we get me from the old apartment to the new apartment?"

"I think I can take you over on the handcart, wrapped in a blanket. You know, Arthur. Like a statue."

"Ah, the statue gimmick again. All right. That sounds good."

The day before the move – and three days after Barbara had come for dinner – a package showed up. It was a long and thin package.

"I wonder what this is," Bach said, coming in from accepting the package.

He opened the first box, to find it was gift-wrapped. There was a card.

"'For future breakfasts,' it says. It doesn't say from who."

Bach opened the gift wrapping and laughed.

"What is it, Steven?"

"It's a two-burner pancake griddle. Big enough to do

pancakes for two."

"Ah. From Barbara, then."

"Clearly. She didn't have to do that."

"It's an invitation, Steven."

"I understand, Arthur. She must have had a very good time, hard as that is to understand."

"Why is that hard to understand?"

"I'm hardly the Adonis type. I mean, I'm not overweight, and I'm in pretty good shape from all the bike riding and all, but I'm not particularly handsome. The Rugged style works for me, but even so."

"I heard your conversation over breakfast, Steven. It seems to me that Barbara is unimpressed with looks. With her own, certainly. What was most important to her is that you listened."

Bach's realization came back to him then, and he nodded slowly.

"OK. I see it now. I think you're right. Mostly listening made it easier on me, because I didn't have to think of what to say. But that's exactly what she said was most important to her."

"Now that may be specific to her, but I don't think so. Her comments about men were pretty all-inclusive. Which probably means she's not the only one. It may be a general complaint among women."

"Can it really be that simple, Arthur?"

"Sure. Why not?"

Moving went about as Bach had predicted. It became much easier, however, when Vegan offered to pack the boxes.

"This is easy, Steven. No problem at all."

He said that as he was packing a box, all four arms taking items and loading them into a box. Vegan used the simple expedient of packing things as they fit in the box, without regard to whether they were related items or not.

"Not worried about packing related items together, Arthur?"

"Why should I be? Aren't they all going to get unpacked right away anyway?"

"Fair enough. I guess that makes sense."

"You take those first four boxes over to the new apartment, Steven. By the time you get back, I'll have another four packed for you."

"All right."

Bach stacked up four of the boxes on the hand cart and set off for the new apartment, about a block away.

He had already inspected the new apartment. They had done a nice job cleaning it up for its new tenant.

This apartment had a larger living room – furnished with a couch and two big armchairs, not just one – and a larger kitchen. There were two bedrooms, one to either side. The master had an en suite bath, while the other had access to the only other bathroom off a short hallway from the kitchen. That hallway also had the equipment and storage rooms.

Of course, Bach could use the whole second bedroom as a storage room. The furnished bed was in the way, but they could take that apart and lean it against the wall.

He unloaded the four boxes from the cart onto the floor in the corner of the big living room and headed back to the old apartment, dragging the hand cart behind him. When he got there, Vegan had six more boxes ready to go.

Bach loaded up four boxes and set off once again for the new apartment.

After five trips – and one each for the bicycle and the television – the old apartment was empty except for one blanket and a bunch of bungee cords Bach used for carrying things on his bicycle. The status of the apartments as furnished apartments near campus had made things easier. There was no furniture to move.

"OK, Arthur. Get on the hand truck."

The alien stood on the nose plate of the hand cart, and Bach wrapped him in the blanket, using bungee cords around the alien to hold the blanket in place. Several more bungee cords bound him to the rails of the handcart.

"All right. Whatever you do, don't move," Bach said. "That would be hard to explain."

"I understand, Steven."

The trip itself went without incident, and soon Bach was unwrapping the alien in the living room of the new apartment.

"That all went well, Steven."

"Yes. As good as I could have hoped. I'm going to take the hand cart back and turn over the keys to the old apartment."

When Bach returned, Vegan was busily unboxing all Bach's things.

"I got the contents of the refrigerator first," Vegan said. "That seemed important. Then I just sort of kept going."

"That's fine."

Bach jumped in, and soon he was completely unpacked. The miscellaneous items they put in the dresser drawers and on the top surface of the dresser in the second bedroom. The bike, too, went into the second bedroom.

"I probably ought to get some storage shelving for all this stuff," Bach said.

"How about we move the shelving in the storage area out into the second bedroom?" Vegan asked. "Then you could use the storage area for your bike. Make things a lot easier."

"Good idea."

They moved the shelving, then Bach ran his bike into the

storage area, which was deep enough to take it. He just leaned it up against the wall.

He walked out into the living room.

"That worked great, Arthur. And the nice thing is the apartment isn't cluttered anymore."

"Yes. Enough signs of habitation to be homey, but without the clutter typical of a bachelor pad. Very attractive. It should make things even easier with the ladies."

"And I can have you hide out in the second bedroom when I'm entertaining."

"That will work, Steven. I have very good hearing in the human vocal range, and, if you leave the bedroom doors open, I can advise you on your conversations with your woman friends."

Bach got a beer out of the fridge, and got an extra one for Vegan. They both sat in the armchairs in the living room.

"I meant to ask you about that, Arthur. I currently have a relationship with Barbara, which she is clearly interested in pursuing on some level. I could, I suppose, date her steadily, to the exclusion of others.

"At the same time, I'm very new to this game. I have no idea what is important to me in a relationship. What I want in a partner.

"And, were I steady with Barbara, I worry I would grow jealous of her. She will always attract other men. Her looks guarantee that. At some point, we would likely break up, and I would be seriously torn up about it.

"So I don't know what to do. Do you have any advice for me?"

"I've been reading up on this, Steven, and I think there are several options. One is to be a ladies' man. A Casanova, if you will. Uncommitted sexual relationships with women on a catch as catch can basis. No commitments. No relationships, really, beyond sex.

"Another is what one might call serial monogamy. Going out with one woman at a time, steadily, until it breaks up, then doing the same with another, then another. Very romantic in each case, until the inevitable breakup.

"There is a third option. Being friends with women – much like their women friends, someone they can talk to – but with the option of sex on the table. If you are having sex regularly, having sex with any particular woman or on any particular evening is not crucial. What is crucial is being someone they can talk to.

"In this third scenario, breakups aren't an issue. If their pursuit of a sexual relationship with someone else becomes exclusive, you remain dear friends even if sex is no longer an option."

"But what if I find the woman of my dreams, Arthur? A true soul mate?"

"How would being friends prevent you both from pursuing that relationship as an exclusive one at that point, Steven? Wouldn't being friends first make it even more special, and more likely to be a successful long-term relationship?"

Bach nodded. That made sense.

"Won't women find me less desirable if they know I'm seeing other people as well?"

"Some, perhaps, Steven, but my reading suggests the opposite is true. If a woman finds you desirable, but no other women do, well, she may think perhaps she's wrong. Whereas if a woman finds you desirable, and she knows other women do as well, that means she's correct."

"Interesting."

Bach thought about it, and decided Vegan was likely correct.

Which, with the move done, made him think about tonight.

"Hmm. I think I'll see what Laurie is up to tonight."

"The bartender?"

"Yes. She works weekends, but tonight and tomorrow night are her nights off."

"Sounds good. One thing, Steven."

"Yes?"

"If she stays for breakfast, do not use your new griddle. Save the first time using your present for the next time Barbara is over. To use it with some other woman first would be, um, inconsiderate."

"Good point. Thanks."

"No problem."

Laurie was the popular and attractive bartender at a campustown restaurant. Not a student dive, it was more upscale, attracting faculty, staff, and parents.

She never dated people she met through the restaurant, keeping work and her personal life very separate. Bach, however, had met her through a mutual friend.

"Hi, Laurie. Steven Bach."

"Oh, hi, Steven. What's up?"

"Hey, it's your night off. You don't want to cook. Come on over and I'll cook for you."

"Deal. Did you move yet?"

"Yes. Today, as a matter of fact. The new place is 21-E."

"OK. See you at six?"

"That works."

Dinner was simple fare, hamburgers and a salad. Laurie could have all the fancy meals she wanted at the restaurant during her work week.

She talked about work, both her interactions with the customers and the other staff. She ran across a broad slice of people in her job, and some of her stories were pretty funny.

With dinner over, and time to leave or stay pending, Bach proposed a solution.

"You know, if you just want someone to cuddle with tonight, I won't hassle you for your body."

She tipped her head.

"That sounds nice, actually. What do we do till then?"

"Movie?"

"Sounds good."

After the movie, Laurie got up from the sofa where they had been cuddling.

"I'm off to bed."

"I'm going to putter the kitchen a bit. I'll be along."

"OK."

Bach cleaned up from dinner and started the dishwasher. Then he went into the bedroom. Laurie was sleeping on her side, facing away from him. He pulled the covers back and saw she was nude.

Bach stripped down and climbed into bed behind her, curling up to her like spoons. She mewed and pushed back against him until she was comfortable. Bach was asleep in minutes.

Bach woke up to her getting frisky, playing with his equipment. He responded in kind, and soon they were into heavy petting.

"I thought you weren't interested in my body."

"Oh, no, milady. I said I wouldn't *hassle* you for your body."

"Well, I have to get going. I have a doctor's appointment this morning. This is going to have to wait for tonight."

"All right."

"No argument?"

"I just had a beautiful woman promise to make love to me tonight. Why would I possibly argue with that?"

She laughed and kissed him, then got out of bed and got dressed while he lay back in bed and watched.

She kissed him once more, then turned toward the door.

"See you tonight."

"I'll just wait right here."

She laughed and was gone.

Vegan came into the kitchen as Bach ate cereal for breakfast.

"No sex last night?"

"No. She had a doctor's appointment this morning. I took a rain check for tonight."

"So being comfortable friends is working for you."

"Oh, yes. Amazingly so."

That night, Bach fried up some ground beef and onions, then made a gravy. He served it over rotini. He started broccoli in the microwave, then finished it in the skillet.

It was comfort food, pure and simple.

Laurie came over as he was finishing up the broccoli.

"Just in time," Bach said when he let her in.

"Oh, good. I'm hungry."

Tonight Laurie talked mostly about her family. It was an epic disaster. Broken marriage early in her life, growing up with her mother, with whom she was still close. Her mother's inability to attract another husband. Her brother's ongoing failure to get his act together.

Bach was a sympathetic listener throughout. It was easy to be sympathetic, the circumstances were so bad. Laurie's family was working class, and it made Bach feel lucky to be in the comfortable middle class. College had never really been on the charts for Laurie, though she probably had the brains and the grit to do it if she had persisted.

Another movie and then they went to bed. While Laurie was perhaps not quite as beautiful as Barbara, she was an enthusiastic and experienced bed partner, and they had a very good time.

For breakfast, he retrieved the skillet from the dishwasher and made one-eyed sailors – a piece of bread, buttered on both sides with a hole in the center made by punching it out with a drinking glass, then an egg in the hole. Over easy, they were simple and hearty, with the extra circle of bread from the punch-out, also toasted.

He served them both, then sat down to eat.

"Sorry I went on so long last night about my mom and all."

"That's OK, Laurie. Sometimes you just need to let it out."

"That's it exactly. Oh, things aren't so bad now. I have good money coming in, my brother's finally putting the pieces together, and my mom's happy enough. But those hard times hang on in your memory. You know? Anyway, thanks for listening."

"It's what I'm good at."

"You really are, Steven. It's nice."

She helped him with cleaning up the dishes, then headed toward the door.

"OK, I'm off. Thanks for everything, Steven."

"No problem, Laurie. You take care."

A quick kiss and a hug, and she was gone.

"So what's on the agenda for today," Vegan asked as he came into the living room.

"Starting to read textbooks ahead for the summer session. Classes start Monday. Also, I need to do the read-through on my book."

"And today's Wednesday. Any company this weekend?"

"Not sure. Maybe. I haven't had Candace over yet."

"What about Barbara?"

"Well, there are two nights on the weekend, Arthur."

The Vegan chuckled but made no comment.

Summer Session

They brought Bach's book out a month into summer session. There was a bunch of effort involved in that, including getting a cover artist, and he could only do the work so fast while attending his summer classes.

Bach put the book up for pre-order, to get a bunch of sales the first day, thereby bumping it up in the charts. He advertised the book during pre-order, on the theory that people couldn't buy something they didn't know about. His income from Vegan's rental payments gave him, for once, extra money he could use for some advertising.

Bach set the categories for 'Hairy Scary, Deeply Creepy' to first-contact science fiction and monster science fiction, both of which it fit, as well as to the more general adventure science fiction.

The book sold well for a first-effort self-published work, and he continued to advertise it with about thirty percent of royalties. He was cash-flow positive on the book once it came out.

He also started thinking about the next book.

Bach kept up on his appearance and personal hygiene as well, refusing to sink back into dweebiness. He had his hair and beard regularly trimmed by the same stylist, and made regular use of the toiletries Vegan had convinced him to purchase.

He was comfortable in his new persona, and he kept it up.

As far as Bach's womanizing, only four of the women whose

phone numbers he got during spring semester were on campus for the summer. Three of the four ended up in his coterie of sexual friends – Barbara, Candace, and Diana – as well as Laurie, whom he had met outside of classes.

All of them knew they had a friend in Steven Bach. They could stay over the night after dinner, or not. That could include sex, or not. Usually they did, and usually it did, but they also knew it didn't have to.

Halfway through summer session, Laurie dropped out.

It was after dinner that Laurie brought up the subject.

"Steven, is it OK if we just cuddle tonight?"

"Of course. You know that."

"Well, I was hoping. I've met this fellow, and I'm kind of sweet on him. I want to give the relationship a chance and see if it goes anywhere."

"I hope it does, Laurie. I hope he's the answer to your prayers. I only want the best for you, you know that."

"You're sweet."

They cuddled and watched a movie, and then went to bed.

In the morning, lying there together as it brightened outside, she had a request.

"Steven, how about one more go? For old time's sake."

"Of course."

They made love then. Slow, tender love. A goodbye kind of love.

After breakfast, he had an admonishment for her.

"Stay in touch, Laurie. We'll always be friends. You know that."

"Yes, I know, Steven. You take care. And thanks for everything."

The new relationship worked out, and Bach was sincerely

happy for her. After what she'd been through, she deserved it.

"Steven, did you know there is a science-fiction convention in town between summer session and fall semester?"

"Yes, I guess I did."

"I think you should go. You know, new author and all that."

"That's only six weeks off, Arthur."

"Yes, but I'm pretty sure you can still get in. You know. As a guest author."

"You think I should go, huh?"

"Yes, Steven. And get a table in the dealer's room. You can sell your book."

Vegan handed him a flyer he had printed off the net.

"Hmm. That's the weekend before fall classes start. No conflict there."

"Yes, and it means all the students will be here and not busy. It's a great opportunity, I think."

"OK, I'll do it."

Steven thought about it.

"Maybe I can get Barbara to help with the dealer's room table."

"She would be terrific for that, Steven. That would likely be a great boon to sales."

The next time Barbara was over, the next morning, Bach was up watching the dappled sunlight play across her magnificent body.

She stirred, looked at him and smiled.

"G'morning, handsome."

"Good morning. Barbara, can I ask you a favor?"

"Sure."

"I'm going to the science fiction convention the weekend

before fall classes start. I'll have a sales table in the dealer's room. Would you help me with the sales table?"

"Oh, you mean do the whole 'booth bunny' thing? Sure, Steven. I can do that."

"I'd appreciate it. I can use the attention for my book."

"Yeah, I have some outfits that would be perfect for that. You know, the 'come hither' outfits."

She thought about it.

"That's funny, Steven. You've never seen any of my 'come hither' outfits."

"That's because I'm already hither."

She laughed.

"Well, it's early, so come over here and hither me again before we go do breakfast."

"Your wish is my command, milady."

He loved the sound of her laugh.

The next time Barbara came over, she brought a big backpack. Packed in it were all her 'come hither' outfits. After dinner, she showed them to Stephen one at a time.

One of them really caught his eye. A pair of Ferrari red skin-tight hot pants that emphasized just how long her legs were, and a long-sleeved painted-on iridescent-blue top that had a lot of cleavage.

"Oh, try those on, Barbara."

She stripped down on the spot and changed into the outfit, which was fun to watch all by itself.

"No undergarments under these," she said. "They would show through."

The outfit covered everything but left absolutely nothing to the imagination. The dimple of her navel, the twin bumps of her nipples, the twin dimples above her ass – even the split mound of her groin – were completely covered, yet completely visible. It was the next thing to body-paint alone.

"That's perfect, Barbara. You look like one of the babes on the cover of a 1940s science-fiction pulp magazine. If you'd be willing to wear that, that would be fantastic."

"Sure, Steven. It's my outfit, after all. And it's all in a good cause."

"We need to get you some shoes like on one of those 1940s covers. Some boots or something."

"Show me."

Bach did a search on cheesecake images of 1940s pulp magazine covers on his laptop, then streamed his display to the TV. Barbara watched as he scanned down the images.

"Wow. That outfit of mine is pretty close, isn't it?"

"Oh, it's perfect, Barbara. We just need the boots."

"There," she said, pointing. "Will those boots work?"

She was pointing at a pair of Ferrari-red ankle-high boots.

"Sure. Those would work."

"I think I've seen those on-line recently. Let me see...."

She dug out her phone and fiddled with her past searches.

"No. No. No. Oh, here it is."

She broadcast the link, and his laptop displayed it on the TV. Ferrari-red ankle boots in a Peter Pan style.

"Those are perfect, Barbara."

She bent back to her phone.

"Done."

"I should pay for those. It's deductible."

"Don't be silly. They finish out my outfit."

She looked back to the screen, where the current pulp cover showed a couple.

"We should get you an outfit like that, Steven. Then we would match."

The fellow on the cover was wearing a Ferrari-red long-sleeved shirt, open at the neck, and navy-blue pants with black, mid-calf boots. The shirt and the trousers were skin-tight, the bulge of his equipment clearly visible.

"Can I get away with that, Barbara?"

"Sure. Why not? Compared to my over-the-top outfit, that's conservative."

"I meant in the looks department."

Barbara looked him over.

"Yes. I think so. You might want to have your beard trimmed quite a bit shorter for that outfit, but otherwise you're good."

"Now to see if we can find it."

They found the boots quickly enough. They were lost on the pants – modern styles were all very loose – until they honed in on bicycle pants. They found a navy-blue pair and added that.

The top, though, was impossible.

"Wait a minute," Barbara said. "What that looks most like to me is a woman's leotard top."

She switched sites and started scrolling through pictures of women in various form-fitting tops. She stopped on one with a V-neck.

"What's your chest measurement, Steven?"

"Thirty-eight."

"Hmm. It should go that big. Let's see. Yes, here we are. What's the smallest cup size? AA. That should do it."

"Is that going to work?"

"Sure. You have pecs, Steven. It'll work fine."

Steven ordered the items.

"Oh God. Look at the time. I've gotta go."

Barbara peeled out of her outfit, then redressed in her street clothes. She jammed her convention outfit back into her backpack, then grabbed a quick hug and kiss from Bach.

"OK, Steven. See you later."

When the outfit came, Bach tried it on. It felt weird to get into the bicycle pants. They were cut for a male and had a pouch for his equipment. He arranged himself into them and was dismayed by how 'out there' he was.

If that felt weird, trying on the leotard top was ridiculous. The thing looked like it was made for a child, but it was super stretchy and he actually got it on. He was glad to see it didn't have any extra sag or space in the chest.

He put the boots on, pushing his socks down so they didn't show over the tops of the boots.

Bach felt completely ridiculous, and more than a little exposed. Then he went over to the mirror on the inside of the bedroom door to take a look.

There he was, the spaceman from the 1940s pulp magazine covers. It was perfect.

"Huh. I guess this'll work after all."

He walked back into the living room. Vegan was there.

"That looks excellent, Steven. Right off the magazine covers. That'll play really well at the convention."

"Yeah. I originally thought it was too over-the-top, but, checking it in the mirror, it looks good. Surprising."

"It looks really good, Steven. You and Barbara will be the hit of the convention."

Bach raised an eyebrow at him, and Vegan shrugged.

"I stole a peek at Barbara when she wasn't looking. You guys will look great together."

The Convention

Saturday before fall semester classes started, the big day for the dealer's room at the convention, Bach was dressed in his costume and ready to go at eight in the morning. He had twenty-four copies of his book in a box to take with him.

"How are you getting to the convention, Steven?" Vegan asked.

"I called an internet ride service. They'll be here shortly."

Vegan nodded.

"Well, break a leg. That is the correct formulation, isn't it?"

"Yes, that's right. Oops. There he is now. Bye, Arthur. See you later."

Bach hefted the banker's box and headed for the door. Vegan opened it for him and closed it behind him.

When Bach got to the convention area of the hotel, he stopped and picked up his badge at the registration counter. There was no line, it being early.

He went on into the dealer's room, which was a complete zoo as everyone was preparing their booths and tables.

"Steven!"

Turning at the sound of his name, Bach saw Barbara waving from a table. She was wearing a beach cover-up over her outfit. He walked over.

"This is our table," she said.

"Excellent. We'll get a lot of action here."

"What did you bring?"

"Twenty-four copies of the book."

"That's all?"

"If we sell out, I'll be happy. But I think it's unlikely."

Bach put the box of books down on the table and walked around the table to stand with her. She turned to block the view from the room.

"This outfit looks really good on you," she said, while running her fingernails up and down his already prominent bulge.

"Hey, cut that out. I can't afford to get excited in this outfit."

"Why not? Women buy books, too, you know."

"Even so."

Barbara went and got some refreshments for them both, and they sat behind the table waiting for the doors to open at nine. They set out some copies of the book as display items, and Bach had a ball point pen handy.

"How do you take people's money?" Barbara asked.

"I have a credit card reader on my phone."

"Ah. Handy."

The commotion all died down as the vendors completed getting ready, then the doors officially opened and the first fans came in.

"Showtime," Barbara said.

She took off her beach cover-up and stashed it in her backpack behind the table. Then she stood up behind the table to await customers.

Her outfit was even more outrageous than Bach remembered. Something about it being in public, not just in his living room. She was the next thing to naked, and on her that looked very good indeed. He was glad he was sitting behind the table, autographing books as she sold them.

Customers soon started hitting on their table, as much to talk to Barbara as anything else. They didn't all buy books, of course, but some did.

Based on the state of her nipples, Barbara was in a constant state of arousal being so scantily dressed in front of so many people, which also didn't hurt the attention she brought to their table.

It was going to be a good show.

After the message came in at noon, Vegan didn't know what to do. He certainly didn't want to simply disappear. Not be here when Bach got back from the convention.

But what choice did he have?

He looked at himself in the mirror in the master bedroom. Elaine had been convinced that Vegan was simply a human in a costume. It almost could be.

Because of their evolution of a respiratory and circulatory system, the Vegans' thorax was much bigger than it might otherwise be, and their waist and neck thicker.

Also, the circulatory system had made musculature possible exterior to the chitinous and thin legs of a normal insect. His arms and legs could indeed conceal a human.

Vegan made his decision, and called an internet ride service.

When his ride showed up, Vegan walked out of the apartment and down the walk to the waiting car. He got in the back.

The driver looked at him in the rear-view mirror.

"Let me guess. The science-fiction convention?"

"Got it in one."

The driver nodded and pulled away from the curb.

Vegan paid the admittance fee from the small leather purse he wore over his shoulder, and went on into the dealer room. No one paid him any mind, other than the occasional 'Nice costume.'

He looked around, and saw Bach and Barbara at a table. He almost didn't see them due to the swarm of fans hovering around Barbara.

Vegan walked over and up to Bach, who stood up and addressed him in a whisper.

"Arthur, what are you doing here? Everybody can see you."

"It's not a problem, Steven."

A fan walking by called out, "Hey, man. Nice costume."

Vegan turned to say, "Thank you."

He turned back to Bach.

"You see, Steven. Not a problem. But I had to see you."

"Why? What's happened?"

"My hive has been in touch with me. They're very upset."

"Oh, no. Why?"

"Apparently there's another Vegan on Earth who has an interest in science fiction. He read your book, and, well, some of the references to an insectoid alien lifeform struck too close to home. He sent it on to the hive, and they tracked it to me."

"So what happens now, Arthur?"

"They're coming to get me. I have to answer to the hive queen."

"Hide. Hide so they can't find you."

Vegan was shaking his head.

"I can't, Steven. I have an RF beacon on me. In me. They implant it so, if I die, they can find me and rescue the body before humans find me. But they can track me anywhere."

"They won't take you here, though, right? In public and all?"

"They probably could, and everybody would just think it was some elaborate cosplay skit, but they're unlikely to think that way, so no, I wouldn't expect them to."

"Well, stay here with us while I think about it."

"All right, Steven. Maybe I can help sell books."

Barbara swapped positions with Vegan and sat next to Steven. She pushed back from the table so she was still on display as an attraction.

"Steven, what's wrong? You look really upset."

"You wouldn't believe me if I told you."

"Steven, if you swore it was true, I would believe you if you told me aliens were invading."

Bach turned around in his chair to face her.

"Lady, you must be psychic."

"What? Aliens are invading?"

"In a manner of speaking."

He ran his hand through his hair. How to approach this?

"Look. Arthur here? He is my roommate, as I said. He's also a Vegan, from the planet Vega, as I said. That's not a costume."

"Steven…"

"Honest. Cross my heart and hope to die. Since early in spring semester. It's really important you believe me, Barbara."

She looked over at the alien, then back to Bach.

"OK. Proof later. So why are you upset?"

"He was not supposed to reveal himself to humans. At all. Study them from a distance. He broke the rules revealing himself to me, but he wanted to do closer study of humans. Follow me?"

"Sure."

"What's happened now is they found out he broke the rules. The other aliens. And he's in serious hot water over it. They're coming to get him."

"How did they find out?"

"That's the nasty bit. I have insectoid aliens in my book.

A GENT OF VEGA

Some other Vegan on the planet read my book and figured out some Vegan must have revealed himself to me, the author. All the Vegans on the planet have an implanted transponder so they can retrieve the body if one of them dies. So they figured out he was the only one close to where I was."

"Then they could follow him here."

"Yes, but they won't try to pick him up here. Too public."

"But if you go back to your place...?"

"Yes. They'll pick him up. And I have a problem with that."

"What's that, Steven?"

"He's my best friend."

Barbara went back to selling books, standing next to Vegan. They were a great hit. Several people wanted photographs of all three of them.

Bach mostly sat and autographed books as they were sold.

"Well, that's it," Bach said. "Six o'clock. The dealer's room is closed."

"It's a good thing, Steven. We just sold our last book."

"Really?"

"Yeah. That last one you signed was the last one, period."

"Well, then, I guess it's time to face the music, eh, Arthur?"

"Yes, Steven. I have to go. If they try to take me somewhere else and are discovered by one or two people, they may just kill them. I can't let that happen."

"All right, Arthur. I'm going with you."

"Steven, I can't recommend that course of action. It's very dangerous."

"I will accompany you, my friend, into whatever awaits us."

"I'm going, too," Barbara said.

"No, Barbara. It's too dangerous."

"Steven Bach, you are not going to go gallivanting off and

leave me wondering what happened to you. Is that clear?"

"Yes, ma'am. But I really don't recommend it."

"We better go, before they come for me here," Arthur said.

"All right, Arthur. Let me contact a ride service."

Bach fussed with his phone, then looked up.

"On the way. Let's go."

Barbara grabbed her backpack and the three of them headed for the entrance to the convention hotel.

They got to the apartment without incident, and there were no other Vegans there when they arrived.

Barbara immediately ran into the master bedroom.

"Back in a sec."

She went over to the dresser and opened the top drawer, Steven's underwear drawer. She knew he kept women's panties and hygiene products there in case someone needed them. She grabbed the box of tampons and shoved it in her backpack. She also grabbed a couple six-packs of panties in her size.

Wherever they were going, it didn't hurt to be prepared.

Thinking about it, Barbara grabbed a dozen or so pairs of briefs for Steven as well. While she was doing that, she came across a small 9mm pistol in a pocket holster, hidden under the underwear. She hadn't known he had a pistol, but it might come in handy now.

Her father had various guns, including small pistols, and he had seen to it that his daughter was trained in their use.

Barbara shoved the pistol in her backpack as well, in a side pocket.

She moved down a drawer, and added a tee-shirt, then one more drawer, and added a pair of blue jeans. Her backpack was full now.

A GENT OF VEGA

Barbara headed back into the living room and was confronted with a bizarre scene.

After Barbara ran off to the bedroom, there was an almost immediate knock on the door. Bach set his phone camera, peeking out over his waistband, to record. Vegan opened the door, and two more Vegans entered the room, closing the door behind themselves.

Bach couldn't tell the three of them apart. They spoke to each other in Vegan, which sounded like a combination of German and Arabic, but with more spitting.

<You are to come with us at the order of the hive queen.>

<I understand. I will come with you.>

<Who is this monkeyman? Must we kill him?>

<I think we must.>

Barbara came into the room from the bedroom.

<Oh. There is a second monkeyman. Do we kill them both?>

"What are they saying, Arthur?"

"They are trying to decide whether they have to kill you."

"I'd like to see them try," Barbara said, producing the pistol from her backpack.

"Arthur, you'd better convince them not to kill us or Barbara will kill them both."

"I will try, Steven."

<You cannot kill them.>

<Why not?>

<I demand Right of Witness, and these are my witnesses.>

<Monkeymen?>

<If I am charged with revealing myself to the monkeymen, who else could be my witness?>

<He has a point.>

<I hate to admit it, but you're right.>

<All right. They come along. Let's go.>

"They've decided not to kill you, Steven. Instead, you're both going along."

"Good job, Arthur. OK. Let's go."

Barbara put the pistol back in the pocket holster in the side pocket of her backpack.

"I'm ready," she said.

Vegan grabbed a twenty-four ounce sirloin steak out of the refrigerator.

<I'm ready,> he told his captors.

In Transit

The two new Vegans opened the apartment door and looked out. It was dark, and there wasn't anyone about. There was a minivan parked at the curb directly in front of the apartment door. It looked like a cargo model, with porthole windows in the back.

They hurried to the minivan and opened the side door as Vegan, Bach, and Barbara walked out to the minivan. Bach locked the apartment door behind him.

"We're going in a minivan?" Barbara asked.

"I don't recognize the brand. It looks like it's a Chinese model," Bach said.

Vegan picked up on various cues.

"No, it's one of ours."

"You're copying the Chinese?" Bach asked. "Good. Serves 'em right."

They all piled into the back, the two captors facing back and Vegan, Bach, and Barbara facing forward. One of Vegan's captors closed and secured the door with some sort of mechanism.

The interior didn't look at all like a minivan. It was just different, in a strange way. Part fifties plastic and part modern stainless steel.

"Who's driving?" Barbara asked as it pulled away from the curb.

"My captors are. I think I saw a human-looking puppet in the front seat."

Vegan looked around.

"I've never seen one of these before. Drop-offs were always

done in the country. Of course, that was a long time ago."

"How long have you been on Earth, Arthur?" Barbara asked.

"Fifty years or so."

Bach gaped at him. That was one question he hadn't thought of asking the alien.

Barbara was looking out the side window as they went along.

"Looks like we're headed out into the country," she said.

"Of course. The pickup would have to be in the country," Vegan said.

Bach, seated between them, leaned over to look out the side window next to Barbara. He was uncomfortably aware of her desirability in the skimpy outfit she still wore, and had to rearrange his bulge.

"We're turning onto a farm road now, Arthur," Bach said.

A weird vibration started in the minivan, and grew in intensity.

"Oh, it's a disguised shuttle," Vegan said.

"A what?" Barbara asked.

"You'll see."

The vibration ran up in pitch and intensity, and then the minivan leapt clear of the road and into the air. Bach and Barbara watched the world sink away beneath them.

"Holy shit," Barbara said. "That's pretty amazing, Arthur."

"Yes, it won't be long now."

"Until what, Arthur?" Bach asked.

The Vegan turned to him.

"Until we're at the ship."

"A ship? In orbit?"

"Yes."

"They're not worried it will be detected?"

"Oh, your detection technology can't penetrate our stealth

technology, Steven. Not yet, at least."

"I would think the heat signature alone would give you away, Arthur."

"Heat signature?" Barbara asked.

"Space background temperature is about two and a half or three degrees above absolute zero, Barbara. Anything one does in space releases heat – life support, if nothing else – and it should be really obvious. Like a spotlight."

"Correct, Steven. We release the heat radiation in the other direction."

Bach looked at him sharply, and Vegan just shrugged.

"We do, and so Earth can't see us."

"How far out is the ship?" Bach asked.

"Beyond synchronous orbit. Too many satellites below that level. If a satellite ran into our ship, that would be hard to hide."

"That's twenty-two thousand miles above the surface, Arthur."

"Yes, but we're already doing thirty thousand miles an hour, Steven. It won't be long."

"Why aren't we feeling the acceleration, Arthur?" Bach asked.

"That is a very long story, Steven."

Barbara continued to look out the window.

"Thirty thousand miles an hour in a minivan," she said. "Gosh."

It hadn't been an hour from taking off from the farm road when Barbara had news.

"Something big coming up. Looks like we're going to hit it."

"That's the ship," Vegan said from the other porthole window. "We'll dock inside it."

"Inside it?" Bach asked.

"Yeah. It's like a little garage."

"I hope it has air."

"Yes, Steven. It is an airlock."

They were soon inside the airlock. Once the door closed, lights came on. It was, in fact, like a little garage.

"The air will be equalizing now. It is going to be cold, though."

A tone sounded outside, and one of Vegan's captors undogged the door. There was a slight sighing sound as the door opened. Probably not exactly the same air pressure in the ship as on the ground.

One captor exited, while the other gestured them ahead.

When Barbara got out of the shuttle, she shivered.

"Brrr. One thing this outfit is not is warm."

"The ship will be much warmer," Vegan said from behind her.

They passed through an airlock door into the ship proper, and it was immediately warmer. Bach guessed it as eighty degrees.

Vegan's lead captor became their guide as he led them through the ship. They passed down various corridors until they came to a door. Their guide pushed a button on the wall and the door slid open. He waved them inside.

<These are your quarters.>

<Thank you.>

The two other aliens turned around and left, the door sliding shut behind them.

It wasn't much. There was a necessary of sorts in the corner, clearly designed for the aliens. It would make do for the humans, as long as they were willing to squat rather than sit. There was no privacy at all.

There also was a chair and a couch of sorts – more a loveseat actually – with a table between them. And there was a display on the wall.

"So are we confined, Arthur?"

"No, I don't think so, Steven."

Vegan turned around and pushed the door button on the wall. The door to the corridor slid open. He hit it again and the door slid shut.

"It is more a case that there is no other place to go. There are service facilities aboard ship, like environmental, and engineering, and drive systems, and there are crew quarters, like this. And where would one go otherwise? There is no leaving the ship."

"Yes, and no desire to sabotage a ship in which I'm riding."

"Well, I don't know about you guys, but I'm going to get out of this silly outfit. Maybe I'll put it on again when we meet with the alien queen. I have an emergency change of clothes in here."

With that, Barbara stripped down and started digging in her backpack. She came up with a pair of panties first, from Steven's stash, breaking open one of the packages. Digging further, she came up with a pair of stretch terry-cloth hot pants and a micro tube top.

A pair of flat slip-on sneakers finished out her change of clothes.

"That's not that much different, Barbara."

"No, but it's much less revealing and it's less tight on me."

"Fair enough. You got anything in there for me?"

"Yes. Jeans and a tee-shirt. Oh, and a bunch of pairs of briefs."

"Well, that's welcome."

Bach stripped out of his outfit and put on briefs, jeans, and a tee-shirt. That felt much better.

Then a thought occurred to Bach.

"Barbara, what else do you have in your backpack?"

"Well, more briefs for you and I. Maybe a dozen each. I stole your box of tampons. I found your pistol when digging in your briefs, so I brought that. My spare outfit, and one for you. My phone and my laptop and power supply. That's about it."

"You have your laptop? It's too bad we can't connect to the net from here."

"But, Steven, you can. Connect to the internet, that is. For the first three days, until we slip into the crease. The round-trip transmission times will get longer and longer, but that's not a problem for uploads and downloads. The frequency will also shift a bit, but the system here is designed to correct for that."

"Wi-Fi?"

"Yes. Through that display connection. I had heard that we stole the technology from you. It was just too handy."

"The problem is I don't know how much charge my machine has on it, Steven," Barbara said.

"There I can be no help, Steven," Vegan said. "You will not find one hundred twenty volts alternating current shipboard."

"What do you have, Steven? Surely there is power."

"Yes, but it's one hundred eighty volts direct current."

"Barbara, let me see your power supply."

Barbara handed Bach the power supply for her laptop. It was a line-switching supply, good for anything from forty volts to two hundred fifty volts, from direct current to a hundred hertz.

"We're in business, Arthur. Assuming we can figure out how to plug it in."

"The connections are here, Steven."

Bach took a look. Banana-plug sort of thing, with spin-on

nuts that could also captivate a spade terminal or bare wire. He bent the prongs out sideways on the line cord plug, then bent the ground pin out of the way.

Bach put the line cord prongs on the terminals and spun the nuts down. The pilot light came on as if it were home in his living room.

The other end of the power supply was a USB-C connector, which would work with the laptop or their phones.

"Let's try one of the phones first. If it blows up, it won't leave us without the computer."

Bach pulled his phone out of his jeans pocket and plugged it in. He got a charging update message. No problem.

"Ya gotta love line-switched power supplies," Bach said.

"So we're good for charging?" Barbara asked.

"Yup. We're good. Which means I have a request for you, Arthur."

"Name it, Steven. If I can do it, I will."

Bach raised an eyebrow at that unequivocal statement, and Vegan responded.

"You have stood by me at a time of great danger. I owe you."

"Very well, Arthur. What I want you to do is describe your space drive technology. In detail. On camera."

"What will you do with it?"

"I'm going to take those videos and upload them to a file-sharing site. I'll set a timer for, say, two months out. If I don't get back to Earth to disable the timer, the download pointers for those videos will be sent to the big players at all the top physics spots. MIT, Caltech, Stanford, Berkeley, Urbana, Jet Propulsion Laboratory. Everybody."

"To what purpose, Steven?"

"I need some cards to play here, Arthur. If the queen doesn't release all of us and return us to Earth, she's going to have to deal with an invasion of monkeymen on the near to medium term. And, since we've presumably been killed, they'll come with an attitude."

"Oh, my."

"Yes. I'm thinking she won't want that."

"I think you're right, Steven. Of course, she could respond in another way. Kill all the humans on Earth."

"I'll handle that one a different way, Arthur. She won't want to go there, either."

"Very well, Steven. She won't want to go there in any case. It's against Vegan moral principles to completely destroy another intelligent species, anyway. That's not a decision she would make by herself, as a single queen."

"How many queens are there, Arthur?" Barbara asked.

"Several per planet, Barbara. So she wouldn't make that level of decision by herself. It would only be reached after consultation among all the queens, at a convocation."

"All right, Arthur. You ready to begin recording once my phone is recharged?"

"Yes, Steven. I'm ready."

"Let's start with some introduction, Arthur. What are you?"

"I am what we call a—" Vegan made a sound like someone blowing his nose while humming 'Für Elise.' "—and which I have translated for you as Vegan. That is, from a planet orbiting the star you call Vega.

"We are an insectoid race, which has also evolved respiration, circulation, and musculature, all of which are inter-related. We are divided into three types, queens, drones, and workers. There are at least several queens per planet, each queen has perhaps a dozen drones, and the rest of us – the vast majority – are workers. I myself am a worker.

"Personally, I am an academic, and have been assigned for the last fifty years or so to studying Earth and humans. I am primarily an anthropologist of sorts, specializing in primitive races. We generally consider humans a primitive race, because you do not yet have interstellar travel.

"For the most part, our people are content to leave primitive races be, isolated on their sole planets. The study of such primitive races is generally considered to be something of an academic backwater, but I find it interesting."

"What is our situation now, Arthur? The situation you, and I, Steven Bach, and our companion Barbara Nowak, now find ourselves in?"

"We are aboard an interstellar ship bound for Vega, to see the hive queen of my hive. The rules of my study on Earth were not to make myself known to the humans there. That, of course, limits the extent of my studies, although social media has made it a lot easier. I did not have to expose myself as a Vegan to interact on social media.

"Then I broke the rules. I exposed myself, as a Vegan, to you, Steven. I chose you carefully. An academic. A loner. Someone without many friends, so it would be easier for you to keep the secret. All with an eye to deepening my research on humans. It has been successful in that regard. In fact, we became friends.

"But I was discovered. Another Vegan with an interest in science fiction read your recent novel. The description of an insectoid alien race was perhaps too close to home, and he reported it. They determined that I was the only Vegan on Earth in proximity to the author.

"So I am being taken to the hive queen to answer for having broken the rules. You both volunteered to go, against my recommendation because of the danger. I invoked my Right of

Witness to secure your passage, or they likely would not have taken you."

"What is the likely outcome of this trip, Arthur?"

"I have been thinking about this, Steven. The hive queen could do one of three things. She could return us to Earth, perhaps giving me further instructions on how to proceed. She could retain us there, on Vega, thus isolating the problem. Or she could have us killed."

"Killed – all three of us – for having contact between Vegans and humans? What is she afraid of?"

"Yes, Steven. She is afraid that, if humans knew interstellar travel was possible, and something about how to do it, that humans would achieve interstellar travel early, and come out into space to challenge the hives."

"What about friendship, Arthur? Does the queen see no possibility of friendship?"

"That would not be her first reaction, Steven. We are different, therefore we must fight."

Bach thought about it, then pursued another line.

"If they killed us, Arthur, what would they do with the bodies?"

"Your bodies, like mine, would be eaten, Steven. The hive does not waste protein."

"Are Earth mammals, generally speaking, good eating, Arthur?

"Yes, Steven. I especially like cows. They're wonderful. Better than anything back home."

"Are humans tastier even than cows, Arthur?"

"Yes, Steven, they are. Very much so. A true delicacy."

"How would you know that, Arthur?"

"When I first arrived on Earth, I was still getting set up. I was hungry and homeless. A homeless man discovered me.

Bearing in mind the rules against revealing ourselves to humans, I killed him. I didn't realize at the time that a homeless man's statements about discovering an alien would not be believed.

"Having killed him, I ate him, consistent with my culture, and as a way to hide the body.

"I wouldn't do any of that now."

"Let's suppose for a moment that, upon arriving on Vega, the queen decides to kill us, and they eat our bodies. Finding us to be so tasty, would the Vegans then be tempted to farm humans? Use the Earth as a breeding ground for humans as some sort of livestock?"

Vegan seemed truly taken aback by that, but considered it carefully.

"I hate to say it, Steven, but they might. Vegans, as I say, consider humans to be a primitive race. There are some compunctions about killing intelligent life, but they are not very strong. They could do just that. Breed humans as a delicacy."

"That sounds cruel, Arthur."

"Do you know how veal is made, Steven?"

"Let's take another tack, Arthur. Describe how your interstellar drive works."

"It's not my primary field, Steven, but I do know something about it. As someone who was given an interstellar assignment, I looked into it a bit before I left for Earth.

"Our interstellar drive is what you might call a dark-matter Bussard ramjet. The problem with a Bussard ramjet is that the density of ordinary matter in interstellar space is very thin. The resulting scoop must therefore be very large. The ubiquitousness of dark matter in interstellar space within galaxies gets away from that problem, and makes the intake scoop of the ramjet pretty small.

"As one picks up velocity, and is disturbing dark matter in this way, something like a crease develops in spacetime. The ship drops out of normal space time into a channel of its own making. Accelerations become very high, and velocity is not limited to the speed of light. In fact, speeds of thousands of times c are routinely obtained.

"As an example, we are bound for Vega, a star twenty-five light-years distant. While we will have three days accelerating and decelerating from velocities well below c on both ends, the bulk of the trip will be made in the crease in something like three days."

"But a Bussard ramjet doesn't work. They've proved it."

"Not with ordinary matter, Steven. But a Bussard ramjet with dark matter works very well."

"How do you manipulate dark matter, Arthur? We can't even detect dark matter. We just see its gravitational signature."

"Yes, Steven, but that means dark matter is affected by gravitons. Once one can manipulate gravitons, one can construct a dark matter Bussard ramjet."

"How do we not feel those accelerations, Arthur? I notice no difference in gravitation now, and we are under way, are we not?"

"We are under way, Steven. But if one is manipulating gravitons to impel dark matter through the ramjet, one can arrange that one's one position within the graviton field is at one gravity."

"Talk to me about manipulating gravitons, Arthur."

"Of course, Steven. The first thing one needs to realize is that gravitons differ from the particles that mediate the other interactions in several important ways...."

Interstellar

"OK, it's all uploaded. Now I just need to set up the time-dependent email transmission."

"Is there a way to do that, Steven?" Barbara asked.

"Yes. Commercial emailers do it all the time. Companies don't actually have someone sit there and send junk mail all the time. They have an emailer program do it for them."

"That makes sense. What about the mailing list? Who do you send it to?"

"There are several technical working groups that consider potential interstellar drive mechanisms. I would think that would be a good place to start."

"What if none of them take it seriously?"

"They don't have to take it seriously, Barbara. I just need the threat of them taking it seriously to move the queen. I need to impress on her one thing."

"What's that, Steven?"

"Don't mess with the monkeymen."

"Arthur, what can we see in this display?" Barbara asked, gesturing to the display on the wall.

"The usual shipboard things, Barbara. Engine status, velocity, acceleration, fore and aft camera views. All that sort of thing."

"We can see camera views?"

"Oh, yes."

Vegan went over to the display and turned it on. He selected the forward camera view, and there was a spectacular image of Saturn.

"What about the aft view, Arthur?"

Arthur switched the view aft. There was the sun, off-center in the view, and a tiny blue crescent in the center.

"That's Earth? In the center?"

"Yes," Arthur said, pointing to the blue crescent. "Right here."

"My gosh. So far already."

"Well, we have been traveling a full day, accelerating hard all the way."

"I have a question, Arthur. Can Earth not see us? Our rocket plume or whatever?"

"With dark matter, Steven? No, Earth cannot see our exhaust."

Bach nodded.

"Makes sense, I guess."

Bach and Barbara had tried sleeping on the loveseat last night. It hadn't worked out. There just wasn't enough room. They ended up sleeping separately, she on the loveseat and he in the big chair.

There were no blankets, and no need of any, the temperature being close to eighty degrees aboard ship.

The food, which was brought twice a day, was bland and uniform, but it did satisfy them. Probably best not to inquire about what it was or how it was made.

To pass the time, they studied. Barbara downloaded the reading lists and the books for their courses, and they spent the time working on the classes they were missing. In the event they made it home, they would not be hopelessly behind.

So passed the second day, and the third.

The fourth day, about the time they had been on board for

seventy-two hours, Arthur had some news.

"Now's the one thing that's interesting about the trip."

"What's that, Arthur?" Bach asked.

"Transitioning into the crease."

"You can see that happen?"

"Oh, yes."

Vegan turned on the display and set it to the forward view. There was nothing in that view now but stars, the bright light of Vega centered in the screen.

For a while, nothing happened. Then, as they watched, a black circle formed around Vega and the stars around it, several inches wide in the display. It grew as they watched, looking as though it was the end of a tube getting closer to them.

When it passed over them, the felt gravity in the cabin wiggled a little bit, down then back up. Arthur turned to the aft camera view, and they could see the tube extending past them, back toward the sun behind them.

"Wow," Barbara said.

"What was that wiggle there, Arthur? That gravity wiggle?"

"Yes, Steven. That was the navigator accommodating the change he needed to make in the Bussard ramjet as we passed into the crease. Some navigators are better than others. This one's pretty good. That was a minor fluctuation."

"And now we're in the crease."

"Yes, Steven. Or the tube. Whatever one wishes to call it. Our acceleration now is tens of thousands of gravities. Now we really start to cover ground."

"How can it be tens of thousands of gravities, Arthur? Force equals mass times acceleration."

"Yes, Steven. But our spacetime mass in the crease is effectively zero."

"OK. That works. And we keep this up for three days?"

"Yes, although there is a difference halfway. The navigator redirects the exhaust stream forward."

"He turns the ship around?"

"No, Steven. I said it precisely. He redirects the exhaust stream forward. The Bussard scoop must remain forward, in the direction one is traveling, whether you are accelerating or decelerating. It is much easier to redirect the exhaust than try to reconfigure the scoop."

"Got it. Well, that's certainly interesting. And then below a certain velocity, we drop out of the crease on the other end?"

"Yes, Steven. That's it exactly."

After three days in the terry-cloth shorts and tube top, they were getting pretty rank for Barbara's taste. There was water in the room, and some sort of soap, so she washed them out and set them to dry. She waited for them dressed in panties and the beach cover-up.

When they were dry, she shrugged and continued to wear just panties and the beach cover-up. It was just easier.

She also washed out her used panties.

Bach washed out his used briefs as well. Might as well have clean laundry along.

"We have another problem, Steven."

"What's that, Barbara?"

She held up a pill carrier. A round pill carrier with twenty-eight positions.

"Sixteen days left. A month after that, I start having babies. It didn't occur to me it was a problem until I started adding it up. Nine days there, nine days back, however long we're on Vega. It adds up."

"That's not a problem. We'll just stop having sex."

"That's OK with you, Steven?"

"Of course. Barbara, before that first time between you and I, it had been six *years*. Four days or four weeks – even four months – is not a long time."

"Huh. I thought of you as something of a ladies' man."

"Me? No. I was just actively looking. Not knowing what I wanted in a woman, having no experience at it, I was actively looking. That's all."

"And do you know what you want now?"

"Yes."

Bach thought about it, then went on.

"Barbara, will you marry me?"

"Is this just a way of getting around the babies problem, Steven?"

"What? Oh. No. We still shouldn't have sex after your birth control runs out. We should have babies when we really want them, not just because of the timing of your prescription. That wouldn't be fair to the baby."

"Agreed. Why the question now then?"

"Combination of things. One is that you're not totally freaking out about this whole Vega thing."

"Oh, I'm totally freaking out, Steven. Trust me."

"Yes, but it's not keeping you from thinking. When we got back to the apartment, you went stuffing your backpack with essentials. You packed essentials for me, too. When you saw the gun, you packed it."

"It just made sense."

"Yes, it did. And you saw that. When the aliens were talking about killing us, you drew the weapon. You didn't hand it to me, you were ready to do business yourself, right there and then. You recognized the problem with birth control and brought it up."

Bach shrugged.

"You've been a competent partner all along, Barbara. That's what I want in a woman. A competent partner. I see that now."

"And it's not just my looks."

"No. Oh, it's a bonus. Icing on the cake. But not the essence."

Barbara thought about it, then nodded.

"Very well, Steven. Yes, I will marry you."

"Excellent. Assuming we survive this, that will be great."

"You think that's a real issue?"

"Yes. Arthur and I were talking while you were napping. If the hive queen had merely wanted to send him new instructions, she could have done that through minions. If she simply wanted to recall him, she could have done that through minions. That he's been called to meet with her means death is very much on the table."

"Really."

"Yes. He's never met her before. With him a worker, she is as far above him as the president is above a garbage man. Even worse, because she's not elected. It's going to come down to a parlay. Between her and me."

"That's why you wanted extra cards to play."

"Exactly. I need to deflect her from her plans. Force her down a different path."

"Good luck with that, fiancé of mine."

"I'll put a ring on it when we get home, Barbara. Promise."

"That's OK, Steven. As you say, icing on the cake. Not the essence."

"I love you, Barbara."

They made love that night, on the loveseat while Arthur slept.

Sex with Barbara was always special, but that night it was—

more. More satisfying. More gratifying.

Just, more.

On the third day after transitioning into the crease, they came out of it. The ramjet had been exhausting forward – decelerating – for a day and a half.

They were watching in the forward camera as the end of the tube seemed to grow. The end of the tube was coming toward them. It passed the ship and then, in the aft camera, they watched as it receded toward Earth's distant sun.

There was the slight bobble of gravity as the end of the tube passed the ship, as before.

"We are now back in normal spacetime," Vegan said.

"Just like that?" Bach asked.

"Just like that."

"Wow. Nice," Barbara said. "Well, back to studying."

They spent the three days on the way to Vega in local space as they had the rest of the trip – studying the materials for their classes.

Barbara often lounged on the loveseat in her panties while reading. Sometimes she wore the beach cover-up, but mostly not. Bach used the armchair while reading, preferring to sit up while he read. He spent most of the time just in his briefs.

They used their phones for most of the reading, though some portions were better done on Barbara's laptop. They shared that resource, depending on what they were doing.

Even with limited wardrobe, limited furniture, and the bland food, it was a comfortable time.

They were together.

Arthur was there as well, of course. They all chatted during meals. While for them, Vega would be all new, for Arthur much of it would be new as well. He had been gone a long time, and, even when he had lived on the planet, he had never been to the queen's palace.

On the third day, they could see on the display of the ship's cameras that they had achieved orbit around the planet, which for simplicity they also called Vega.

They packed everything up in Barbara's backpack to be ready for anything. Bach was dressed in the blue jeans and tee-shirt, and Barbara wore the terry-cloth shorts and tube top.

It wasn't long before two Vegans came to their cabin.

<We will now transport you to the surface.>

<Very well> Arthur said, then to the humans, "They're taking us to the surface."

"We're ready," Bach said.

Barbara put the backpack on and nodded.

The two Vegans led them through the corridors of the ship as before, back to the little garage with the shuttle. They got in the shuttle and one of the Vegans closed and dogged the door as before.

Barbara and Bach watched out the porthole window as the shuttle descended. The planet was largely agricultural, with warrens of residences spotted throughout the fields. Some of those fields had animals grazing, but they looked, even at this distance, like no animals Bach had ever seen.

The warrens thickened as they approached a magnificent structure, the only thing of its kind they had seen.

"The palace of the hive queen," Vegan said. "I've never been there. I saw it once, from a distance."

"You've never been there, Arthur?"

"No. Never."

A GENT OF VEGA

The shuttle approached the palace, then was over it. It landed on a lower level of the multi-tiered structure. One of the Vegans undogged the door and got out. The other waved them ahead.

They got out of the shuttle to find another two Vegans waiting. The one who got out before them got back in the shuttle and closed the door.

<You will come with me,> said one of the waiting Vegans.

He led them through a doorway into the palace, then generally upward through a maze of corridors. Finally, they came to a doorway. He waved them through.

<You will wait here for the queen's pleasure. She will see you when she awakens.>

And with that, he left.

"What did he say, Arthur?"

"We're to wait here until the queen awakens, then she will see us."

"How long is that likely to be?"

"Oh, it could be days. The queens spend most of their time sleeping."

"Really?"

"Yes. But they live over a thousand years, Steven. Their metabolism is much different than mine."

"So do we get taken to the throne room, then?" Barbara asked.

"No, Barbara. We will be taken to her chamber. The queens do not move. They are unable to move. We will therefore see her in her chamber. It serves as her sleeping chamber, her dining chamber, her audience chamber."

"Well, we might as well see what we've got. It looks more comfortable than the ship, anyway."

Looking around the room, Steven saw multiple couches. Full

couches, not loveseats. There were other chambers attached, one of which held the sanitary facilities, similar to aboard ship, but more elaborate and private.

While he looked around, Bach noticed a display. He had another idea. He turned to Vegan.

"Arthur, is there Wi-Fi here as well?"

"I believe so, Steven. We found it very useful. It may not be the latest version, however."

"That's fine. Do you have access to the planetary data net?"

"I should have. We don't really practice data security the way you humans do. We are all part of the hive."

"Does that mean you can access technical and scientific data about graviton manipulation and the interstellar drive?"

"Of course. I could fifty years ago, when I studied up for my trip. Why? What do you want to do, Steven?"

"Steal the technology. Barbara, get out your laptop."

Barbara removed the laptop from its pocket in the backpack.

"Got it, Steven. What do you want me to do?"

"Fire it up. Then remove all of our textbooks and such. All your school data. All of the apps, too. Word processor, spread sheet, calendar, pictures, everything. Just leave the operating system. Like it came from the factory."

"I think I can just reset it to factory defaults, Steven. That will leave it as I got it. But why?"

"We're gonna steal everything that isn't nailed down. Their whole technology base, starting with the interstellar drive."

"But, Steven," Vegan said. "It will all be in Vegan."

"So which is easier, Arthur? Inventing gravitonics from the ground up or translating the files?"

"You have a point there, Steven."

"Start downloading stuff, Arthur. You know what we need."

The Queen

Over the course of the next two days, Vegan downloaded everything he could fit on the laptop. A textbook on gravitonics. The design of the interstellar drive, right down to the mechanical drawings and metallurgical specifications of the parts. The early experimental setups, where the field of gravitonics was developed. Absolutely everything.

"That's all I can fit, Steven. Even though Vegan is smaller than English for text data, that's all I can cram into the laptop."

"Do we have everything we need, Arthur?"

"Yes, I think so, Steven. Everything I would need, in any case, to duplicate the technology."

"Excellent. Then we're set."

"For what?"

"For whatever happens."

On the third day, a Vegan came to their chamber.

<The queen will see you now.>

"The queen will see us now, Steven."

Bach and Barbara had been waiting for this. They were completely packed, and were wearing just briefs and panties in the eighty-degree temperature. They stripped out of those and put on what they thought of as their 'Flash Gordon' outfits. They'd washed them and hadn't worn them since the convention and trip to the ship.

Bach shoved the 9mm pistol, in its leather pocket holster, into the bulge in his pants, tucking himself carefully to one side of it. When he had asked Vegan how to conceal the weapon, the alien had answered simply.

"We don't wear clothing, Steven. Anything tucked into clothing is effectively invisible to us."

<You need to come now.>

"He says we have to go now, Steven."

"Lead on. We're ready."

<You may lead us.> Vegan said.

The palace Vegan led them through the corridors of the palace, higher and higher, until Bach figured they must be in the central tower.

There the palace Vegan led them into an antechamber.

<Wait here.>

He left by the door they had come in.

There were couches, and they sat and waited.

Perhaps twenty minutes had passed when a drone came in. At least Bach assumed he was a drone. He was every bit of eight feet tall, and a spermipositor nearly two feet long hung between his legs.

"Just call me Gifted," Barbara said sotto voce, and Bach cracked a grin.

<The queen will see you now.>

They got up and went into the queen's chamber. There were several drones about. Some of them stood motionless, and Bach assumed they were asleep. Other moved about, servicing the queen.

The walls looked like they were picture windows out onto the landscape around the palace, but the blinds were down now. The room was rather dim.

The queen herself was built on the same scale as a drone, but her abdomen was the size of a small SUV. She lay on a large couch – more of a bed – and was turned to one side so she could see her guests. It was clear the bed rotated.

A drone began reciting in Vegan.

"What's going on, Arthur?"

"He's laying out the case against me for breaking the rules. Oh, and he's saying that the two of you are the monkeymen to whom I exposed myself."

When he was finished, the queen considered.

<Very well. Kill them.>

"She's told them to kill us!"

"What about your Right of Witness, Arthur? Demand your Right of Witness."

<I demand Right of Witness, Your Majesty.>

<I see no Witness. Where is your Witness?>

<He is my Witness, Your Majesty.>

Vegan pointed to Bach with this last.

<A monkeyman?>

<If the charge is that I exposed myself to the monkeymen, who else could it be, Your Majesty?>

<Oh, very well. What language does it speak?>

<English, Your Majesty.>

The queen signaled one of her drones, and he brought a device to her. It looked like headphones, but was more of a skullcap device.

"What's she doing, Arthur?"

"Learning English, so she can speak with you."

"Did we get that device in the downloads, too?"

"Oh, yes."

"Good."

After maybe ten minutes, the queen waved the device away, and the drone who brought it to her took it away.

"So, monkeyman, you stand as Witness for—" She made a noise like someone gargling with ball bearings, which Bach took to be Vegan's name in Vegan.

"Yes, Your Majesty."

"What can you possibly say that will amend my will in this matter, monkeyman?"

"I think you must consider that the defendant only exposed himself to me, Your Majesty. A known loner, with no friends, who had no opportunity to pass this knowledge on to another. That he did so in order to better study humans, the charter to which he was assigned, for the benefit of Your Majesty. And that I did, in fact, keep his secret."

"And what of this other?"

"She was exposed only in consequence of your agents appearing to bring the defendant to you, Your Majesty."

"Nothing you say alters my will in this matter, monkeyman."

"Does the defendant then have no rights, Your Majesty? You consider yourself an advanced society. Is there no consideration of motive? Of impact? Of rehabilitation?"

"Workers do not have rights. Only queens have rights."

"Oh. Yes. We once had such a system, Your Majesty. We overthrew it centuries ago. That's a very atavistic point of view for an advanced society."

"Queens are necessary for procreation, monkeyman. We're special in that sense."

"Yes, of course. But are queens not replaceable, as well, Your Majesty? Were a queen to die, is she not replaced? What is to prevent the workers from rebelling against such a rule? Could they not keep a queen in captivity for procreative purposes alone, and rule themselves?"

"Nonsense."

"Your Majesty, where I come from, one of our most popular political slogans is 'Workers of the world, unite!' Could that not happen here, if workers rights are not respected?"

"I have heard enough. My will in this matter is decided."

"In that case, I am saddened to have to kill Your Majesty."

"You cannot harm me."

Bach drew the pistol.

"On the contrary, Your Majesty. Do you know what a firearm is? A pistol?"

Clearly she did, for her antenna stood straight up.

"Please tell your drones to keep still, Your Majesty. If I get nervous they are moving against me, I might shoot while I have the opportunity."

<Remain still.>

"She told them to remain still, Steven," Vegan said.

"Thank you, Your Majesty. I think Your Majesty is making a terrible mistake, and I should like to tell you why."

"The floor is yours, monkeyman."

"The first thing is that, on the way here in your ship, I recorded a series of conversations between the defendant and myself about your interstellar technology. How it works and the like. I then uploaded those conversations to a computer back on Earth.

"I've set those interview files to be sent to all of Earth's most prominent scientists in two months. If I do not return to Earth, to stop that transmission, those interviews will be enough to set them on the path to an interstellar drive.

"Within ten, or fifteen, or twenty years, hordes of monkeymen will be out among the stars. You will have visitors here on Vega.

"On another point, the other human here with me is a queen. A young queen, to be sure, but a queen nonetheless. I am her primary drone. Were you to kill a queen...? Well, what I will say about that is that humans hold a terrible grudge, Your Majesty. They will not come out among the stars as your friends.

"And yet, Your Majesty, being friends is possible. The defendant and I have proved it. He is my best friend, and I volunteered to appear before you on his behalf knowing full well the danger.

"Humans will eventually discover gravitonics and the interstellar drive, Your Majesty. Whether we are friends when we do is largely in your hands here and now."

"There is another alternative, monkeyman. We could put an end to the threat of the monkeymen by incinerating their world while they are still constrained to a single planet."

"You could, Your Majesty, but I provide two caveats.

"One is that we are very hard to kill. Oh, not individually, no. But together we are very difficult to kill. Every one of us is drone or queen. There are no asexual workers. That means we reproduce quickly. You must be sure to kill every single one of us. If even one pregnant queen survives, we will be upon you within a short number of years.

"The other is that, while your authority is vast within your own hive, Your Majesty, I understand you cannot act in such a way against the monkeymen on your own authority."

"That last is true."

The queen thought about it, then decided.

"Very well, monkeyman. Have it your way."

<Return them all to Earth. I will take it up with the Convocation.>

"Steven, she's returning us to Earth."

Bach replaced the pistol in its pocket holster and bowed to the queen. For her part, she made a shooing-away gesture, and a drone came to guide them back to the anteroom. The palace guide came to escort them back to their chamber.

<You will remain here while transport is prepared.>

He left them there.

"I must say, Steven, that was well played," Barbara said. "And you gave me my rightful place as your fiancée, as a queen."

Bach shrugged.

"It was the terminology she understood. And it's true, for that matter. Men are much more upset about the killing of a woman than a man."

"But you've only delayed her, Steven," Vegan said. "She will take it to the Convocation. The united queens may decide to incinerate Earth."

"How often are the convocations, Arthur?"

"Every two hundred years, Steven. It is a major disruption moving the queens. They don't travel well."

"When's the next one, Arthur?" Barbara asked.

"The last one sent me to Earth. That was fifty years ago. So we only have a hundred and fifty years left."

Bach threw back his head and laughed, while Vegan looked concerned.

"A hundred and fifty years, Arthur? A hundred and fifty years ago we were just getting into electricity. We didn't even have cars yet."

"So you don't think it's a problem, Steven?"

"Arthur, I will be very surprised if I don't see the queen again, after I travel to Vega in a starship of my own making."

The day after their interview with the queen, a palace Vegan came by their chamber. He dropped off two small suitcases, setting them inside the doorway. He left without a word.

"Good," Vegan said. "My luggage is here."

"Your luggage, Arthur?" Bach asked.

"Yes. On the chance that our audience with the queen proved successful, I requested more gold with which to finance our efforts."

"How much is there, Arthur?"

"Three hundred pounds. That's about as much as I can carry."

"Three hundred pounds?"

"Yes, Steven. Will that be helpful? We could leave it here if not."

There were about fourteen and a half troy ounces per pound, so three hundred pounds was, hmm, call it forty-three hundred and fifty troy ounces, which at current prices of around thirty-five hundred a troy ounce, was a bit over fifteen million dollars.

"That will be very helpful, Arthur. We'll take it with us."

"Very well."

Barbara walked over to the suitcases. She tried to lift one and failed.

"Wait," she said. "That's all gold?"

"Yes, Barbara," Bach said. "In one-troy-ounce bars. Over four thousand of them."

"That's ridiculous. How does Arthur get them?"

"It's a waste material here, Barbara."

"I need to finance my studies on Earth, and so they let me take gold bars with me," Vegan explained. "I can take as much as I want. They have no use for them here."

"That's over ten million dollars," she said.

"At current spot prices, it's over fifteen million," Bach said. "And Arthur has another ten million already on Earth."

"A little over twelve million, Steven. I don't spend much."

"So we have twenty-seven million dollars?" Barbara asked.

"And change," Steven said. "That should come in handy, eh?"

"Oh, I would think. That's ridiculous."

"We're going to need it, Barbara."

She raised an eyebrow at Bach.

"You don't think the graviton research is going to be free, do you?"

Her eyes got very wide.

"Good job, Arthur," Bach said to the alien. "I didn't even think of that."

"Your mind was on other things, Steven."

Return To Earth

As they waited for transport, they began to wonder whether the queen would go back on her word. At least the food was much better here in the palace than it had been aboard ship.

"Has she gone back on her word, Arthur?" Bach asked.

"That would be unusual, Steven, if not unprecedented. The queen need never go back on her word. Her word, after all, is law."

"OK, but I'm getting nervous."

It was toward the end of the second day after the interview with the queen that a palace Vegan showed up.

<The ship to Earth is preparing to depart. You will come with me now.>

"The ship is ready, Steven," Vegan said.

"All right, Arthur. Just a minute."

Bach and Barbara had been lounging in briefs. He now put on the blue jeans and tee-shirt and Barbara put on the terry-cloth shorts and tube top, all freshly washed. Bach placed the firearm, in its pocket holster, in the front pocket of his jeans. He tucked the spare magazine in his other front packet.

"All right, Arthur. Let's go."

With Bach watching for trouble, Barbara with the backpack, and Vegan carrying his suitcases, they followed the palace Vegan down, down, down through the palace. Eventually, they arrived at the landing pad on the wing of the palace, where the shuttle waited.

Two Vegans waited with the shuttle. Bach had begun to

think of them as the pilot and the load master. The pilot got in first and they followed, as the load master put Vegan's suitcases in the storage compartment in the back. Barbara kept her backpack with her as carry-on.

The load master got aboard and closed and dogged the door, then the shuttle began to whine with the weird vibration as before. It leapt into the air, and the palace fell behind them.

The load master from the shuttle showed them to their cabin. The cabin he showed them to was larger by about half again than the cabin they had had previously. The necessary and sink were in their own compartment, and the furniture was different. In particular, there was a full couch, with a deeper seating surface.

"Well, this is better than before," Bach said. "Different ship?"

"Not necessarily, Steven," Vegan replied. "I think this is the VIP cabin."

"Why the VIP cabin?" Bach asked. "Not that I'm complaining."

"Because you told the queen I was a queen," Barbara said.

"That could be, Steven," Vegan said.

"OK, that makes sense," Bach said. "She's hedging her bets on us going forward as friends, pending the decision of the Convocation."

"Oh, that couch looks good," Barbara said.

"I think we can both fit on there," Bach said.

"That's why I like it."

"I'll just sleep in the sanitary compartment," Vegan said. "Give you guys some privacy for a change."

"You're going to sleep in the bathroom, Arthur?" Barbara asked.

"Yes. When I'm sleeping, it doesn't matter to me where I am."

"All right. If you're sure it's OK."

"What's your birth control situation, Barbara?" Bach asked when they were alone.

"I have four more pills left. There's four more days to Earth from that point. I'll get right back on when I get home. My prescription is mail-order, and it'll be waiting for me. But we're OK. I shouldn't be able to get pregnant for a month after going off."

"No. It doesn't make any sense to take chances on stuff like that, Barbara. I can wait."

"I love you, Steven."

She kissed him before continuing.

"But that means we have four days left. We should make the most of it."

And they did.

The couch was great.

When the food came in the morning, it was the better food of the palace, not the ship's rations of the trip out. It was the VIP cabin, and that was that.

They spent most of their time lounging in briefs and panties. There was no homework to do on the way home, as Barbara had deleted all the textbooks and study materials to make room for as much of the Vegan tech database as they could steal.

Mostly they cuddled and napped on the couch. The removal of the nervous apprehension of the interview with the queen had left them exhausted.

Sometimes they played solitaire on their phones, or talked with Vegan.

They watched the crease form on the third day out, and watched it recede on the sixth day. After that, they watched the Sun, and eventually Earth, grow in the forward view screen.

They abstained from sex the last four days, but there were many other forms of amorous play than just coital sex, and Barbara was good at all of them. Bach, for all his lack of experience, did his best.

They were comfortable, and content.

They were going home.

<The shuttle is ready for you.>

"The shuttle is ready."

"And so are we. Lead on, Arthur."

The load master put Vegan's suitcases in the storage compartment as before, and they rode down to the surface. The shuttle landed on the deserted farm road, and then they drove on into town, dropping them all at Bach's apartment.

Having spent nine days in transit each way and five days on Vega, they had been gone twenty-three days. Where they had left on the Saturday evening of the convention, their phones, back in contact with the network, let them know it was Monday evening of the fourth week of classes.

For all that it was a short time, they had both changed a great deal.

They had faced execution, stared down an alien ruler, and made her see their way of things. They had grown in their relationship, come to a deeper understanding and appreciation each of the other, and formalized their bond.

It was two different people who entered Bach's apartment that night than had left it three weeks before.

Arthur Vegan, for his part, had also changed. His long association with humans, especially the six months spent with

Bach, had allowed him to see his own race from outside itself. His summary sentence of execution at the hands of his hive queen had soured him on the system as it was. There must be a better way.

He now thought of other Vegans as 'they.'

A man without a country, he lived between.

Returned to the apartment, the shuttle having departed, they took stock of their situation.

"Steven, I have *got* to get into some truly clean clothes. And I need to get to my BC pills. And I have a full schedule tomorrow. Can we just say goodbye for now, and I'll see you tomorrow night?"

"Sure, Barbara. I have a bunch of things to do here before the place is habitable again. And I have some classes tomorrow as well."

"All right. Thank you."

She came over and kissed him.

"I love you, Steven."

"I love you, Barbara."

As she prepared to head out, Bach had another idea.

"Barbara, take a ride share. Don't walk it. Money's not an issue. Not anymore."

"All right."

She fiddled with the phone, then they cuddled on the couch for the few minutes it took for the ride to show up.

"OK. I'm off."

"See you tomorrow, dear."

When she left, Bach went into the bedroom and changed into fresh jeans and tee-shirt. Shower later.

He went to the fridge and got a beer. He also grabbed one for Vegan.

"Here you go, Arthur."

The alien was seated in the big armchair, and accepted the beer with a sigh.

"One thing I really missed the last few weeks, Steven, was the simple act of having a beer."

He opened the can, inserted his proboscis, and sucked at the foamy liquid.

"Ahhh."

"You almost never had another one, Arthur."

"Yes, I know, Steven. If not for you, I would be dead. And you volunteered to come along, knowing full well the danger."

"You would have done the same for me, Arthur."

"Yes. I likely would have. You know, Steven, I never fully understood that quote before. I feel it now."

"Which quote?"

"'Nothing in life is so exhilarating as to be shot at without result.'"

Bach nodded. After his own recent experience, he couldn't disagree.

"So what now, Steven?"

"On the short term, we need to replenish the refrigerator. All our stock of fresh meat and vegetables is dead. And I need to pay the rent. It's several days late as it is, and I'll have to pay the late fee.

"On the medium term, I need to finish my degree, which I will complete this semester assuming I can catch up.

"And on the long term, we need to develop gravitonics and deploy interstellar ships before the hive queens decide to destroy us all."

"Let's start with the refrigerator."

Bach chuckled. He checked the time.

"OK. I think I can still get a shopper if I'm willing to pay the surcharge for the evening bunch."

"Do it, Steven. I could really use a nice steak right now. There's just nothing the Vegans have that tastes like beef."

After dinner, Bach made an early night of it. He took a shower and went to bed. It was great sleeping in a real bed again, although he missed Barbara.

The next morning, he took another shower – a luxury they had not had for three weeks – and performed all his normal personal hygiene. He used shampoo and conditioner, shaved his neck, used deodorant and after shave – everything he had learned under Vegan's tutelage and had to forego for three weeks.

It felt good to be able to do again what had at first seemed such a chore.

On his way to his first class, he stopped by the rental office and paid the rent, including the late fee. Between classes, he stopped in at the stylist and had his hair and beard trimmed.

She noticed something different about him.

"What have you been up to? You seem different somehow," she said.

"Overseas trip."

"That'll do it. Makes you grow up in a hurry to see how other people live, doesn't it?"

"Oh, yes. It sure does."

Returning to his apartment after his final class, Bach called Candace and Diana to apologize for not being in touch for three weeks, and also to tell them he had gotten engaged. Both of them were philosophical about it, but Candace offered more.

"Just so you know, honey. You'll always be my 'the one that got away.'"

"That's sweet, Candace. Don't you worry. There's a guy out

there for you, and he'll be one lucky bastard to get you."

"You always say the sweetest things, Steven. Take care now."

"You, too, Candace. Be good."

"I'm always good. Ta."

Bach couldn't argue with her there.

Barbara came by that evening. She came with a ride share and she brought two shopping bags of stuff with her.

"I brought some things, Steven. Clothes, toiletries, that stuff. Unless I'm being presumptive?"

"Oh, no. Not at all, Barbara. I hadn't thought to suggest it."

"Oh, good. So who's cooking tonight, me or you?"

"I'm already started."

"Great. How can I help?"

After dinner they sat on the sofa with beer. Vegan joined them.

"How are your classes going to be?" she asked.

"Good. I won't have any trouble catching up. What about you?"

"I may have to put cost accounting off a semester. I have a bunch of slack in my last semester, so I can do that if I have to. It's just a completely different way of looking at things."

"Well, it's a good thing I don't have to do that. I don't have a next semester. I graduate in January."

"Lucky you to do it all in three and a half years."

"Uh, six and a half years. I've been a part-time student while I had a job all the while. Barbara, I'm twenty-four years old. Twenty-five by the time I graduate."

"Ooo. You mean I'm marrying an older man? Exciting."

The next morning, Bach made pancakes for them both on the

two-burner griddle she had bought him as a present after their first evening together. He had used it with her before, of course, but today it was extra special.

They were back on Earth, they were together, and together they would stay.

Finances And Family

As fall semester carried on, several things came up. First was finances, between Bach and Vegan.

They had carried on with Bach's second novel. It seemed anti-climactic, in some sense, after the interview with the Vegan hive queen, but Bach was only part-time in this, his final semester, and he needed something to do. At the same time, he was not yet free to dive into the gravitonics, which he predicted would consume him.

As he was finishing up the second novel, Vegan brought up their finances.

"Steven, I no longer think it is appropriate that I pay you rent. You need much more financing to undertake the gravitonics project."

"What do you suggest, Arthur?"

"That you simply consider my gold supply to be ours, Steven. That we work together on the project, and we use the gold supply as necessary to get the project done."

"Arthur, did you just give me a half share in twenty-seven million dollars?"

The Vegan chuckled.

"I guess I did, Steven, unless it is your intention to turn it down."

"Well, that wouldn't be my first option, no. But are you sure, Arthur?"

"Of course. Now that we've been blessed by the hive queen, if I ever need any more, I can just ask for it and they'll bring it to me."

That was a new one on Bach. Gold on demand. It made

sense if you knew how worthless it was in Vegan space, but even so.

"All right, Arthur. If you're good with it, I certainly am."

"We're a team, Steven. We have a project, and we have funding. What more could I want?"

The second thing that came up was the need for an engagement ring. Bach had promised to put a ring on his question, and he felt some urgency about it.

He asked Vegan about it.

"Take three ounces of gold to the jeweler's and get her a nice ring, Steven."

"Ten thousand dollars worth, Arthur?"

"Yes. Don't skimp on her. We need her."

"Well, I need her. That's sure."

"Yes, but we need her. Steven, what do you know about money?"

"Well, …."

"Strike that. What do you know about corporate finance?"

"Nothing," Bach said.

"And what is Barbara's degree in?"

"Corporate finance."

"And what is your degree in?"

Bach's degree was in Engineering Physics. The application of physics principles in the engineering world. That was a perfect background for working through the issues likely to be associated with the development of gravitonics and the interstellar drive.

Corporate finance it wasn't.

"All right, all right. I understand. But that's not why I want to marry her, Arthur."

"Of course, it isn't. Then again, we're sitting on over twenty-seven million dollars. You do *not* want to disappoint her."

"OK, that's probably fair. Though I think it won't matter to her. She may even get pissed about me spending so much money on her."

"At least that's being angry in the right direction, Steven. Trust me on this one."

So Bach had gone out to a jeweler. He selected them on the basis of a recommendation from a professor he had asked. They were more than willing to take three bars of gold bullion, at two percent below spot, against a suitable engagement ring.

He even got significant change back.

It had to be sized, of course. Bach got her size from a ring she wore, one evening while she was in the shower and had set the ring on the vanity in the bathroom.

When he had picked it up, in its black velvet case, he kept it in his pocket. That evening, after dinner, they were sitting on the sofa winding down from the day. Vegan, by prearrangement, was in the second bedroom, so they were alone.

"Barbara, will you marry me?"

"I already said yes, silly."

"But I didn't have the right to ask the question. Now I do."

He produced the jewelry case.

"Oh, Steven."

"Open it."

Barbara took it and opened it, and she gasped.

"Oh, Steven. It's beautiful."

Barbara took it out of the case and put it on. It fit perfectly, of course.

"It's like it was made for me. But, Steven, can you afford such an extravagant ring?"

"Yes. Besides, you're worth it."

"Oh, Steven. I don't think I've ever been happier."

The third thing that came up was family. Before getting married, they had to do the rounds, of course. Neither family knew anything about the person their son or daughter had chosen.

There was apprehension about that at both ends, and on both sides of the aisle.

"I hope my parents like you, Steven."

"I hope my parents like you, too, Barbara, but if they don't, they don't. C'est la vie."

"Oh, I know. But it would be so much nicer if everybody liked everybody."

Bach nodded. There was no disagreement there.

Then there was the logistics. Barbara was also a statie – that is, an inside-the-state student. They both had gone to the state university and took advantage of lower in-state tuition.

Their parents even lived in roughly the same direction, forming a big triangle on the map.

Barbara's parents made a big deal of Thanksgiving, whereas Bach's parents didn't. Bach's parents made a big deal of Christmas Day, however, while for Barbara's parents the Christmas season was one long holiday.

"So it's decided, Steven? We do my parents on Thanksgiving, and your parents on Christmas Day, but we hit my parents on the way home from Christmas."

"That works."

"Oh, it'll be so fun to introduce you to Daddy."

"We'll see."

There was another wrinkle. Barbara, who had brought boyfriends home before, knew that her parents would be happy to have the kids stay over – in separate bedrooms. So they planned on staying at a local hotel the Wednesday and Thursday nights of Thanksgiving weekend.

Bach's parents – after his studious ignoring of the female sex for so many years – were so happy to see him settling down, his mother just asked, 'One bedroom or two, dear?' She took the answer – 'One.' – in stride.

The remaining question was how to get there. He took that question to Vegan.

"Buy a car, Steven. Get a new one, so you're not inheriting someone else's problems."

"Really, Arthur?"

"Yes. You're going to need a car for the company anyway. Make it a company car. Talk to Barbara about it. She'll know how to handle it."

"That makes sense."

"Get a US make, so you've got dealers all over. A premium brand from one of the majors. Cadillac or Lincoln. Something like that. Makes you look successful. Get the smaller model, but something that seats four. Smaller model will be sportier, everybody will get that."

"You sound so sure."

"I am sure, Steven. Go buy a car. Talk to Barbara first."

"That makes a lot of sense, Steven. It really does. But to have a company car, you need a company, so I'll have to run the incorporation papers through."

"Is that hard?"

"No. I'll have a lawyer do it. There's one outfit in town most people use for that. We'll use them. Then we set up a bank account, and run everything through that, including buying a car. That'll be a hundred thousand or so."

"Will they sell a car to a brand-new company, Barbara?"

"Of course. Taking a car and not paying for it is grand theft auto. They know most people aren't going to do that. It'll be fine. One question is lease or buy. I lean to buy for the first car, maybe lease for the second."

"The second?"

"There's two of us, remember. So what's the company name?"

"Graviton Dynamics."

"Ooo. I like it. Graviton Dynamics, Inc."

She made a note in her laptop.

"Now I've got another question. What have you been living on since you quit your job?"

"Arthur's been giving me sub-rent."

"Sub-renting at a profit?"

"Yeah. A big profit, actually."

"OK. I can handle that. Going forward, we need to give ourselves salaries. Like, a hundred thousand a year for you, fifty thousand for me part-time until I get my degree, then a hundred thousand for me, too."

"Two hundred thousand a year and a company car, Barbara?"

"That's not that much. Not for high-flyer entrepreneurs. I'm thinking it maybe should be half again or double that."

"But what'll we do with all that money?"

"Where are you going to do graviton research, Steven? The spare bedroom? The kitchen table? No, we need to move to a much bigger place, maybe with an industrial space. Some of that the company can pay for, but it's going to increase our spending by a lot."

"Gosh. I guess I hadn't even thought that far ahead."

"That's OK. That's what I'm for. I'll get the company incorporated and set up a bank account. Then you can buy the car. Decide what car you want. It won't take me long."

The next day, Bach got a call from Barbara.

"Who's the president of Graviton Dynamics?"

"You are. The president should be a finance person. Make me the chief technology officer."

"Got it. Thanks."

Bach shook his head. They weren't even married yet, and he was already working for her.

Stanley Nowak watched the car pull up the driveway. A sleek new Cadillac sedan, black, with darked-out windows. He was prepared to dislike someone who drove such a car – especially a fresh college graduate – but he set that aside.

The young man who got out, by contrast, looked like the sort of man Nowak instinctively trusted. Blue jeans and blue denim jacket over a plaid flannel shirt. Tallish, and in shape. Shortish to medium-length hair and a beard, well trimmed.

Nowak walked out to meet them.

"Well, here we go," Bach said as he put the car in Park.

"Oh, c'mon. It'll be fun," Barbara said.

They got out and Stanley Nowak came up to greet them.

"Daddy!"

Nowak got a big hug and a kiss from his daughter.

"Daddy, I want you to meet Steven."

The men shook hands.

"It's good to meet you, sir."

"Call me Stan."

Nowak turned to Barbara.

"Your mother's in the kitchen getting Thanksgiving dinner started."

They turned to walk to the house. Twenty feet from the car, the car beeped and locked itself. Bach started a bit at that, and Nowak noticed.

"Rental?" he asked.

"Company car. I wanted to go for the Corvette, but our company president here—" He indicated Barbara. "—said No."

"Have to have room for company," she said.

"As company president, it'll be her car more than mine anyway," Bach said.

Nowak relented on his feelings about the car. Buying his daughter a Cadillac was OK with him, and the blacked-out windows made her safer. No one would see it was a woman traveling alone.

As soon as they got inside, Barbara went into the kitchen to help her mother with dinner, while the men sat in the living room.

For a young man, Bach was unexpectedly mature. He had the air of having seen the elephant, unusual in a new college grad. For that matter, Nowak had noticed the same thing about his daughter. Both of the youngsters had matured, had a quiet confidence about them that usually came from having prevailed in a very tight spot.

He found himself liking Steven Bach. Not a boy, like the ones Barbara had occasionally brought home, he was a man.

"Unusual, to start a company so young," Nowak said.

"Yes, Stan, but we have a compelling technology."

"What's that?"

"Manipulating gravity."

"I haven't heard of that, Steven. Some new breakthrough?"

"Yes. It's unique to us."

"Sounds expensive."

"It will be, but we have our first funding already."

Nowak nodded. Impressive. There must be something to it.

"And you made Barbara president."

"Yes, Stan, the finance side is all hers. I'm the technology guy, she's the financial whiz."

"She has other skills, too, Steven. We never had a son, and I'm afraid I took it out on her. Taught her how to shoot, for one thing."

"Yes, I know. That's already come in handy."

"How so?"

"That's nothing I'd like to share, Stan."

Nowak nodded. Being able to keep one's mouth shut was a positive trait.

"Were the police involved?"

"No."

"Good. Very good."

The women came in then, the big first push toward Thanksgiving dinner completed. Bach was introduced to Barbara's mother, and the conversation turned lighter, with talk of the wedding and their plans to buy a house.

But Stanley Nowak already knew what he had wanted to know about this young man. Whatever had happened to them, it had been serious, they had prevailed, and they had done it together.

That was good enough for him.

Later that evening, on the way back to their hotel, Barbara had the results.

"Daddy likes you, Steven. When you were out of the room, I asked him. He said, 'He's a good catch, honey. He's a good man.' He always called the other people I dated 'boys.'"

"I like him, too, Barbara. I understand him."

One day between Thanksgiving and Christmas, when Bach and Barbara were both at classes, Vegan got a phone message from the Cadillac saying someone was messing around with the car.

Vegan looked out the window and saw some young man trying to get into the car, parked right in front of the apartment.

Vegan walked out and confronted him.

"May I ask what you're doing?"

"Fuck off, asshole."

Then the young man looked at him. Vegan leaned forward and gnashed his mandibles while reciting the Vegan alphabet, which sounded like someone had dropped a couple of live hamsters into a blender.

"Holy shit!"

The young man actually shit himself while getting away. Vegan chuckled and went back into the apartment.

The word got around, and the Cadillac wasn't messed with after that encounter.

The Christmas visit with Bach's parents was much less fraught, at least from Bach's point of view. Barbara was beautiful, she was smart, and she loved their son. What was not to like?

Bach would always treasure the memory of sitting around the kitchen table early on that first Christmas morning over coffee with his parents, with his mom and Barbara both in their flannel pajamas.

They stopped through at Barbara's parents on the way

home. Bach was surprised when Barbara told him they didn't need to stay at a hotel anymore. Her parents had relented, and they were allowed to stay in her bedroom the night they stayed over.

It had been Stanley Nowak who had overruled his wife on the issue.

"They're adults now, Kate. Their sleeping arrangements are none of our business anymore."

Reverse Engineering

Barbara pretty much took up residence in Bach's apartment once they got back from Vega. While Bach and Barbara were in classes, Vegan worked on translation of the materials they brought back from Vega, beginning with the textbook on gravitonics.

The anthropologist found it slow going. He had all the words, but they didn't make sense to him. It wasn't his field, and quantum mechanics was hard enough to understand even if it was your field.

He finally took the issue to Bach.

"It's not going very well, Steven. It's just not my field. I have all the words, but they make little sense to me."

"Yeah, that would make it tough."

Bach thought about it, then had an idea.

"Arthur, didn't you tell me the learning widget – the headset the queen used – would work on humans?"

"I believe so, Steven. It works for workers, drones, and queens, and they are anatomically very different. That's not my field, either, however."

"If it did, would it work to teach Vegan to English as it does to teach English to Vegan?"

"That's certainly true. The dictionary it contains is not one-directional."

"So could we build that first? Teach me Vegan?"

"Yes, Steven, but a human can't pronounce Vegan. We have many more sounds than humans, and you can't even make most of them. We can make all of yours, but not vice versa."

"But I don't need to be able to speak it to translate the book, Arthur. Just read it. And quantum mechanics is my field. Part of it at least."

Vegan opened his mandibles to speak, then closed them. He started again.

"You're right, of course. I had discounted humans' ability to learn Vegan because of the speech issue, but that doesn't apply to reading."

"So how do we make this machine, Arthur?"

Vegan worked on the language teacher while Bach and Barbara were at classes throughout November and December of that year.

There were two major pieces to the device. One was the headset and the circuitry that drove it. The other was the software that prepared the signal to the headset from the Vegan-English dictionary. This last could be done on a laptop.

Vegan concentrated on the software. He made good progress on it and was able to replicate the signal diagrams given in the Vegan design specifications for the device.

It was refreshing after having made so little progress on the gravitonics textbook.

The hardware would have to wait for Bach's availability, after classes ended for the semester.

Fall classes ended just before Christmas.

When Bach freed up after getting back from Barbara's parents, they dove into the hardware specifications together. Bach had taken an electronics course as part of his studies.

"This is the circuit diagram, Steven."

"All these symbols are strange, Arthur."

"Of course, the symbols are different. Some of them I got

right away. Others not so much."

"Yes, I can see that. These ones with three leads are probably transistors. Most of them anyway. They have a consistent symbol. Mostly. Probably the difference between NPN and PNP transistors. This looks like an H-bridge, so I can figure out which is which from that."

"It's the two-lead components that are hard, Steven. I tried to translate the units. I think I got them all right."

"OK. Ohms, farads, henrys. Those I get."

"The units on this one translated into volts. I don't get that one."

"Probably a zener diode, Arthur. That looks like a zener clamp right there."

"So you understand this diagram?"

"Mostly. I want to get it in my own familiar symbols and then analyze it. What's surprising to me is that it isn't one of those widgets with everything built into a single chip."

"We don't have a consumer market, Steven. There's no advantage in all the cost needed to do that for a limited run."

"OK, Arthur. I can see that. So let's redraw this with the proper symbols."

Bach redrew the circuit on the laptop, using the standard component symbols.

"I don't know, Arthur. Something doesn't look right, but I can't put my finger on it. It doesn't make any sense that this would be a PNP transistor."

"Would it make a difference that Vegan voltage is backwards from human voltage, Steven? We label 'plus' as the side that has the extra electrons, which are positive in our nomenclature."

Bach looked at him dumbfounded for a second, then flipped the diagram upside-down.

"OK. That makes sense. So this H-bridge has got the NPNs here, and the PNPs there. Which makes this transistor an NPN. Hmm. That means I have the zener diode backwards, too."

He stared at it the corrected diagram.

"Yeah, that makes a lot more sense, Arthur. I think we're pretty close."

Bach looked at the mechanical drawing for the headset.

"And these inductors here at the right end of the circuit diagram are the coils in the headset, shown here. Which is how the thing affects the brain. Much is clear now. I think we can build this device."

"But how do we test it, Steven?"

"Normally, one would do animal testing first. To test for safety and effectiveness. We can test for safety, I suppose, but what would indicate effectiveness? That's the puzzle."

The other thing Bach was doing was looking at real estate. What he wanted was a property that was private – so Vegan could roam around outside – and that was zoned for residential and light commercial, like an office park. Hopefully it had a house on it already, but it didn't need to be much for the three of them.

That said 'county' to him. That is, a property not inside city limits.

Bach and the real estate agent went around looking at properties, and he soon found a viable option. Half of a quarter quarter-section – twenty acres – that was wooded. It had a small vacation house on it, with three bedrooms.

The small house and no garage meant it was cheap as such properties go. Half a million or a little more.

Bach had been looking without Barbara. She had managed

to complete cost accounting last semester, so she had a light semester, but looking was time-intensive.

They made a trip out to the property together, along with the real estate agent. They picked him up in the Cadillac. When Bach drove the driveway to the house, nestled among the trees, Barbara was enthusiastic.

"Oh, it's so pretty. And in among all the trees? Steven, it's perfect."

"Better yet. There are several hundred acres of state forest behind the property. It's like having the woods, without having to buy them."

They toured the house. Barbara was happy with it.

"I was afraid it would be too small."

"After living in an apartment, Steven? It's perfect. And that extra bedroom means we actually have a guest room."

"No garage for the Caddy."

"Yes, but you're going to put up a steel building, right? Put a garage door in it."

"Company storage for the company car?"

"Yes, of course. Make it a two-door garage. Make the building a little bigger if you have to."

"The other issue is we don't actually have half a million dollars. Or the credit rating to get a mortgage."

"No. The company buys the property, Steven. The company has the money. Then we rent the house with the money the company is paying us."

"You're kidding."

"Nope. Perfectly good with the tax man."

"What about the building? The company builds that, yes?"

"Yes, on the front five acres. We lease the back fifteen acres with the house on it. We even have right of way on the driveway."

"What about if the company goes bankrupt? The creditor gets the property."

"Yes, but we write a lease binding on heirs and assigns. We can even make it five years. Typical corporate stuff. And we can put in the lease an option to buy at a specific price if the property changes hands. None of this is a problem, Steven."

She glanced aside to where the real estate agent stood, just out of earshot, as they talked.

"The bigger problem is going to be converting a million dollars or more worth of gold bars without attracting attention. I'm still working on how to do that."

The answer, when Barbara got it, surprised Bach.

"You have the government convert it?"

"Yes. I talked to the Treasury Department on the recommendation of one of my professors. You know, a hypothetical question.

"It turns out the reason the government keeps such a close eye on cash transactions – everything over ten thousand dollars gets reported – is that they want to track down terrorist and cartel money. Well, terrorists and cartels don't want to convert gold to cash, they want to convert cash to gold.

"In order to keep that from happening, the Treasury Department is willing to buy gold bars in bulk for cash. At the spot price, no questions asked. To keep them away from the terrorists and the cartels.

"So the answer is to sell them to the Treasury Department. It doesn't even go on the federal budget, because it's not a spending item."

"But doesn't the million-dollar deposit that results get reported?"

"Of course. But it gets reported as a government transfer. No problem."

"That's insane."

"Welcome to government."

The net result was that, one day in February, an armored car marked with "U.S. Treasury" stopped by their apartment. The armored car men took delivery of over twenty pounds of gold one-troy-ounce bars – three hundred of them, to be exact – in a briefcase Bach had purchased for the transaction.

They insisted on transferring them to a container of their own – not wanting to take the briefcase! – as they counted them. They then issued Bach a receipt from a computer in the truck.

Neither Bach nor Barbara mentioned that they had another three hundred and forty pounds of gold in the spare bedroom.

Two weeks later, Bach received an email that the bars had assayed at over 99.99% pure gold. They gave him the spot price on the day of the transfer, a little over thirty-six hundred dollars a troy ounce.

Bach checked the balance of Graviton Dynamics' bank account, and saw a transfer from the U.S. government of one million, eighty thousand, and change U.S. dollars.

"What's your answer as to where the gold came from?" Bach asked Barbara.

"If they ask? From a foreign investor."

"Don't they have the right to know who?"

"Of a privately held company? Don't be silly."

With cash in hand, Graviton Dynamics bought the property for its worldwide corporate headquarters, and immediately leased the back fifteen acres with the pretty little house to Steven Bach.

Now to build the building. Barbara had an opinion on that.

"Buy a Morton steel building, Steven."

"They're the more expensive option, Barbara."

"Yes, but they guarantee the building. If a tornado takes it down – or you accidentally generate a five-gravity field and pull it down – they will replace it, no questions asked."

"Really?"

"Yes. Their attitude is, You bought a building, you get a building. They'll replace it within a week. That's why all the farmers own Morton buildings. You only have to buy it once, and you don't have months dealing with insurance adjusters and the like while your crop rots in the field."

"Fair enough. Where do we build it?"

"On that little meadow at the front of the property. There's no setback requirements in county. Oh, and Steven?"

"Yes?"

"Make it big enough. We need some front office space."

"How about we start small and set it up to be expanded?"

"That works."

Waiting for the property to close, while the building was being ordered and the plans finalized, Bach concentrated on getting the headset device built. He contracted for someone in the electrical engineering department to build the prototype.

As the intellectual property of university professors was normally owned by the university, Bach contracted with a graduate student to do the work. That work included analyzing the circuit and sizing the components for voltage levels, power consumption, and heat dissipation.

He delivered toward the end of March. The question now was how to test it.

The property also closed the end of March, which meant the

house was theirs.

"Time to move, Steven."

"But it's a ways out from the university. You have to be able to get back and forth to classes."

"Have you forgotten about the Cadillac?"

"No, but there's no good parking on campus."

"There is if you're willing to buy a permit."

"Those are pricey."

"Several hundred dollars a month? Not a problem."

Bach shrugged.

"OK. I guess it's time to move, then."

"Keep the apartment here, though, Steven. At least for the time being."

"Why?"

"As a place to keep the gold that's not associated with our activities. More secure, I think, by being sort of anonymous."

"All right."

They moved both of their apartments into the pretty little house. Bach's apartment was rented furnished, so they had no furniture to move there. Barbara owned her furniture, so they had a sofa and armchair for the living room, and a single bed for the guest room, at least for the time being.

They bought a king-sized bed for the master bedroom. They brought Barbara's dresser. They also bought a second armchair for the larger living room. They combined kitchen items, like pots and pans and utensils. They standardized on Barbara's more upscale flatware and dishes, and bought an additional set of each to fill out their holdings.

It was all in the 'early marriage' style, but they were happy.

The final element of the move was to move Vegan. They had him sneak out to the Cadillac in a raincoat and hat, and from that point the darkened windows did the rest.

Before they did that, however, there was one thing Vegan wanted to take care of. The Vegans generally were pretty ignorant of Earth customs and habits, and could not follow Vegan's movements except using the transmitter that had been subcutaneously installed in the alien when he left Vega.

Vegan did not want his fellows to be able to follow him, so, the week before they moved him, he removed the transmitter. He actually cut into himself at the location – in the armpit of his left lower arm – and removed it. They left it in the apartment.

When they ultimately abandoned the apartment, Bach set the transmitter into a pocket of the drywall behind a short piece of baseboard in the second bedroom closet, and replaced the baseboard.

If they came looking for Vegan, they would have to deal with whoever were the new tenants of the apartment.

Bach wondered how that would work out for them.

In any case, the aliens could no longer track Vegan out to the pretty house in the woods, and that's the way Bach and Vegan both wanted it.

No more visits to the hive queen except on Bach's own initiative.

Testing

With the move accomplished, Bach was back to the testing issue. How did they test the device? He didn't want to take the chance of being turned into a mental vegetable if it didn't work.

Barbara was more concerned about the security issue. When she, and Bach, and Vegan were in the house, who kept an eye on the commercial building? What did they do to keep the gold safe? Relying on Bach's empty apartment was not a solution.

"Steven, we need to talk about the security issue."

"What do you think we should do? Any ideas?"

"Yes. I think we should get a dog."

"A dog?"

"Yes. A trained watchdog. You know. A German shepherd who knows all the commands and stuff. Burglars hate dogs. He can stay in the building. Then we can move the gold to the building."

"Well, the building isn't up yet. They're almost ready to put it up, but we don't have a building yet."

"He can stay here in the meantime. Or outside. It's summer coming up, after all. If one of us walks the property perimeter with him every day, he'll know his territory."

"OK. I'll look into it. In the meantime, I'm still trying to figure out how to test this device."

"Yes. That's a big problem."

They sat quietly for a moment. Then Barbara gasped.

"Steven, could we test the device on the dog?"

"Sure. That would prove safety, I suppose. If the dog remains undamaged – you know, still responds to all the commands and stuff – it would likely mean it's safe for a human as well. That doesn't test efficacy, though."

"Wouldn't it, Steven? If the dog took the training for English to Vegan, wouldn't it then understand all the commands in Vegan? I mean, if it worked. Arthur could test him on those."

Bach stared at her for several seconds, and she shrugged.

"I hadn't thought of that, but you're likely right. Arthur?"

Vegan looked up from the desk – also one of Barbara's things from her apartment – where he was still banging away at translating the gravitonics textbook.

"Yes, Steven?"

"If we tested the headset device on a guard dog – you know, one of those dogs that know a dozen or more commands in English – and it worked, would the dog then understand those same commands in Vegan?"

"I would think he would, Steven. I understand that the device was originally tested on animals in that way. We would probably have to relocate the coils on the headpiece, but the drive circuitry would all be the same."

"By the way, Arthur. I always meant to ask you. Why was the device developed, anyway? Not to teach English, surely."

"No, Steven. It was developed long before our involvement on Earth. What we have been calling Vegan is one variation of the language of our species. There are several others across the planets we colonized. It was developed so we could speak to each other. Especially the queens, who speak something you could call High Vegan at their convocations."

"And you just added English to the dictionary when you started working here?"

"Yes, Steven. English, Mandarin Chinese, Hindi, and Spanish."

"All of those are in the dictionary, Arthur?"

"Yes. We've had agents in all those cultures."

Barbara sat stunned.

"Arthur," she said, "say that again slowly. What human languages can the dictionary teach?"

"English, Mandarin Chinese, Hindi, and Spanish. From any language to any other."

"Did you bring the entire dictionary with you, Arthur?"

"Of course. You had that extra two-terabyte flash drive along with your laptop on our trip, and, while the dictionary is large, I managed to fit the whole thing on your flash drive."

"What are you getting at, Barbara?"

"Steven, don't you understand? If the device you're building works, we can teach – in minutes, mind you – any or all of those languages to anybody who speaks one of them already."

"Yeah. So?"

"So how many Hispanic or Indian or Chinese immigrants to the United States want to speak English? How many American businessmen want to speak Spanish, or Chinese, or Hindi? How many Chinese businessmen? How many Hindi businessmen? How many of anybody wants to speak another language, and with no effort involved? Steven, the market is huge."

"Yes, but what I want the device for is to learn Vegan so I can reverse engineer the interstellar drive."

"Of course, Steven. I get that. But how much easier would it be if there were no financing worries? Wouldn't it be easier to develop your interstellar drive if we had billions of dollars a year coming in from teaching languages?"

"Billions of dollars a year?"

"Easily. Even a million people at, say, five thousand dollars apiece is five billion dollars. And it's all margin, Steven. Other than customer service and office space, there's no cost involved. It's like free money."

A GENT OF VEGA

"Gosh."

"We need to get that dog, Steven."

"I'm on it."

Bach found the dog at a trainer's in the next town. They both had to go pick him up, as there was some owner training. What to do – and what not to do – with a dog trained in that way. He was a reject from police training, which was very strict, and would not impact their use of the dog.

Bach surreptitiously recorded the training with the phone in his shirt pocket so Vegan could watch it when they got home.

The dog, whose name was Todd, was sweet enough when allowed to relax, but was all business in carrying out commands.

The brought him home – after paying a substantial amount of money for him – in a cage that he knew was his. He rode in the cage in the back seat of the Cadillac.

When they got home, they put the cage in the guest bedroom, and made sure Todd knew it was there. There was a command for him to go to his cage, at which point he would happily stay there. They locked him in the cage at night, which Todd didn't mind.

That first day, Bach walked the perimeter of the property with Todd, a one-mile circuit. He took the dog without him being on a leash, and whenever the dog crossed over the line, Bach called out, 'No. Come.'

Over subsequent days, there were fewer instances of him crossing the line, until there were none whatsoever.

Todd's reaction to Vegan was interesting. On first seeing the alien, he snarled and growled. Bach announced Vegan to be 'Friend.' Vegan greeted the dog with, 'Good boy. You're such a good boy. Come.'

Todd came to Vegan then, slowly and tentatively, and the alien petted him and played with his ears, after which they were friends.

They actually got to be very good friends, as Vegan was more available than either Bach or Barbara to walk the perimeter of the property every day with Todd, and the alien was glad to be able to walk outdoors again. With empty wooded properties to either side, and the state forest behind, there was no issue of him being seen.

Bach had planned on waiting a month for things to settle down, but after they had had Todd for three weeks, he was ready to go for it. His urgency to be about the gravitonics was pushing him.

The building was up now, and the septic field had been installed. A presby system, it was pretty small. But Barbara was parking the Cadillac in the building now, and they had moved the dog's cage out to the building. They didn't lock him in the cage at night, giving him free rein of the building.

They had the device set up in the building, on a work table. They were still using Bach's laptop for now. They also had a special headpiece for the dog.

All of them were present when they tried the device on the dog.

"Sit. Stay," Bach told the dog, then kept an eye on him while Vegan fitted the headpiece.

Bach also had him on the leash.

When the alien was done fitting the headpiece, he looked to Bach. Bach nodded.

"English to Vegan. Here goes," Vegan said.

Todd tilted his head and whimpered a bit when the device started, but quieted down. Ten minutes later, there was a ding from the laptop.

"All done," Vegan said.

Todd was quiet, so Bach took off the leash.

"Todd. Get the ball," Vegan said.

Todd ran over to his cage and got the ball, ready to go outside and play.

"Looks like no damage," Bach said. "So safety is probably OK."

"Let's go see if it worked," Vegan said.

They all went outside, Todd leading the way.

"Todd. Sit. Stay."

Todd let Vegan take the ball. The alien threw it hard, and Bach reflected that, if they ever got peaceful relations with the Vegans, they would have to put limits on them playing professional sports. Vegan could probably pitch a hundred-fifty mile-an-hour fastball.

The dog watched intently, switching back and forth between Vegan and the ball. He had been told to stay, but he was so tempted.

Then Vegan made a sound like a V-8 engine with a half-race cam throwing a rod.

<Fetch!>

Todd took off like a shot after the ball. He retrieved it, then came trotting back with it. He let Vegan take it, ready for another throw, but Vegan had other ideas.

<Sit.>

Todd sat.

<Down.>

Todd stretched out and lay on the ground.

<Stay.>

Vegan threw the ball again, but Todd did not take off after it until he got the go-ahead.

<Fetch.>

Todd jumped up and spun around, tearing off after the ball.

"I would say efficacy has been proven, Steven. At least insofar as a dog is concerned."

The dog came trotting back with the ball, and Vegan praised him. In Vegan.

<You're a good boy. Such a good boy.>

The dog came up to him, wagging his tail, for pets and treats.

The next question was, Which of the humans should use the device first? It was an open question, and Bach and Barbara sparred about it.

"I should use it first, Steven. If something happens to you, I have no chance with the gravitonics issues."

"That you can hire out," Bach said. "I have no chance whatsoever with finance. I wouldn't even know if I was being cheated."

Barbara turned to Vegan, who was trying not to be involved.

"Arthur?"

"In human society, historically, if there is potential danger, the men undertake the task. Much as the queen's drones are her food tasters. The female is never unnecessarily put at risk."

He turned to Bach.

"Sorry, Steven. I think it's on you."

Barbara wanted to object, but she couldn't. She knew Vegan was right.

They watched Todd for the next week, but the dog seemed unchanged. He responded in all the same ways. He acted in all the same ways.

The only difference was that he now knew all the commands

he had been taught in Vegan, and he responded when Vegan talked to him in Vegan.

It was time to go ahead with a human trial.

As the one thing that was different, Bach carefully checked the headpiece they would use for humans. That was one thing that was different than the one they had used with Todd, and he needed to make sure it was correct.

Then came the big day.

It was Saturday again, a day they would all be available to watch and see what happened. It was the beginning of May, and Barbara had exams throughout this period, but she had none on Saturday.

Bach sat in a chair by the worktable in the building. Vegan mounted the headpiece and made sure it was on properly. Then he set the machine for English to Vegan.

"Are you ready, Steven?"

"Yes, I'm ready, Arthur."

"All right. We're set for English to Vegan. Active."

Bach's head filled with the sound of voices – thousands of voices – speaking Vegan. It seemed to go on for an hour or more. Then it was over.

<It's completed, Steven. How do you feel?>

"I feel fine, Arthur."

It was only then that Bach realized the alien had spoken to him in Vegan.

<Well, apparently, it's worked.>

"Yes. It worked fine. I can understand you completely. How long was I under?"

"About ten minutes," Barbara said.

"Geez. It felt like an hour."

"All right, Arthur," Barbara said. "Reset the machine. I need you to spin me up for Mandarin Chinese and Hindi."

"Chinese and Hindi?" Bach asked.

"Yes. I need to get in touch with the Indians and Taiwanese, so we can get them to ramp up the production of these machines. We're gonna need a bunch of them."

"Where do you put the first office, Barbara?" Bach asked.

"Right here in town. Get new grads in business trained locally so they can run our various outlets."

"And the second office?"

"Washington, D.C."

"Washington?"

"Yes, Steven. I would think the State Department would have an interest, don't you?"

Commercialization and production of the prototype device would be expensive. They would also need to expand the building again, to have office space for their big expansion.

They arranged the transfer of forty pounds of one-troy-ounce gold bars to the Treasury Department. Six hundred in all.

They met the Treasury people at the apartment, as they had the first time. The Treasury men counted them out into their own container as before, and gave them a receipt off the computer in the armored car they arrived in.

After the Treasury people left, they transferred the rest of the gold into the Cadillac and took it out to the company building. It would now be safer there, with Todd on watch at night.

Expansion

Bach was now able to read Vegan, and he read the gravitonics textbook with interest. He could see why Vegan had had problems. It was written on the physics grad-student level. But he made good progress in reading it. He corrected Vegan's translation where it needed it, which helped the alien see where he'd been going wrong.

Free from her exams, Barbara concentrated on getting the language-teaching machine commercialized. The Indians were more geared to the smaller projects – which theirs certainly was at the moment – if she could get past the sexism problem. The Indian engineers were just not taking her, a woman, seriously.

She thought about getting Bach involved, but he was busy with the gravitonics issues.

In the end, she paid a premium to go with a Taiwanese firm, thinking it would be cheaper in the long run. Her excellent facility in both Hindi and Chinese helped a lot during these negotiations.

They expanded the building. The addition was twice the size of the original, and was all office space except for a second garage space. The original building was left for Bach's workshop, the big garage door being helpful for getting anything big in or out, which Barbara anticipated needing.

Barbara also started hiring people for customer service, and teaching them using the prototype machine. It was the end of spring semester, and too good a chance to pick up new grads to pass up. They practiced by running each other through the machine, until all five new hires had learned the other three human languages.

Hiring presented a new difficulty. The language company would be a wholly owned subsidiary of Graviton Dynamics.

That meant they had to decide what to call it.

"Another C-corp? A wholly owned C-corp?"

"Yes, Steven. S-corps are a cheat. They allow the government to treat you like a taxpayer, while calling it a corporation. You get liability protection and very little else. Being a C-corp means we can do anything the big boys can do."

"And that saves money?"

"Oh, yes. On things like medical plans, company cars, all that sort of thing, the tax treatment is totally different."

"And a separate corporation?"

"Yes, so if we want at some point to sell it off, or sell stock in it, or have it go bankrupt, we can do that without impacting the graviton effort."

"Why would we ever want it to go bankrupt, Barbara?"

"Well, let's say there's a big liability lawsuit, and we just want to concentrate on the gravitonics work...."

"OK. Got it."

Lawsuits were magic to Bach. They usually didn't make any sense, and he was beyond the point where he expected them to.

"What do we use for a name, Steven?"

"Language Dynamics?"

Barbara bent to her laptop.

"It's taken."

"Translation Dynamics?"

"It's taken."

"Really, Barbara?"

"Yeah. It's a medical term and has something to do with mRNAs in live cells."

"Wow. Hmm. How about LangWitch?"

"No, it would turn off some devout Christians. Like my parents, for example. Nothing to do with witchcraft."

"Wait a minute. Our big claim to fame is the time, right? And it's a retail outlet. How about Ten-Minute Fluency?"

"It's taken. Something about ten minutes a day."

"How about Lingo Quick?"

"It's taken."

"Speedy Spanish?"

"It's taken."

"Geez. This is hard. All the reasonable things are taken already."

"Now you know why I asked. The good news is it indicates the size of the market. Lots of stuff out there."

"Wait. How about Lingua Zinga?"

Barbara looked up from her laptop.

"That one's actually OK, Steven."

"Trademark it. Use it. It says what it's about, and indicates it's fast."

"You got it."

It was two months before the first commercial units came in from Taiwan. They had compressed the circuitry down into a programmable analog array and a few power components. Bach's foot-on-a-side prototype had become a module of three inches by two inches, half an inch thick.

The headpieces came in at the same time. They, too, had been cost-reduced, without giving up effectiveness. The hand-tooled adjustable leather skullcap was now a stretchy nylon unit that required no adjustments.

Barbara had already arranged for quantity pricing on laptops, and they took delivery of their first twelve laptops as the headsets came in.

It was the beginning of July when they opened their small shop in campustown. They advertised with flyers on telephone poles, and with ads in the student newspaper.

Business was initially slow, but it really picked up the beginning of August. New students coming to campus were looking for a leg up on the language requirement. When their clients, with no previous experience, passed language proficiency exams, bypassing the language requirement entirely, word quickly got around.

Professors started turning up for language instruction, often in languages they thought they already knew. Soon, people were coming into town from other universities. That spread further, and businessmen from the nearby state capital started showing up, often for multiple languages at once.

They expanded from twelve booths to twenty-four, and kept them busy ten hours a day on strict appointment schedules. With twenty-minute turnarounds, they were running upwards of seven hundred people a day through their system. Ten minutes of instruction in what to expect, ten minutes in the booth, and out the door.

At five thousand dollars a class, they were grossing over three million dollars a day, six days a week.

Barbara brought on an office staff to do all the accounting, customer inquiries, and appointment scheduling. She also brought on personnel staff to keep up with employee acquisition and payroll. The existing staffers became an in-house training crew to train additional people to give the classes.

Barbara planned a further expansion of the company building – a two-story section – and construction started in September.

Then Barbara opened the DC office. She found a location on F Street NW, just blocks from the State Department. She advertised on telephone poles on the Georgetown University campus nearby, and in the Georgetown University student newspaper. She started with twenty-four booths.

It started out with a trickle of Georgetown students. As word got around, business picked up, especially among the international relations students, many of whom took multiple languages. Professors followed.

The international relations students included some people working for the State Department. When word got around in the State Department, a number of young go-getters from State came in for instruction.

That quickly turned into a flood as more senior personnel started showing up. Soon, people were showing up from NSA and CIA.

Barbara expanded the DC office to forty-eight booths, and they were booking appointments a month in advance.

By the end of November, Lingua Zinga was doing over ten million dollars a week.

Keeping up with personnel acquisition and training was a big issue, and Barbara brought on more personnel to handle it. They started running a shuttle from campus to the company location for her employees, most of whom didn't have a car.

Barbara's next round of expansion was New York City, Chicago, and Los Angeles.

The president of the United States had a request for his security staff.

"I need you to check out this company. Lingua Zinga. Get me background on the principals. All of that stuff."

"Yes, Mr. President."

When the report came back, the president listened with interest.

"Lingua Zinga is a company that has a revolutionary new way to teach foreign languages. They can teach English, Spanish, Hindi, and Mandarin Chinese, in any combination. Reportedly, they do it with a headset arrangement that directly infuses the language into the brain. It apparently takes ten minutes to achieve complete fluency.

"Principals are an engaged couple, Steven Bach and Barbara Nowak. Both recent graduates of a Big Ten university. Neither is politically active. Their fathers both served for a time in the U.S. military. Honorable discharges. Neither is politically active, though one is a registered Democrat, one a registered Republican. Similarly with their wives. Working middle class."

"The salt of America."

"Yes, Mr. President. We found no negative influences or anything else troublesome."

"Thank you."

"Of course, Mr. President."

"We need more room, Steven."

"Buy an office building in town."

"Really?"

"Sure. You can use it for all the personnel stuff. Training and all that. Just keep accounting and central office functions here. You can get rid of the shuttle buses then, too."

"What if there's no suitable building available, Steven?"

Bach shrugged.

"Then build one. Some standard design you can get off the ground quickly."

"I guess I'm having a hard time getting my head around

that."

"Barbara, this thing is taking off in a really big way. You'll end up with shops in every university town. You're going to go international soon. It's as big as anything I've ever seen."

"Yeah. It's kinda wild."

"As a matter of fact, you should probably be looking to hire a new president. Somebody who's done this before. Taken a company huge. Just offload the whole thing. Move it all into the new building."

"That sounds like an abdication. An abandonment."

"No. Think about it. It's the smart thing to do. Offload the whole thing, and let it make us money while we go on about our business."

"Hmm."

The corporate phone rang then. It was an extension off the main switchboard in the company building, and they had a conference phone on this end, in the living room of the house.

"Yes," Barbara answered.

"Ma'am, I have a phone call for you."

With that she patched it through with no further explanation. Barbara would have to talk to her about that. Everybody in the company was new, however, and such things happened.

"Hello, this is the White House switchboard, placing a call for the president. Is Barbara Nowak or Steven Bach available?"

"Yes, we're both here."

"Hold for the president, please."

There was a delay and a click before a familiar voice came on the line.

"Barbara Nowak?"

"Yes, Mr. President. Steven Bach is also here."

"Oh, good. I wasn't sure which one of you to talk to. I have a situation, and I think you two can help me out."

"Whatever we can do, Mr. President."

"Well, I'm meeting with the premier of China in two weeks, and I thought it would be wonderful if I could just sit down with him and talk. You know, in Chinese. Without translators and all of that nonsense. Now, that's never been possible before, but it is now, isn't it?

"Yes, Mr. President. It is."

"Excellent, Ms. Nowak. Now, it's a big deal whenever I go anywhere. Disrupts everybody and everything. Is this training something you can do here? In the White House?"

"Yes, Mr. President."

"I'll need the names of staff for the Secret Service to check them out and everything first."

"We would be honored to do it ourselves, Mr. President."

"Excellent. They've already checked you two out. And I'll take care of the billing and all, and see that you get paid."

"We would be happy to do it free of charge, Mr. President."

"No, Ms. Nowak. That's not how it works here. Then it's a gift and there's all sorts of rigmarole about it."

"Very well, Mr. President. You know, if you had the Secretary of State drop by, we could do you both at the same time."

"An excellent idea, Ms. Nowak. I'll do that. Now let me connect you to my appointments secretary, and she can set up a time that works for both of us."

"Of course, Mr. President."

"Well, that doesn't happen every day," Bach said when they got off the phone.

"A call from the president? It sure doesn't."

"And on a Saturday?"

"That way he can keep it off his appointments schedule. I think he wants it to be a surprise."

"So you go out there and come back same day?"

"We go out there and come back same day. Yes. I'm not going alone. I need the moral support. You can do the Secretary of State."

"We can do all three languages while we're there."

"Yes. Except for the Secretary of State. He's already fluent in Spanish."

Bach nodded.

"You know, Steven, I think you're right. About a new president. Offload the subsidiary onto a new guy, and you and I can go after the gravitonics business."

"I think that's smart. You think business is going great guns now. What do you think is going to happen when the president starts speaking fluent Mandarin?"

"Oh, my God."

"Yup. And there's something I just saw in the business news that you need to see."

He typed on his laptop, then turned it toward her.

"George Fuller? You have got to be shitting me. He grew them into an international brand."

"Yes, Barbara, but it's become a commodity business now. The board's going with someone else."

"You think I can get him?"

"Only one way to find out."

"George Fuller."

"Good morning, Mr. Fuller. My name is Barbara Nowak. I am the president and chairman of the board of Lingua Zinga."

"Good morning, Ms. Nowak. How can I help you?"

"I want to make you a job offer, Mr. Fuller. As president of

Lingua Zinga."

"Never heard of it."

"Oh, but you will, Mr. Fuller. You will. I would simply suggest you do your due diligence on our company. You can call me back on this number."

"Very well, Ms. Nowak. I'll do that."

George Fuller called back two hours later. Barbara could tell from the calling number.

"Yes, Mr. Fuller?"

"Ms. Nowak, is it true you're doing over a million dollars a day right now?"

"Mr. Fuller, we're doing over *ten* million dollars a day right now, it's all margin, and I can't expand the company fast enough."

"Well then, Ms. Nowak, assuming we can work out the details, I'd say you have a new president."

"Excellent, Mr. Fuller. Welcome aboard."

The business news picked up on George Fuller's new position as president of Lingua Zinga.

Then the president met with the Chinese premier, and the two engaged in conversations in Mandarin Chinese, without interpreters. The president mentioned Lingua Zinga in a press conference on his return to the United States.

George Fuller knew how to grow a company fast, and with a launch like that, Lingua Zinga couldn't miss.

Fuller brought in his whole team. They bought a big office building in the nearby state capital, moved the company, revamped the company logo, and opened two dozen new locations.

In the first month.

A GENT OF VEGA

Fuller also put in place an employee stock option program. Barbara had made a deal with Fuller that gave him a few percent of the company for himself, and let him use more as 'spreading around' money. Eventually there would be an IPO.

As long as Graviton Dynamics maintained control, they didn't care.

There was one wrinkle that came up during this period. The IRS started getting curious about where the initial five million dollars in gold bullion had come from. Bach and Barbara had cashed in gold a total of three times – a total of a hundred pounds – before Lingua Zinga took off.

They got nowhere. In fact, they got shut down pretty hard.

If IRS took Lingua Zinga down, a whole bunch of people and agencies would be affected.

The State Department, for one, was not amused, and made its position clear to the Secretary of the Treasury.

Treasury, for its part, was glad to have the gold bullion off the market and away from the drug cartels. And IRS was part of Treasury.

NSA and CIA didn't want Lingua Zinga shut down, either. They still had thousands of staff waiting for classes.

"But where did the bullion come from?" IRS asked.

"That is a matter of national security, and none of your business," the Secretary of State answered.

The IRS pushed back, and then the director of the IRS got a call from the president of the United States.

"On Lingua Zinga? Cut it out. If some of your people don't have better things to do, they can look for another job. Just let me know."

That was the end of the IRS' interest in the gold bullion.

Gravitonics

While Barbara launched Lingua Zinga, Bach and Vegan were working on the gravitonics side of things.

It was slow going.

Bach was clawing at the edge of his quantum mechanics understanding to make sense of the gravitonics textbook. It was one level deeper than he had seen before, maybe two.

But it was important he understood the theory enough to ensure their experiments weren't dangerous. Unlike the language teaching device, messing around with gravitonics had the potential to make things go boom in a big way.

Like if he generated a five-gravity field, for instance, and pulled the building down around his ears. Or neutralized gravity over a wide enough area to have things whizzing about under the slightest impulse.

So Bach and Vegan took it slow, figuring it out a piece at a time.

It was clear early on that they would be making devices, and that most of those would be out of metal. Bach started working with a retired tool & die maker in town, Fred Durham, paying him top dollar as a consultant. Durham welcomed the pay for very part-time work.

One thing Bach told Durham to do was to equip a small machine shop, good enough to do tool & die work. Durham bought a Monarch engine lathe and a Bridgeport vertical milling machine with digital readouts, an industrial air compressor and cutoff saw.

Other tools occasionally showed up, and Bach paid for them,

originally with gold-conversion money, then with the dividends coming into Graviton Dynamics from the Lingua Zinga subsidiary.

They started by building a very small device, something that would negate gravitation within a very small volume – about a single cubic inch. Durham built the device up from steel and brass stock he had purchased.

The electronic part of it was built by Bach at the workbench. He had acquired all the necessary tools now, and he built this one up himself rather than call in an electrical engineering grad student from the university. This one was mostly big analog stuff, and he felt comfortable with that.

It was a big cumbersome device, with a lot of power used up by the large electrical circuit that powered it, but it was just a proof of concept, nothing more.

When it was time to test it, that night at the end of September, Bach and Vegan were present. No one else. They did it after hours, when all the others – all the Lingua Zinga people – were out of the building. Barbara was doing paperwork in the house.

Bach turned the device on, and it generated an evil hum coming up to power, then grew silent. A faint blue glow surrounded the test space, the volume in which gravity had been negated by steering gravitons around the volume.

Todd decided his best personal strategy was to make himself scarce, and he retreated to his cage.

Vegan walked forward with a quarter-inch steel ball bearing in a wooden spoon. He inserted the ball bearing into the device, and then lowered the spoon and pulled it out.

The steel ball bearing floated there, not attracted by the planet's gravity. After several seconds, it floated out of the test volume, moved by a slight air current of the HVAC system.

Then it fell to the device and bounced from there to the floor.

"It would appear to work, Steven."

"Yes, Arthur. I think you're right."

It had taken them months of study, and tens of thousands of dollars of machining and electronics, but they had done it.

For the first time, man had manipulated gravity itself.

The second device was planned to be much bigger. It would negate gravity in a volume of a single cubic foot.

Durham began machining the pieces of this bigger machine while Bach started working up the much more serious package of electronics to drive it.

The parts were getting big – and expensive – but Lingua Zinga had serious money coming in now. Bach could buy whatever he wanted.

When Bach and Barbara went out to DC the weekend after Thanksgiving, the new, larger unit was not yet complete, but it was getting there.

"So you put this thing on my head, and you run that machine there, and after ten minutes I know Chinese?"

"Yes, Mr. President."

"Do I feel anything while it's working?"

"You'll hear what sounds like voices, Mr. President. Thousands of voices, talking all at once, in Chinese. It will seem to you like it goes on for an hour, but it's really just ten minutes."

"And then I know Chinese."

"Yes, sir."

"All right, then. Proceed, Ms. Nowak."

Bach was standing by with the Secretary of State, there in the Oval Office. They were seated on one of the facing couches, and the president and Barbara were seated on the other.

"Yes, Mr. Bach. Proceed," the Secretary of State said.

They put the headpieces on each of their charges.

"Just close your eyes and make yourself comfortable, gentlemen. Here we go."

Barbara and Bach selected English to Mandarin Chinese from the menu and hit the 'Go' button.

The ten-minute wait felt like hours. They had had no adverse events, and had, by this point, used the devices on tens of thousands of people, but still Barbara worried. This was the President of the United States, after all.

When the machines dinged, one after the other, the president and the Secretary of State opened their eyes.

<What do you think, Bob? Did it work for you?> the president asked in Chinese.

<Yes, sir. It sure did.>

<Me, too.>

He turned to Barbara.

<Thank you, Ms. Nowak.>

<You're very welcome, sir.>

"Oh, I'm sorry. I said that in Chinese."

"No worries, Mr. President. I've taught myself Chinese with the machine. I understood you."

"That's an amazing device, Ms. Nowak. How did you come up with it?"

Barbara was torn. Could she lie to the president? She decided the truth was best.

"It's an alien technology, sir. We stole it from aliens."

The president looked at her for a second, then nodded.

"It's OK that you don't want to tell me, Ms. Nowak. I was just curious."

"Yes, sir. Would you like to learn Hindi and Spanish as well, as long as we're here?"

"Ten more minutes each?"

"Yes, sir."

He looked over at the Secretary of State, who shrugged.

"Sure, Ms. Nowak. Let's do it."

"Yes, sir."

Barbara and Bach both set their devices to Hindi and hit the 'Go' button. Barbara didn't worry as much this time, and both the president and the Secretary of State emerged from the training unharmed.

"And now Spanish, Ms. Nowak."

"Yes, sir."

"I don't need this one, Ms. Nowak," the Secretary of State said.

"Are you sure, Mr. Secretary? If you take the Spanish anyway, it will make sure you know all the modern technical terms of art. It should also make Spanish easier to slip into without having to think about it."

"Oh? Very well, then, Ms. Nowak. Proceed."

"Yes, sir."

Once more, Barbara and Bach set their devices and hit the 'Go' button. Once more, after ten minutes, the president and Secretary of State emerged from the trance unharmed.

"That is a remarkable device, Ms. Nowak," the president said.

"Yes, sir."

"And you and Mr. Bach own the company?"

"No, sir. Not exactly. Lingua Zinga is a wholly owned subsidiary of Graviton Dynamics. We own Graviton Dynamics."

"And what does Graviton Dynamics do?"

Barbara turned to Bach.

"We are experimenting with manipulating gravitation, Mr. President," Bach said. "We intend to build an interstellar spacecraft."

"Really?"

"Yes, sir."

"More stolen alien technology?" the president asked, with a wink at Barbara.

"Yes, sir."

"I would be very interested in that, given your success with the language business."

The president wrote briefly on a card.

"This is my private number, Mr. Bach. I would be pleased if you would contact me when you have something to show me. I need to get out to the Midwest soon, anyway."

"Yes, sir. I'll be happy to."

"Good. And now, do you have an invoice for me, Ms. Nowak?"

"Yes, Mr. President."

Barbara had prepared several versions, depending on whether they had taken the other languages or not, and whether the Secretary of State had taken Spanish. She took the correct one out of her bag and handed it over.

"I will take care of this, Ms. Nowak. Thank you very much. I predict the meeting with the Chinese premier will be much more productive now."

"You're very welcome, sir."

The same White House car that had picked them up from Reagan airport this morning dropped them off back at the airport, and they were home in time for supper.

Vegan was interested in their meeting with the president.

"This is the hive queen of your hive, right?"

"In a manner of speaking, Arthur," Bach answered. "He's the highest-ranking person in the United States' government."

Vegan nodded.

"What did he think of the training?"

"He liked it a lot. He and the Secretary of State both took all three languages."

"Did he ask you where the technology came from, Steven?"

"Yes, Arthur. Barbara told him it was alien technology we had stolen."

Vegan's antenna shot straight up at that, and he turned to Barbara.

"You didn't."

"Oh, yes, I did. I couldn't lie to the president. Relax, Arthur. He took it as a joke. He said he could understand why I didn't want to tell him."

Vegan relaxed then and he nodded.

"Sometimes the truth is the most effective lie of all," he said.

Work on the larger device continued through December and January. The device was bigger, which presented its own problems, but they had learned a lot building the smaller device and made good progress.

The parts were expensive as well, but by now George Fuller was on-line and rolling out outlets for Lingua Zinga. Money was coming into Lingua Zinga in prodigious amounts, and Bach could request whatever dividends he wanted to be paid to Graviton Dynamics to fund the effort.

Graviton Dynamics also ponied up for another company car for Steven Bach, and he finally got the Corvette he wanted.

Whenever the three of them went anywhere, though, they went in Barbara's Cadillac. It had the room, and it had the darkened windows that allowed Vegan to ride along.

A GENT OF VEGA

The place Vegan most liked to ride to was the local ice cream shop. He didn't get out of the car, but waited while Barbara and Bach got ice cream in cups, plus a shake for him. Vegan really liked milk shakes.

He didn't even need a straw.

Bach had some setbacks when they started testing subsystems in January. The problem was that going from a one-inch cubic volume to a one-foot cubic volume was not a twelve-times bigger problem. The volume difference was twelve cubed, so it was a seventeen-hundred-times bigger problem.

On the power supply side, he had to get much bigger components even than he had planned.

Eventually, though, they passed subsystem tests and it was time to test the new device.

It was the beginning of February, just over a year after he had graduated and a year and a half after visiting Vega.

Barbara was running the checklist, Vegan was standing by to assist, and Bach was running the experiment.

"First up, turn off everything in the building except the lights in this room," Barbara said.

That included the HVAC system, despite it being February in the Midwest. The building would hold heat for as long as this would take.

Vegan nodded. The main breaker panel for the building was in this large experiment room, a bit of foresight. Vegan turned off all the breakers except the one for the lights in this room and the big breaker for the experimental device.

Todd, aware that something big was going on, retreated to his cage. This was not his kind of problem. Intruders, yes.

Gravitonics, no.

"Safety glasses," Barbara said.

Everyone put safety glasses on, including Barbara. They had had to rig up something for Vegan from the bubbled visor of a motorcycle helmet.

"Main switch on."

Bach nodded and turned on the main switch for the power supply. Nothing big yet. The device itself wasn't enabled.

"Check power supply output."

Bach looked at the meters, both voltmeter and ammeter.

"Power supply nominal."

"Check test volume for obstructions."

Bach visually checked the test volume.

"Test volume clear."

"Enable device."

Bach enabled the device with another control. The system let out a truly evil hum, and the lights in the room dimmed for a few seconds before returning to normal brightness. The hum subsided.

"Check power supply output."

Bach looked at the meters again.

"Voltage holding. Current within expected range."

"Check gravitation within the test volume."

Bach held a big wooden spoon several feet long, a stage prop for a witch's cauldron scenario, such as in Macbeth. Vegan placed on the spoon a one-inch steel ball bearing, actually the ball from a pinball machine.

Bach inserted the spoon into the test volume, then lowered it and pulled it out. The ball bearing hung in mid-air, unaffected by the Earth's gravity.

Bach bumped the ball bearing with the spoon, and it lazily traveled across the test volume before reaching the edge of the test volume and falling. It bounced off the device and the table, and landed on the floor.

"Test complete. Disable device."

Bach disabled the device, at which there was a crackle and a pop.

"Shut off power supply."

Bach shut off the supply.

"Restore power to the building."

Vegan went over to the open circuit breaker panel and turned the breakers all back on.

"Test complete. Congratulations, gentlemen," Barbara said.

Intermezzo

They were having a celebratory beer in the living room of the pretty little house in the woods.

"So what's next, gentlemen?" Barbara asked.

"First is to invert the operation of the current device. See if we can generate a five- or ten-gravity field in the test volume."

Bach looked to Vegan, and the alien nodded.

"After that," Bach said, "We need to see if we can generate a field that includes the device. Have it go up in the air on a tether."

"Why on a tether?" Barbara asked.

"Because we need the power. To do more than that, we need a portable power source."

"We also need to work on focusing the field, Steven," Vegan said. "We have to focus the field to manipulate dark matter."

Bach nodded.

"Ah. Actually, though, I was thinking more near-term than that, Steven."

"Like what, Barbara?"

"Well, I think there's someone in Washington, DC, you ought to show your current device to."

"Oh. Yes, that would probably make sense."

"You want to keep him interested, Steven. He'll be the source of your portable power supply, if I'm not mistaken, and you're also going to need clearance to space at some point."

Bach nodded.

"Second, I've gotten a request from George Fuller wondering if we can add a dictionary for some other languages to the Lingua Zinga device. French, Arabic, Russian, Japanese."

Bach looked to Vegan.

"It is possible, Steven," the alien said. "You start by processing the existing language dictionaries. I can spend some time on that as we're working up to the next gravitonics test."

Bach looked back to Barbara.

"I hate to take the time away from the gravitonics project."

"You're going to need billions for space," Barbara said, "and if you want to keep those billions coming in, we need to keep George happy."

"I suppose you're right, Barbara."

"And the other thing on our schedule is marriage. We've been engaged for a year and a half, Steven Bach, and if you think I'm gonna wait for you forever, you are mistaken."

The first item was the easiest. Bach watched the president's social media accounts in the evening. On the second night, he saw the president post something, so he called the number the president had given him.

"Hello," the familiar voice said.

"Good evening, Mr. President. Steven Bach here. The Lingua Zinga guy."

"Of course, Mr. Bach. I remember you. Have you got something to show me?"

"Yes, sir. It's sort of small, in a way, but no one has ever done anything like it before. It's a proof of the concept. We now know we can do what we planned."

"Which is, make an interstellar spaceship."

"Yes, sir. We now know that it's possible."

"That is something I want to see, Mr. Bach. Very well. I'll arrange a Midwest event at some point coming up. And when I'm out there, I'll come by and you can show me. Deal?"

"It's a deal, Mr. President."

"Excellent. We'll be in touch, Mr. Bach."

The second item was on Vegan. The third item was hard.

When Barbara brought up a wedding to her parents, they were off to the races, talking in terms of a huge event. The big church wedding, the reception with anyone closer than fourth cousin once removed invited, the cake, the food, the band.

Of course, Bach and Barbara at this point had as much money as they wanted. They could foot the bill for anything.

But problems came up immediately. Which church, for example. Barbara's Polish Catholic parents had their druthers, of course, and, as the bride, Barbara had the right of way. But what about Bach's German Lutheran parents?

For that matter, neither Bach nor Barbara was religious, and it seemed disrespectful of other's beliefs to carry on that way since they weren't.

Which city was another problem. Again, the bride had the right of way, but their current friends were all either here or in the nearby state capital where Lingua Zinga had located, not back home.

The final part of it, though, was privacy. The reclusive couple, now billionaires, who had founded Lingua Zinga had become an item of press curiosity, and they didn't give interviews. Everybody they had to their wedding would become a target of the media – for pictures of the event, for public statements about it, for harassment generally.

They talked about it with Vegan while the three of them played pool on the regulation table Bach had had installed in the big experiment room of the company building. He'd always liked pool, and now he could indulge such small pleasures.

"Can't we run away and get married, Barbara?"

"My mother would have a coronary. It has to be special."

"Can we make it special in a different way than having it be a hoopla affair?"

"I don't know, Steven. What did you have in mind?"

"Well.... Just throwing something out here. Let's say we have it in the state capital. We rent the top-floor penthouse suites of that fancy hotel. You know. The really expensive one."

Barbara nodded.

"The Ritz-Carlton."

"Yeah. Just us, and your folks, and my folks. We take the penthouse suites. Like a bunch of interconnected suites on the top floor. We have one suite all dolled up for the ceremony and stuff. We get the judge to come in to marry us.

"Then we have them cater the best food they have directly to the suite. No press. No relatives. Nobody else. Just the six of us. Everybody else is secondary anyway. We can even have music and dancing if we want."

"Well, my dad's not big on dancing, so losing that would be OK by him. Maybe live music during dinner, though. Chamber music. You know."

"What do you think? Will they go for it?"

"They might. When I brought up the press, they got worried about security and all. What about Arthur? He's why we have all this money in the first place."

"And the fame, too, I'm afraid," Vegan said. "It really helped when you bought the twenty-acre properties either side of this one. Todd loves the extra room to roam in, and he positively detests the press."

The big dog had been essential in their keeping their privacy from snooping press. The topology of the property and the density of the woods kept anyone from getting within sight of the house without violating the property line, and several cameramen had beat a hasty retreat when Todd arrived at a run to enforce the property limits.

Bach and Barbara didn't let him keep the ones he caught, which the big dog took with only mild disappointment, but he remained up for the chase anytime someone tested him.

Barbara chuckled at the memory of one such incident, and Vegan continued.

"But you need not worry about me in planning your wedding, Barbara. I'm pleased that you are both happy. I need no more than that."

"You're a sweetie, Arthur. A true friend."

Barbara turned back to Bach.

"I'll try it out on them, Steven, and see where I get."

"I can't ask for more than that."

Both sets of parents agreed, with two major motives – one, the added security, and the other, that it could happen sooner, without all the planning. One request was to include the grandparents, which Bach and Barbara thought was a good idea.

"Yeah, my mom's parents, that's a good idea," Barbara said. "Dad's parents are both gone. And your grandmothers."

Both of Bach's grandfathers were gone as well.

"OK, so ten of us all told, right?"

"Yes, and a total of six bedrooms."

"Got it."

They got married the second weekend in March. They made the weekend of it, sending two liveried cars out, one to each hometown to pick up the family, on Friday afternoon. They had all of Saturday and Sunday, with the liveried cars returning their families home on Monday morning.

Barbara and Steven took liveried cars both ways as well. It

was just easier, as they were both nervous as cats.

Saturday afternoon, everyone got all dolled up for the event, with a photographer coming in for the pictures. The judge showed up and married them under state law. They had an exquisite catered dinner with soft, live chamber music. Barbara and her dad did one dance together, as required.

They even had a wedding cake, sized to the party, with enough to take home as souvenirs and leftovers.

The rest of the weekend they spent slumming in the suites, in jammies or casual clothes. It was great fun, and everyone got to know one another.

Then it was over, and time to get back to work.

The newspaper carried a public notice of the wedding by the judge, after which the best the media could do was report that Steven Bach and Barbara Nowak, the billionaires behind Lingua Zinga, had wed in a private ceremony.

The president came into town the last week in March. Bach and Vegan were still planning the next step, and hadn't torn into the big device yet, so it was available for demo.

The president gave his big speech at the university, and headed out to their site almost like an afterthought. The press was not invited, which drove them crazy. The state police did a good job in keeping the press cars moving on the rural road, however, so they were ultimately stymied.

"Hello, Mr. President. It's good to see you again."

"And you, Mr. Bach. I understand congratulations are in order since the last time I saw you."

"Yes, sir. We were married two weeks ago."

"Well, congratulations," the president said, shaking Bach's

hand.

"Thank you, sir."

"And to you, Ms. Nowak. Or is it Ms. Bach now?"

"Ms. Bach, Mr. President."

"Barbara Bach?"

"Yes, sir. A coincidence. No relation."

The president had come in with his National Science Advisor, as well as half a dozen Secret Service people. Todd looked anxious, not knowing what he would be called on to do. But Bach announced them all friends to the dog, after which he calmed down. The president ruffled his ears, and Todd loved it.

"That's a well trained dog, Mr. Bach."

"Yes, sir. Trained guard dog. We got the best."

"So what do you have to show me, Mr. Bach?"

"Here, sir."

Bach led them over to the apparatus.

"I will create, in this test volume, a space of zero gravity. That is, this device will shield the Earth's gravity from acting on this test volume."

The president looked to his science advisor.

"An incredible accomplishment if true, Mr. Bach," the science advisor said.

"Yes, sir. We agree. We're quite happy about it."

Bach turned to Barbara.

"Ready with the checklist?"

"Ready."

Bach looked to the president, who nodded.

Barbara read down the items in the checklist as before, Bach performing each one, until the pinball sat weightless in the test volume.

"That could be a magnetic effect, Mr. Bach," the science

advisor said. "With a steel ball."

"Yes, sir. It could."

Bach looked around, spied the pool table. He went over, picked up the cue ball from the table and returned. He placed the cue ball on the test spoon, and inserted it in the test volume, bumping the pinball aside.

The pinball bounced down to the floor, but the non-magnetic cue ball floated weightless in the test volume.

"Now *that* is astounding," the science advisor said.

"Excellent, Mr. Bach," the president said.

Bach bumped the cue ball out of the test volume, then retrieved it from the floor and held it out to the president.

"Not even warm," the president said.

He handed the cue ball to his science advisor, who inspected it carefully. It was clearly not metal. The weight was wrong. It was too light to be a ringer.

"Let's have a seat and talk, Mr. Bach."

"One moment, sir."

Bach nodded to Barbara, and she walked him through the rest of the checklist to shut the machine down. Some of the Secret Service people had a little bit of a twitch when the machine popped on power down, but it was clearly from the machine.

They went over to the compound conference table/lunch table/work table and the four of them sat down.

"So this means – to you, Mr. Bach – that you can build an interstellar spaceship."

"Yes, sir."

"How will you do that, Mr. Bach?" the science advisor asked.

"We will manipulate gravity to use dark matter as a propellant, achieving high accelerations, while manipulating gravity in the cabin to keep felt acceleration at one gravity. At a high enough velocity, and with dark matter flux, space-time will open a tunnel for us that will allow us to travel thousands of times the speed of light to our destination."

"How can that be, Mr. Bach? $F = ma$."

"Yes, sir. But the effective space-time mass of the ship in that tunnel will be zero, allowing very high accelerations from a finite force. Also, the speed of light limitation will not apply."

The science adviser mulled that over for a few seconds before turning to the president and nodding.

<And I know better than to doubt you two at this point, don't I, Mr. Bach?> the president asked in Hindi.

<Yes, sir. You do,> Bach replied, also in Hindi.

"Very well, Mr. Bach. At some point, you are going to need things from me. What are those things?"

"I've given quite a bit of thought to this, Mr. President. First, we will need a portable nuclear power station. One of those shipping-container-sized units people keep talking about."

"Which don't exist yet."

"No, sir. But they will soon. We'll need one. Maybe more than one. Second, we'll need clearance to space, worked out with NASA case by case, so we don't run into things during our testing."

The science advisor was scribbling away in a notepad he had produced.

The president nodded.

"What else, Mr. Bach?"

"Cooperation of NASA with radiotelemetry and tracking facilities, so we don't need to reproduce all that."

The president nodded.

"What else, Mr. Bach?"

"That's my wish list at the moment, sir."

"And on what timeframe do you need these things, Mr. Bach?"

"It's hard to say, sir, but I'm planning on two years."

"At which time, I'll still be president. Longer if I get a second term."

He looked to his science advisor, who nodded and put his notebook away.

"Very well, Mr. Bach. When you need those things, you will let me know. I don't think any of those things is a particularly tough pull."

"Excellent, sir. I wasn't sure."

The president nodded and stood up, so everyone else did. He came around the table and shook their hands, each in turn.

"All right, Mr. Bach. Ms. Bach. Thank you so much for such a fascinating demonstration. And congratulations on such a magnificent accomplishment."

"Thank you, sir."

The President of the United States and the National Science Advisor walked to the door, the Secret Service man there opened it for them, and they were gone.

Increasing Gravity

Throughout February and March, as Bach and Barbara worked on their wedding and awaited the president's visit, Vegan worked on the dictionary problem.

There were some issues. It wasn't that there weren't quality bi-lingual dictionaries available, but they were all copyrighted. Vegan solved the problem by using bilingual dictionaries that were out of copyright – the limit being ninety-five years – and compiling them into the Vegan format required for the teaching machine.

Ninety-five years was a long time, however, and there were a lot of new words, such as for technology that had been invented since, like television, computers, and smartphones. Vegan solved for those by searching against a modern bilingual dictionary for the missing entries, and then entering those himself.

Vegan did all of this for one of the easier languages – German – and then documented the process. Barbara sent the bilingual language compiler, the process documentation, and the German dictionary to George Fuller in early April. They had bought another laptop for Vegan to do the dictionary work on, and they shipped that laptop to Fuller as well.

From that, Fuller could hire the appropriate people for each language, and Lingua Zinga could carry out the rest of the languages without help from Vegan.

Over the next year, Lingua Zinga rolled out six more languages: French, Arabic, Portuguese, Russian, Japanese, and German. As language barriers fell, the world economy prospered.

A GENT OF VEGA

And Lingua Zinga continued to make lots and lots and *lots* of money.

The other strange thing that happened is book publishing saw something of a revival. As people learned more languages, they decided to read some of their translated favorite books in the original languages. Copies of Don Quixote in Spanish, and of the works of Jules Verne and Alexander Dumas in French, in particular, became very popular.

Even War and Peace, in the original Russian, was popular, though how many people actually finished it was unknown.

Barbara did the bulk of the work on the wedding weekend, while Bach dug further into gravitonics. The gravitonics textbook was starting to make some sense to him now, where it had been almost impenetrable before.

Bach focused his study now on increasing gravity within a confined space. Where rendering a confined space free of gravity before was a matter of blocking the action of gravitons, increasing gravity was a matter of focusing gravitons. More properly, it was a matter of increasing graviton activity within the space, rather than a focusing per se, but that's how Bach thought about it.

Bach started to relate his study to the plans for the next device in the set of devices for which Vegan had stolen the plans. This would be a variation on the large device they had demonstrated to the president, and they would modify that device going forward to implement the new version.

The original small device Bach saved as a legacy object. The first device man had ever used to manipulate gravity. He would donate it to the Smithsonian when everything went public.

Work on modifying the existing large device began in earnest in April. Fred Durham machined up the new metal pieces required while Bach concentrated on the modifications to the drive electronics.

This variation of the device was much more dangerous than the previous version. The goal was to increase gravity – by a factor of five or ten – within the defined volume. All well and good, as long as the effect stayed within the confined volume. If it did not, very bad things could happen, including flattening the observers.

Bach and Durham proceeded carefully.

During this period, Barbara concentrated on something else entirely: bringing more physicists and engineers aboard the project.

She had brought it up with Bach after the president left.

"Steven, you need more help."

"Fred's doing a great job, Barbara, and I'm not using him close to full time as it is."

"Physics help. Pointy-headed types. And engineers. You need to be directing the effort, not doing it all. It's going to get ahead of you, if it isn't already."

"How do we handle Arthur in that setup, Barbara?"

"Keep him in the house, or out back. You can go to him for assistance when you need it, but aren't you already out of his depth on all this stuff?"

"Yeah. Really, I am. He helps sometimes with the Vegan language stuff, but on the physics he's out of his field."

"So, do you want me to start looking for people?"

"Yes, I guess so, but be very wary of who you're looking at. I don't want the technology to be stolen."

Barbara knew exactly what Bach was talking about, and she

knew who the biggest threats would be.

There was a curious wrinkle to human history. Peoples who had once had an empire held the dream of empire in their hearts. They longed to see it again, and worked toward that goal.

The Chinese, the Russians, the French, the Indians, all held dreams of empire, leftovers of the glorious past. All had long been known for the infringement and theft of intellectual property.

The Persians – modern Iran – had had the most experience of empire of them all. The original Persian Empire had stretched from Macedonia and Libya in the west all the way to the Indus River and the Himalayas, to the very borders of modern China. At various times, Tashkent and Samarkand owed their allegiance to Persepolis.

From 550 BC through all the ages to the present, over a period of almost twenty-six hundred years, a Persian empire had existed for more than half of that time. They had been given separate names, so historians could keep them straight: the Achaemenid Empire, the Seleucid Empire, the Parthian Empire, the Sasanian Empire, the Seljuq Empire, the Safavid Empire.

A Persian empire of one sort or another was the norm throughout history, not the exception, and they remembered.

In contrast, the most famous empire of them all, the Roman Empire, was not an issue. The current inhabitants of Italy were not the same people as the Romans had been.

The United Kingdom was also not a problem. The Brits and Scots had wasted the boldest and brightest of an entire generation, slaughtered on the fields of France. The Scots alone had lost a third of all men of military age in the First World War.

Twenty years later, they had done it all over again.

Knowing all this, Barbara set out to hire the most promising and brightest engineers and physicists she could find. She stayed away from those people of any nationality that had once ruled an empire.

It wasn't racist. It was cultural.

Barbara had no problem attracting people, even to a project as outlandish as building an interstellar spaceship. She was able to pay competitive salaries, offer stock options in a company whose wholly owned subsidiary was wildly successful, and give a sign-on bonus people could keep after working for them for only three months.

By then, they would either be captivated by the project or they were the wrong people anyway.

As physicists came aboard, Bach gave them a single assignment. Spend a month at home with the gravitonics textbook, figure it out, then come in for work.

For electrical engineers, the assignment was to work on the power supply for the next test platform, while for mechanical engineers the assignment was to consider the implications of building the hull of the spaceship.

The electrical engineering problem was pretty wide open. One fellow came up with the brilliant idea of building a line-switched supply that ran off the 220VAC three-phase power that Bach had had brought into the building. With three-phase power, there was always voltage somewhere, and he was able to design a high-voltage, line-switched DC supply that could provide high-current capacity without any sag, even with a small capacitance.

The mechanical engineering people had a simpler problem in some ways. The hull only had to hold one atmosphere of pressure against the vacuum of space, and do so without excessive mechanical stresses on the hull. This last was because the hull would never be subject to anything more than one gravity. It also flew in the face of typical spaceship design because it need not be aerodynamic.

The winning hull design was square in cross-section rather than round, there being no advantage to a round design. There were however many advantages in the utility of the space if it were squared off. No round furniture or anything of the kind was required.

The winning hull design was also flat compared to typical hull designs, getting rid of the need for lots of stairs between decks. It would be a big, square metal box three stories tall, with the human spaces around the outside and the mechanical spaces and drive system in the center.

Cabins were on the bottom floor, command, control, dining, and recreational spaces were on the middle deck, and stores were on the top deck. This way, one went downstairs when one was tired, and stores were moved down instead of up during flight.

The main airlock was on the top floor, moving stores aboard being much more hassle than moving people aboard. There was also a garage/airlock on the upper floor, big enough to hold a minivan.

Computer software people would also be needed when they got closer to launch. All the initial space testing would be unmanned, under computer control, for safety reasons. But that was still quite a ways into the future.

Many of the people coming on board Graviton Dynamics did not originally understand English, but Lingua Zinga fixed that. The international team Barbara hired worked strictly in English beginning day one.

There was plenty of office space for everybody in the two-story portion of the building Lingua Zinga had vacated when it moved to the state capital.

Two months after Barbara's hiring push started, with a dozen or more people working in the building, Bach held his first demonstration. He used the big device, which had not yet been disabled for upgrade to the next design.

When Bach released the cue ball inside the test volume, and it hung motionless in mid-air, there were curses, some excited conversation, and more than a few gasps in the small crowd of onlookers.

Bach's message was simple.

"This is not wishful thinking, people. This is not a theoretical problem. We *can* manipulate gravity. We are going to use this capability to build an interstellar spaceship, on the near term, and you are going to design it.

"You are the very best people we could find in a worldwide search. This is the most exciting project you could possibly be working on.

"We – you and I – are going to do this, ladies and gentlemen. We are going to build this device, and then we are going to go out and look around. See what we see. Find what we find.

"Welcome to the future."

The energy level in the group definitely picked up after Bach's demonstration. The theoretical physicists started arguing about *how* something was possible rather than *if* it was possible. The experimental physicists were whole hog into building the new apparatus. The electrical engineers were working out the details of the three-phase line-switched power supply.

Bach and Barbara talked about it with Vegan one evening in April.

"Sorry that we can't have you involved, Arthur."

"That's OK, Steven. The guys you hired are way out past my training now. It is fun to watch them, however, so thank you for putting the cameras in. How did you get them not to object?"

"We gave them access and told them they were for their own use. To call up a conversation or a statement that they needed to rehear. You know. To get them back into what they were thinking at the time. And we only put them in the conference rooms and the big lab bay. Not in the offices."

"Well, however you did it, it's been a big help. I can stay in touch with what's going on. And I do still get out of doors, out the back of the house with Todd. That is very pleasant."

Todd was sprawled on the floor of the living room. He looked up at the mention of his name, but, as no treats or walkies seemed forthcoming, put his head back down and sighed.

Todd was mostly for security in the house and around the grounds now. The company building had people coming and going day and night, working as it suited them. Some of the younger new hires actually camped out in their offices for the first couple weeks as they looked for apartments in town.

And, given the apparent immunity of some nationalities to comprehensive and enforced traffic laws, they would probably have to institute a shuttle bus from town again.

"I'm glad you can still walk in the woods, Arthur," Barbara said.

"You know, Steven, at some point you are going to have to tell the president about me. Well before you go off and 'discover' Vegans."

"Yes, I know, Arthur. It's still too soon."

"Agreed, Steven. But don't let it go too late. One thing leaders don't like – Vegan as well as human – is to be blindsided by something their people should have told them already."

One thing they had to figure out how to do was measure the field in the test volume. The experimentalists considered this easy. They used an extra cue ball, drilling it at three equally spaced points around its circumference. Installing eye hooks in these holes, they suspended the cue ball with three wires, each of them with a scale on them.

They would weigh the cue ball in one gravity by reading the three scales. Any increase in its weight – due to the increase in gravity in the test volume – would register on the scales.

The day of the big test came in July. Bach and Barbara were observers only. The checklist and procedures were being handled by the emergent natural leaders in the groups.

The leader of the theoreticians read off the checklist as they went. The leaders of the experimentalists and the engineers carried out the procedures.

There was no requirement this time to turn off all the other electricity in the building. The electrical engineers had done their jobs, and their sophisticated power supply was much more efficient than Bach's rather basic effort had been.

Then came the actual test. The field would be adjustable using a heavy industrial control. That would eventually be replaced by circuitry, but for this early testing, they kept it simple.

"Initiate field strength at five percent," the checklister said.

"Initiating field strength at five percent."

"Gravity now reads one point five five."

They had done it. They had increased gravity in the test volume. But the test was not yet finished.

"Increase field strength gradually."

"Increasing field strength."

"Gravity now two."

"Three gravities."

"Five gravities."

"Seven gravities."

"Ten gravities."

"Field strength now at one hundred percent."

"Gravity stable at eleven point five."

"All right. Shutting down now. Reduce field strength gradually to zero," the checklist said.

"Reducing field strength to zero."

The electrical engineering lead cranked the big industrial control back to zero over several seconds.

"Now reading one gravity."

"Shut down power supply."

"Shutting down power supply."

There was no crackle and pop with this supply, but the pilot LED gradually faded to black.

"Power supply shut down."

The audience of engineers and physicists, including Bach and Barbara, now applauded. It was not lost on them what had been achieved.

Bach and Barbara moved through the crowd, shaking everyone's hand.

"Congratulations, everyone."

"Tremendous job. Thank you."

They had cake and champagne, and passed out tee-shirts. Bach had kept it all hidden until the test was concluded.

Shaping The Field

Bach, Barbara, Arthur, and Todd celebrated that night. Bach and Barbara sent out for Italian from their favorite local restaurant, including a double order of tiramisu for dessert. Arthur ate a pound and a half of New York strip steak raw, and Todd got the bones.

Everybody was pretty mellow when they retired to the living room after supper.

"What's next, Steven?"

"Shaping the field."

"Shaping the field?"

"That's what I've been calling it, but it may be more accurate to say externalizing the field. We need to generate the gravity field outside the device, while keeping the field where the device is at one gravity."

"OK. That makes sense. How hard is that?"

"Hardest thing yet. And we have to do it outside."

"Outside? Why?"

"Because otherwise it will pull the building down," Arthur said.

Barbara looked at him, then back to Bach.

"Arthur's right. This is the most dangerous step so far. Pulling the building down is just one of the hazards."

"What are the others, Steven?"

"Well, unlike the previous devices, this one's likely to explode if we don't get it right. Also, if it works, the device will try to fly."

"Oh, my."

"Oh, that wouldn't last long. It would rip out the power

cables and fall back down."

"Steven," Vegan said. "Make the power cable short."

"Yes," Barbara said. "And include pull-out connectors."

"Yes, both of those. But we'll also bolt it down."

"What about the explosion risk?" Barbara asked.

"We need a test cell."

"A what?"

"A concrete pit."

"Ah."

"We may be able to ultimately use it as a launch pad."

"Where are you going to build it? Are we cutting down some of the woods."

"Nah. We'll build it on the adjacent property. Plenty of room out by the road."

"By the road?"

"Well, we may have to have the county close the road during testing. That shouldn't be a problem."

"How long for this phase, Steven?"

"I don't know. I've estimated it at years. Two or three. Four, maybe. We'll just have to see."

"Then I have a proposal for you. For another project."

"Another project? Barbara, you don't think I'm busy enough with this one?"

"Children, Steven. I want to have children."

Bach looked to Vegan, but the alien was busy looking somewhere else. Anywhere else.

"Todd," Vegan said. "Walkies?"

The dog jumped up off the floor and was ready to go, eager and wagging his tail. Vegan didn't bother with the leash. They left, and Bach and Barbara were alone.

"Is it a good time, though, Barbara?"

"No time is perfect, but it's a good time. Steven, in four

years, we can have two kids, and they'll both be walking and out of diapers by the time it's over. And Arthur will be great with kids."

"What makes you think that?"

"Well, he's great with the dog."

"True enough. Umm, I think it's more your decision than mine, Barbara. But I'm good with having kids now if you are. And you're right. The next several years are just going to be one long slog to get to the next step. This is the big one. Once we can do this, we can build a ship. But it's going to take time, so now is a good time. To have children, that is."

"I love you, Steven."

"I love you, too, Barbara."

It was a good thing they had been as careful with Barbara's birth control as they had during the trip from Vega. After her cycles reestablished, she caught on their first attempt.

Bach had more trouble with that attempt than she did. As they made love, his lizard back brain kept shouting, 'No! Don't come in her. You're going to get her pregnant!' Shouting back at the idiot id that that was the whole point did little to shut it up.

Unlike some women, Barbara liked being pregnant, and her body loved it. She was happy, and that's all Bach needed.

While Bach devoted himself to the attempt to shape the field, Barbara took on the job of getting the pad built. Bach specified a hundred-foot by hundred-foot concrete pad with fifty-foot-high walls. Bach also specified a moving gantry crane for delivering items to the surface of the pad, including people. There would be no break in the fifty-foot wall for a door.

Barbara decided to build the pad halfway into the ground,

excavating twenty-five feet and having the other twenty-five feet above ground. This would keep the pad from appearing bigger than the building next door. The excavation dirt would be used to buttress the walls above grade. Siting the pad on the neighboring lot properly also obscured its size. The topography allowed it to appear almost a part of the normal hillside.

The gantry crane would be installed first, to assist with the digging and delivery of rebar for the concrete. Its steel stanchions would be mounted to bedrock, and would become part of the steel reinforcement once the concrete was poured over them. The gantry itself would be over a hundred feet long, to span the pad, and it was fifty feet wide. The rails would be a hundred and seventy-five feet long, so the crane could get completely out of the way of the pad.

First up was drawings and specifications, then requests for bid. The whole setup would be expensive, but Lingua Zinga was making so much money at this point, it wouldn't matter if it was ten times as much.

The construction itself went well. When the construction men saw the obviously pregnant Barbara show up on the site in the supervisor-colored hard hat, they knew better than to mess with her. They were all family men, and they all knew that messing with a woman in nesting mode was not a lot of fun. The result was that she got what she wanted.

The construction itself was massive. Gravel base first, then enough rebar to sink a ship. Steel tie-downs set into the floor, welded to rebar so they couldn't pull out. Twelve inches of interstate-highway grade concrete for the floor. Solid concrete walls, three feet thick at the base tapering to two feet thick at the top, for the side walls, massively rebarred.

Barbara was finished with the construction for the pad before she was finished with the construction of the baby, but it was close.

Barbara woke Bach at five in the morning.

"Steven, it's time."

"How long have you been having contractions?" he asked sleepily.

"Since eight o'clock last night."

That woke him up.

"Why didn't you say anything?" he said as he hurriedly dressed.

"I figured one of us should get some sleep."

Bach drove her into the hospital in her Cadillac, his Corvette being completely the wrong car for her to struggle into and out of. She had her overnight bag with her.

Jared Robert Bach was born at four-thirty-seven in the afternoon that day. Barbara and the baby went home the second day after the birth.

Jared's reaction to meeting Arthur was interesting. His first reaction was to shy away from the alien, but when Vegan made cooing sounds like his mother and father, he reconsidered. Then he tried bugging his eyes out, to match the alien's large, green-faceted eyes. He gave up on that, and simply decided Vegan was a friend.

Barbara, for her part, switched gears as new mothers often do, and decided breasts were for feeding babies, and that was that. She would feed Jared anywhere and anywhen he wanted it, and if someone objected, she didn't much give a damn. Current state law, which had finally stopped being draconian about breast nudity for nursing mothers, backed her up.

Bach delighted in being a father, and spent more time in the house. He still managed the project full-time, but he had good people in charge and he backed down to forty hours a week. He took his lunch at home with Barbara, Jared, and Vegan.

Vegan was very interested in watching the baby human as he grew, and Bach and Barbara always had a willing babysitter for the infant. The alien had never had the ability to watch, over a long period of time, a human infant and its family, and he was professionally interested.

A high-capacity Hyster forklift delivered the test device to the pad just before Jared's first birthday. This was the first test device for shaping the field.

The gantry crane lifted the device and placed it offset toward one front corner of the pad. This was so that any debris from an explosion would not hit the road or the property on the other side of the road, or the neighboring property to the pad. Any debris should land on Bach and Barbara's sixty acres.

Everyone watched the test within the big bay of the workroom. Multiple high-speed cameras were mounted in the pad trained on the device, all of their output displayed on monitors within the workroom. No one was outside.

They brought the machine up to one gravity first. The new, much larger, three-phase line-switched supply the engineers came up with felt this one. Not a one-cubic foot test volume anymore, the test volume was the space around the machine, a hundred foot diameter of the device.

The air for a wide area around the pad was accelerated downward. When it hit the ground, it flowed out, displacing the atmosphere at one gravity around it. That air flowed upward, to fill in the space the downward moving air had vacated. A great toroidal flow of air around the machine started.

The same thing was happening to the dark matter in that

volume, though there was no way to detect it.

At the same time, the gravity closer to the machine continued to measure one gravity. The machine was maintaining one gravity in its near neighborhood, even as it manipulated the gravity farther afield.

The device rose off the pad a foot, to the end of its tethers. It shuddered there, shaking just a bit. Bach recalled the vibration in the alien minivan when they had taken off to meet the alien ship in space.

They took the device up to five gravities, as measured outside the pad. The toroidal flow of air away from the machine increased. So did the shaking of the machine. It strained at its tethers.

When they passed six gravities, the device had had enough. It came apart, and pieces of it flew everywhere. The ones headed for the road or the neighboring property bounced off the sidewalls of the pad and landed in the Bachs' property. Small parts of the device rattled on the roof above the observers.

The biggest piece of debris came down in the backyard, about two hundred feet behind the house.

It had been a test to destruction, but it had been a successful test to destruction. There would be months of analysis of the failure, beefing up some of the parts, and fine tuning of the system, but they had done it. They could shape the field. Generate the field external to the device.

There was cake and champagne.

Months of analysis of the imagery had resulted in a new device. The first device for shaping the field had torn itself apart. There was a way to fix that.

The new device had no fasteners. All the pieces were TIG-welded or MIG-welded together. Every interior corner of the parts had been radiused, to prevent stress concentrations. Every part had been magnafluxed to ensure against microfractures in the materials.

All together, it was a huge step up in the solidity of the structure.

Eight months along, they were ready for another go.

In that eight months, Jared had started talking, and he was well along in his toilet training. Barbara had weaned him off the breast, and she was pregnant again.

Early testing indicated this one would be a girl, and Bach and Barbara were both thrilled about having one of each.

The new device was set up in the same corner as the previous one, and tethered as before. The power supply, as before, was set up just over the lip of the sidewall of the pad, so it wouldn't be exposed to an explosion if it occurred.

But no explosion occurred. They got the device up to eight gravities before the power supply ran out of horsepower. The toroidal movement of air around the pad got truly impressive, picking up dirt and dust as it grew into a roiling grey donut of air.

They shut the device down, and had cake and champagne.

This time, Bach added ice cream.

That night after dinner, Bach, Barbara, and Vegan sat in the living room to review events.

"What's next, Steven?"

"Sizing the device. We need a big one for the ship, and a small one for the minivan. We also need to work on running the small one from batteries, and get a hold of a couple of nuclear power plants for the big one."

"A couple of nuclear power plants?"

"Yes. If it's going anywhere with humans in it, it had better have redundancy on something like that."

"And you start building the ship?"

"The first one. Yes. After that we'll move manufacturing somewhere else. The building will stand empty again."

"Two launches of new companies? Not a bad history there."

"And there's something else we need to do. I think it's time to talk to the president again."

"Well, you're going to have to do that if you're going to get nuclear power plants."

"Yes, but I think it's time we tell him about Arthur."

"Really?"

"Yes. It's time."

Bach looked over to Vegan, who had been watching their conversation quietly.

"I agree, Steven. That is, if you think it's time, I'm good with that. As I said before, the possible error lies in waiting too long."

"OK. Well, I guess that's next up," Barbara said.

"We'll move the device to the center of the pad for that demonstration," Steven said. "It will be more impressive, I think. The toroidal dust cloud will be perfect."

Disclosure

"We have something new to show you, Mr. President."

"What's it been, Mr. Bach? A couple of years?"

"A bit longer, sir. More like three. But we've made a major breakthrough."

"Very well, Mr. Bach. With the election over, I have time to swing by the Midwest. My scheduler will be in touch."

"Thank you, sir."

The presidential motorcade arrived as before. This time, the county sheriff closed off this mile of the county road to everyone except residents. There was no snooping press.

First, Bach took the president and the National Science Advisor to the pad in an electric golf cart. Electric golf carts were also available for the Secret Service detail, and they both preceded and followed Bach's cart.

The president looked up at the gantry crane and at the pad.

"Impressive, Mr. Bach."

"Thank you, sir."

They got to the top of the sidewall of the pad, on the uphill side, and the president looked down into the pad from fifty feet up the sidewall. The device, about the size of two SUVs stacked up, sat in the center of the pad.

"That is the device you're going to show me, Mr. Bach?"

"Yes, sir. We'll actually watch its operation remotely. It's not safe to be here when it's operating, as it affects this whole area. What we have done is build a device that can create gravity around itself, rather than in a small test volume."

"Does the gravity affect the device itself?" the science

advisor asked.

"No, sir. It protects itself and its immediate environs, maintaining one gravity in that area. It generates the high-gravity field outside of that volume. This is necessary for a shipboard application, so the occupants of the ship are protected."

"Impressive."

"Thank you, sir."

Bach drove them back to the building, where staff waited to operate the device. The president, the National Science Advisor, and Barbara, again visibly pregnant, sat in a row of chairs facing the monitors.

"Quite an operation you have here now, Mr. Bach."

"Thank you, sir. I couldn't do it all myself. We've brought on the best and brightest scientists and engineers we could find."

The lead electrical engineer looked to Bach, and Bach nodded. He started the power-up sequence.

"Mr. President, that monitor shows the gravity inside the pad enclosure as well as the gravity outside the enclosure. Also shown is the combined tension on the tethers that hold the device down. That's what's most of interest."

The president nodded.

"All right, Mr. Bach. I get it. We're set."

Bach nodded to his lead experimentalist, and he gradually brought up the field. He stopped when he hit eight gravities. The grey toroidal dust cloud gradually grew in the monitors.

"The toroidal dust cloud is from air being accelerated down nearest to the pad, and then circling up to replace the vacuum created above, sir."

"I've got to see this, Mr. Bach. Is it safe?"

"From here, and for a limited time, yes, sir."

The president and the National Science Advisor got up and

went to the front door. They went out and turned to see the great dust cloud roiling over the pad.

Bach walked up, and the president turned to him.

"I've seen rocket tests before, Mr. Bach, but this is a new one on me."

"Absolutely fascinating," the science advisor said.

"Yes, sir. It's a unique artifact of the gravitonic system."

They went back indoors and the president noted the combined tension number for the tethers.

"Is that real, Mr. Bach?"

"Yes, sir. That reading is in hundreds of tons."

"Excellent."

Bach nodded to the team and they shut down the system, gradually bringing the gravities down, then shutting down the power supply.

"You don't get that thrust number from stirring up the air, Mr. Bach," the science advisor said.

"No, sir. It's from accelerating dark matter through the system. Likely in the same pattern, but we have no way of knowing for sure."

The science advisor thought about it, then nodded to the president.

"This is a tremendous achievement, Mr. Bach. You've discovered another way of achieving space. And without thousands of tons of chemical propellant."

"Yes, Mr. President, but I have something even more important to show you."

"Really?"

"Yes, sir. But for that we need to go back to the house."

Bach, Barbara, the president, the science advisor, and the Secret Service detail headed out the back of the company building and down the path to the house. On getting to the house, Bach turned to the president.

"Mr. President, I need to advise you of two things before we go into the house. First, what I am about to show you is the biggest national security secret of them all. No kidding. It is the most potentially disruptive thing you can possibly imagine. I'm not even sure you want the Secret Service in on this."

"These boys are pretty good at keeping a secret, Mr. Bach."

The president turned to the head of the detail.

"Perhaps just two, though? Your best?"

"We can do that, Mr. President."

The president nodded to him, then turned back to Bach.

"And the other thing, Mr. Bach?"

"There is no danger here to you, Mr. President, but the first reaction of the Secret Service may be that there is. We need to make sure people don't get trigger-happy. The results would be disastrous."

The president turned to the head of his detail again.

"You get that, Mr. Denner?"

"Yes, Mr. President."

Bach led them into the house, and everyone sat in the living room, except for the two Secret Service men, who stood either side of the door.

"So what's this all about, Mr. Bach?"

Bach turned to Barbara.

"Mr. President, years ago, you asked me where we got the technology for Lingua Zinga. I told you we had stolen it from aliens."

"I recall, Ms. Bach."

"But you see, Mr. President, I found I could not lie to the President of the United States. It *is* alien technology, and we *did* steal it from aliens."

"Ms. Bach...."

212

A GENT OF VEGA

"Arthur, you can come in now," Barbara called out.

Vegan walked in from the kitchen. The Secret Service men twitched, but did not go for their guns.

"Good afternoon, Mr. President," Vegan said.

The president sat back and considered.

"Good Lord," the science advisor said.

Vegan turned to Barbara.

"Jared is down for his nap, Barbara."

"Thank you, Arthur."

The president decided, He got up from his seat and walked over to Vegan. The Secret Service men tensed.

"It's good to meet you," the president said, stretching out his hand.

"It's good to meet you, sir," Vegan said.

They shook hands, then the president walked back to his chair and sat. He waved to the last remaining chair for Vegan.

"Why don't you tell me your story?" the president asked.

Vegan sat down and turned to the president.

"Of course, sir.

"My name is unpronounceable by humans."

He pronounced his name, and Barbara laughed.

"It means Bearer of Knowledge. I didn't know Vegan when we met the hive queen, Arthur."

"Yes, of course, Barbara."

Vegan turned back to the president.

"On Earth, Mr. President, I have been going by the name Arthur Vegan. I was sent here from my planet, circling the star you call Vega, some fifty years ago to study human society. I did that, learning what I could without revealing myself, until about five years ago.

"At that time, I revealed myself to Steven here, and subsequently to Barbara. I did that as a way of learning more, and hoping that they would keep my secret, which they have done until now. No one else on Earth knows we aliens exist. And now, you gentlemen know as well."

"Why do you reveal yourself now, Mr. Vegan?"

Vegan turned to Bach.

"I can answer that, Mr. President. Four years ago, Arthur was called back to Vega, for revealing himself to us, in violation of his hive queen's orders. Effectively, a crime. We went along, to defend him. We were all sentenced to death by the hive queen."

"Sentenced to death, Mr. Bach?"

"Yes, Mr. President. Workers, like Arthur, effectively have no rights. Only the queens have rights. Think medieval Europe."

"I see. Carry on, Mr. Bach."

"Yes, sir. I defended Arthur, in part by threatening to kill the queen, with a firearm we had along. She didn't expect that. You see, the race we call Vegans is a multi-planet intelligent species, for all their political structure is medieval. They do not have a consumer society. Nothing is mass-produced, because only the queens and their drones get luxuries.

"They consider us a primitive species, because we aren't interstellar. The queen let us return to Earth, no harm done, until a Convocation of the queens can decide what to do with us. That might include incinerating the planet to get rid of the threat we represent."

"When is this Convocation, Mr. Bach?"

"In a hundred and fifty years, sir. So what we did is, we stole their technology. Everything we could. Everything that wasn't nailed down. The language machine, which was developed so their queens could understand each other despite many different dialects. Their interstellar drive technology.

Everything we could fit on Barbara's laptop."

"Technology theft, Mr. Bach?"

"We have no intellectual property agreement with the Vegans, sir."

"Fair enough."

"So my plan – what I have been working on – is to develop the interstellar drive – make humans a multi-planet species – before the queens consider what to do about us. Go back to the hive queen and present her with a fait accompli. We are now a multi-planet race, therefore not primitive. That changes their options, in their own minds."

"And Lingua Zinga, Mr. Bach?"

"Merely a means to an end, Mr. President. Establish a revenue source for the interstellar effort."

The president nodded.

"Your plan is clear enough, Mr. Bach. I approve. So what's next? Why do you tell me now?"

"Two things, Mr. President. We now have a drive system. I need nuclear power plants to make it fly. That's one.

"The second thing is, the Vegans occupy planets to the north of us. We need to occupy planets they are not on. Avoid contact with them until we are established. So we need to concentrate on spreading to planets south of us. Have a multi-planet species before we confront the hive queen."

"What's your ultimate goal with respect to the Vegans, Mr. Bach?"

"Friends, Mr. President. Partners. We've become good friends with Arthur. There is no reason we can't become friends as species."

The president nodded.

"Friends is always good, Mr. Bach."

Vegan stirred.

"For my own part, Mr. President, I have one more goal."

"And what is that, Mr. Vegan?"

"I want to be a citizen of the United States, sir."

That caught them all by surprise, then Bach nodded.

"That makes sense, sir. He has no rights on Vega."

The president considered.

"There is a test, Mr. Vegan. To be considered, you must pass."

"I already know all of that, sir. My job was to study human society in the United States. You have two houses in Congress. The House of Representatives has four hundred thirty-eight members, four hundred and thirty-five of which can vote. The Senate has one hundred members, two from each state. The Electoral College has the sum of these, five hundred thirty-eight members, which is why it takes two hundred seventy votes in the Electoral College to select the president. I know it all, Mr. President."

"Do you know the Oath of Citizenship as well, Mr. Vegan?"

"Yes, Mr. President. Of course."

The president stood, so everyone else did as well.

"Say it now, Mr. Vegan. Hold up your right hands."

Vegan, now standing, held up both of his right hands and recited the oath.

"I hereby declare, on oath, that I absolutely and entirely renounce and abjure all allegiance and fidelity to any foreign prince, potentate, state, or sovereignty, of whom or which I have heretofore been a subject or citizen; that I will support and defend the Constitution and laws of the United States of America against all enemies, foreign and domestic; that I will bear true faith and allegiance to the same; that I will bear arms on behalf of the United States when required by the law; that I will perform noncombatant service in the Armed Forces of the

A GENT OF VEGA

United States when required by the law; that I will perform work of national importance under civilian direction when required by the law; and that I take this obligation freely, without any mental reservation or purpose of evasion; so help me God."

"Very well, Mr. Vegan. You are, as of now, a citizen of the United States of America. I will see to it that you get the proper certificate to attest to the fact."

The president reached out and shook Vegan's hand.

"Congratulations, Mr. Vegan."

Vegan looked like he was about to cry, which was interesting, because Vegans didn't cry. A human mannerism he had picked up, apparently.

"Thank you, Mr. President."

The president nodded.

"As for you, Mr. Bach, I whole-heartedly endorse your efforts. I will see about those nuclear power plants. Continue on as you have. Since you have the funds you need, I won't be in any hurry to nationalize your efforts and get you bogged down in government red tape. You only have a hundred and fifty years, after all."

"Yes, sir. Thank you, sir."

"And thank you, Mr. Bach, for a very interesting afternoon."

The president was true to his word. Vegan's citizenship certificate showed up two days later, overnight delivery.

Vegan framed it, and hung it on the wall. He also took a picture of it with his smartphone.

"Why the picture, Arthur?" Barbara asked.

"So I will be able to prove it anytime I am asked."

"Who would ask you?"

"No one yet, Barbara. But 'yet' is a big word."

Minivan

One thing Bach could get on with, even without the nuclear power plants, was scaling the existing device. A smaller version was needed for a shuttle – what they had called the alien minivan – and a larger version for the interstellar ship.

Battery technology was improving all the time as continuous work was being done in the area. In particular, one of the electric vehicle companies had recently come out with a new battery that doubled capacity while reducing charge time. It was also a domestic company, which was Bach's preference.

They didn't have a truck-format vehicle, however. Bach wanted a truck so he could fill up the back with enough of the new batteries to run the graviton device.

Another manufacturer had a truck, but it had all-wheel drive, including small electric motors on the front wheels and a large electric motor on the rear wheels. The big electric motor lived under the hood, which volume Bach needed for the graviton device.

The decision was made to get the truck, in a crew cab so it would seat five, and remove the rear-drive motor. The stock vehicle was seriously quick on acceleration, which Bach didn't need. The front-drive motors would be enough to drive the vehicle well enough for what Bach needed.

"OK, so nobody makes what we want," Bach said to his key leaders.

"Right," Anton Cernik said. "We already know that. We can't get enough of the new batteries into any vehicle they make."

"We're gonna have to get them to sell us the batteries so we can put them into the vehicle we want."

"I'm not sure they'll sell the new batteries outside of them being in a car, Steven," Rick Vermat said.

"I'm thinking they will. I'll call the CEO if I have to. Hell, I'll have the president call the CEO if I have to. Failing that, we'll buy several of their cars, strip the batteries out of them, and throw the vehicles away."

"OK, so we get the batteries. Which vehicle do we put them all in?"

"That crew-cab truck."

"There's not enough room under the hood for the device, Steven," Colin Miller said. "I mean, we don't know for sure how the device will scale, but we're pretty sure it won't fit."

"Right. But that vehicle has what? A thousand horsepower? We don't need seven hundred horsepower to the rear wheels. Three hundred horsepower to the front wheels is enough. We strip out the rear-wheel drivetrain, including that godawful huge motor under the hood."

"And the batteries?" Cernik asked.

"We put a topper on the back, and stack 'em up. We fill it, Anton. Plus the existing battery box."

"That'll probably work for capacity. We'll have to see about draw."

"Work up the numbers. Let's see how close we are. We'll extend the bed if we have to."

"All right, Steven," Vermat said. "That's a plan. See about getting those batteries. I'll get the truck."

In the end, Bach figured Barbara would be better at getting the batteries. So Barbara called Cooper Evans, the CEO of the electric vehicle company with the new battery technology.

"Cooper Evans."

"Hello, Mr. Evans. My name is Barbara Bach. I'm the CEO of Graviton Dynamics."

"Hello, Ms. Bach. What can I do for you today?"

"We're very interested in your battery technology for a high-draw mobile application, Mr. Evans. Normal batteries won't work for us, but we think yours will."

"We don't sell the batteries separately, Ms. Bach."

"Understood, Mr. Evans. That's why I'm calling you, and not your sales team."

"The problem is, Ms. Bach, that the new batteries are very expensive. We're currently selling the car model that uses them at a loss, working up the volume to bring the costs down."

"I should mention that this is a national security application, Mr. Evans. Cost is not an issue. We can help with volume, however. We're looking at a dozen or more of those battery packs per vehicle."

"A dozen or more? Per vehicle?"

"Yes, Mr. Evans."

"And this is real?"

"Oh, yes, Mr. Evans. The President of the United States visited our facility last month for a demonstration. He was most impressed. I can have him call you about it if you wish."

"That won't be necessary, Ms. Bach. I saw the news reports, sparse as they were, given that it is a defense application. Let me ask you another question. Would it be helpful if we could package the battery packs to your specification? You know. Form factor, dimensions, that sort of thing? I think you could get higher energy density if we could customize the pack for you."

Barbara looked to Bach, who was monitoring the call. He nodded and gave her a thumbs-up.

"Yes, Mr. Evans. That actually would be helpful."

"Very well, Ms. Bach. Let me get my design people in contact with you."

Colin Miller came by Steven's office two days later.

"I have an idea, and I have bad news, Steven."

"Come on in, Colin. Have a seat."

Miller came in and sat in one of Bach's guest chairs. Bach waved a hand to go ahead.

"The idea is that we move the device from the front of the vehicle to the middle of the vehicle. To the front of the bed, specifically."

"What's the goal there?"

"It gets us closer to the center of mass. I mean, we can shape the field, so it's not a killer to have the device in front, but it makes it easier. Probably more efficient, for that matter."

Bach nodded. Made sense.

"Do we keep the big motor for the rear wheels, then, Colin?"

"Oh, no. We fill up the under-hood area with batteries. As long as they're willing to make battery packs to our specification, we can work around the suspension and all and just fill it up. That also helps with the center-of-mass issue, because those batteries will be way out in front."

"OK. That all sounds good. What's the bad news?"

"It still won't be enough batteries, Steven. Not for the lifetime you want. You figured six hours, right?"

Bach nodded. He had used the time they had spent in the alien minivan, both directions, and doubled it as the time required for running the device off the batteries between charges.

"Well, we're maybe ten percent short. Fifteen. Something like that. We're still working up the numbers on the device."

Bach thought about it. The only limit on the size of the truck was the size of the garage on the spaceship, and they hadn't built the spaceship yet. In the preliminary designs for the spaceship, the easiest direction to go was up.

"How about we extend the topper by a foot? Make it a foot taller. Then we get another topper, cut it down to a foot, and run it out over the crew cab? So we add a foot of batteries, from the top of the windshield all the way back."

Miller thought about it.

"That would probably increase the battery volume by twenty-five percent or so. That should more than do it."

"More is better, less is not so good. Let Anton know, so they can modify the toppers and get the battery manufacturer the correct specs."

"Both items, Steven? Including under the hood?"

"Yeah. Let's do both."

"I'm on it."

They were sitting around after dinner for their typical quiet evening. Jared was in bed, and Daphne had not yet – quite – been born.

"Steven, there's something I don't understand," Barbara said.

"Yes?"

"Something's been bothering me since the president was here and I finally figured out what it is. When we did the demo, we had thrust shown in hundreds of tons, right?"

"Right."

"And he mentioned that an electrical system beat thousands of tons of chemical propellants, right?"

"Right."

"Don't those chemical rockets have thrust in the thousands

of tons? Eight, nine, ten thousand tons?"

"Yes, they do."

"Then how can we make do with hundreds of tons?"

"Ah. Because we've escaped the rocket equation."

"The rocket equation, Steven?"

"A Russian guy named Konstantin Tsiolkovsky came up with something called the ideal rocket equation. It specifies the limits on the performance of any rocket.

"Basically, since you have to carry your propellant with you, that limits what you can accomplish with a rocket. Even if you expel your propulsion mass at the speed of light, you can only accelerate so fast, for so long, because you run out of propellant. Put in more propellant, and now you have to move more mass, and it actually slows you down.

"Ninety percent or more of the mass you can get to orbit with a rocket is propellant and the container you carry it in."

"And that doesn't apply to us?"

"No, because we don't use propellant. Or, rather, we use dark matter as our propellant, and we don't have to carry it with us."

"So hundreds of tons is enough."

"Yes, because none of it is used to accelerate propellant. It's all applied to the payload."

"OK. Got it. Boy, that really makes things easier, doesn't it?"

"Oh, yes. It's the secret sauce for the whole setup. Of course, we have to lift the nuclear reactors to get the electricity. Or, in the case of the truck, the batteries."

Barbara nodded.

"Got it. But that's still a lot less."

She winced.

"Something wrong, Barbara?"

"Daphne's kicking again. She wants out."

"Still a month or more to go yet, right?"

"Five weeks. But I'm ready."

Testing of the small device, when it was ready, was something of an anticlimax compared to the previous device. It barely managed fifty tons of thrust. One difference was testing it in both directions, up and down, but it was still only fifty tons.

The small device did not create the huge toroidal dust cloud of the large device. It was more like the rotor wash of a medium-sized helicopter. Again, it was only fifty tons of thrust, and that was mostly with dark matter, not air.

Then again, the truck, with all the batteries aboard, would weigh only six tons. The small device would be able to accelerate the truck at eight gravities, or something over two hundred and fifty feet per second per second.

That is, in the first second, it would be a hundred and twenty five feet off the ground. After two seconds, it would be at five hundred feet and rising at over three hundred miles an hour.

And still accelerating.

They would have to hold it back in atmosphere to keep from exceeding the sound barrier.

Then again, that was only for the first sixty miles.

The first ten minutes or so.

The weight of the vehicle was actually of some concern. Could they use the standard suspension, brakes, and tires while on the ground?

"What about the weight?" Bach asked. "It's going to be six tons. Plus passengers."

"We're OK, if just barely," said Gary Fram, Bach's chief

mechanic. "The standard vehicle is four and a half tons, and it's a one-ton truck. It actually has twenty-five hundred pounds load capacity. Add to that the trailering capacity, with up to a thousand pounds of tongue weight, and you're just over six tons on wheels. It's not gonna be a sports car, but we're good."

"Excellent."

"Just don't go pulling a trailer with it."

Bach chuckled.

"Yeah, well, that would be a problem when it went airborne anyway."

"I would think so."

Reworking the cabin and the doors so they were airtight was a bigger problem than Bach had anticipated. Oh, cars were pretty tight, but there was a big difference between 'pretty tight' and 'space tight.'

The doors in particular were a problem, as were the windows and the windshield. Gary Fram and his people were all over it though, and, with some help from NASA, they got it done.

They ended up walling off the windows – including the ones in the roof – and the windshield and adding portholes back in. All the doors except one – the front passenger door – were welded shut, and that door was fitted with a double seal and a dogging mechanism.

Various panels also had strength members added, to keep them from bulging in vacuum. Not that bulging was an issue in itself, but stress concentrations going in and out of atmosphere would lead to metal fatigue and, ultimately, failure.

Maneuvering thrusters were also on the to-do list. The graviton device was too gross an effect for fine maneuvering.

More to the point, its effect was all up and down. Oh, they could manipulate the field a bit. Perhaps a forty-five degree angle from straight up or straight down. But fine maneuvering, of the kind it would take to park in the garage on the spacecraft, was not in the cards.

Bach decided on compressed air. Among other things, he could put an air compressor and tank on the truck with little effort. Another thing was that, on Earth, the first fifteen psi of air pressure was free.

Lines, jets, and spool valves was all it took.

Controls were the final issue that had to be resolved. Of course, the truck needed standard driving controls for when it was on the ground, but turning the wheels would not make much difference when in the air.

Bach was sold on the idea of computer controls. When you were coming in from hundreds or thousands of miles in space, it didn't take much of a miss on landing to leave a crater.

Further, much of the initial testing would be unmanned. There was no way people were going aloft in the truck until it had been fully tested, so there had to be some sort of computer control anyway.

Bach worked with his new computer controls group on how to set up the controls until they had an interface he thought was workable. It was much like an elevator, in which one did not control the motor, but instead specified the destination.

The operator of the truck would select the desired location from a satellite map, and the truck would go there.

The truck was fitted with various instrumentation – cameras out the porthole windows, gravitometers, barometers – and prepared for unmanned testing.

A GENT OF VEGA

How the testing would work out, they could not know.

There was some concern initially about how to register the truck with the FAA. It was powered flight, certainly, but not with any propulsion system they had a category for. It was not an airplane that required horizontal velocity to operate. It was not a helicopter that had a powered rotor. It was not a spacecraft, at least not yet.

They registered it initially as a lighter-than-air craft, which was most like the flight characteristics it would exhibit.

As for clearance, they were outside of the controlled airspace of the airport clear on the other side of town. It was a small airport anyway, the commercial flights all using the big international airport in the nearby state capital.

As long as they stayed out of those controlled airspaces, they were good to ten thousand feet.

Testing The Truck

The truck was moved to the pad for testing. With all the batteries topped up, Gary Fram drove it from the work bay of the company building over to the gantry crane. From there, they craned it into the center of the pad.

The device installed in the truck had already been tested, so there would be no static test of the truck.

It would be a flight test, pure and simple.

Bach went into Mission Control, the converted conference room on the first floor.

"All right. We all ready?"

"Yes, Steven. We're good to go," Rick Vermat said.

"All right, Rick. You have control. First test is a thousand feet, then back down."

"And the second is three thousand feet, and the third is nine thousand feet. Yes, I know."

Bach walked back to the door.

"Where will you be, Steven?" Vermat asked.

"Oh, I'll be outside. I'm gonna watch."

"Are you sure that's safe?"

"Sure. If a six-ton truck falls on the building, you won't even see it coming. Outside, I can see it and duck."

Vermat laughed, and Bach headed outside.

He wasn't alone.

They did watch from the front of the building, though, which was quite a distance from the pad. Barbara was there, sitting in a lawn chair nursing Daphne, the infant covered with a blanket against the sun.

There was a big monitor set up on the side of the building, the camera view down into the pad. A voice came from the monitor.

"First test is one thousand feet. Coming up in ten seconds. Five, four, three, two, one, zero."

The truck shot vertically out of the pad, accelerating at eight gravities.

"Holy shit. Look at it go."

The truck stopped a thousand feet in the air – which it reached in four seconds – and simply sat there for fifteen seconds. Then it fell back to the pad.

Except it didn't just fall. It accelerated toward the pad.

"It's gonna crash!" someone called out.

But it didn't. It just ignored gravity and repeated its rapid ascent in the downward direction, slowing hard at the end and settling gently to the pad.

"Wow. That's something."

Several minutes of congratulations and conversation followed, then the voice of Mission Control was back.

"Second test is three thousand feet. Coming up in ten seconds. Five, four, three, two, one, zero."

The truck shot up out of the pad again. It took two seconds to accelerate to three hundred miles an hour at five hundred feet, four seconds to reach twenty-five hundred feet, and two more seconds to decelerate to zero at three thousand feet.

It just hung there for fifteen seconds, stationary in the air.

Then it accelerated down, following the same flight path in reverse. It was a lot more impressive coming toward you at three hundred miles an hour than it was heading away.

Again, it settled gently to the pad at the end.

Several more minutes of congratulations and conversation

followed, then the voice of Mission Control was back.

"Third test is nine thousand feet. Coming up in ten seconds. Five, four, three, two, one, zero."

The truck shot up out of the pad a third time. It took two seconds to accelerate to three hundred miles an hour at five hundred feet, sixteen seconds to reach eighty-five hundred feet, and two more seconds to decelerate to zero at nine thousand feet.

It was a dot against the sky.

Then it was falling – faster than falling, at three hundred miles an hour – but in the last two seconds decelerated and settled to the pad.

"Tests concluded," came the voice.

There was cheering.

There was also champagne, cake, and ice cream.

"So what's the rate of climb of that thing?" Barbara asked.

"Nine thousand feet in twenty seconds? Call it twenty-seven thousand feet per minute."

"That's interceptor territory, Steven. And those aren't from a stop."

He looked at her curiously.

"Daddy's an airplane fanatic, and he didn't have a boy to share his passion with."

"Ah. Yes, it's quick. We didn't want to go over three hundred miles an hour, because we were afraid air friction would tear it apart. It's hardly streamlined."

"Yeah, it's basically a brick of batteries with four seats in it. How was the battery consumption?"

"It went as expected. Which means we could go from a ship in orbit to the surface, and back, on one charge, with change. Alternatively, it has about a three-thousand-mile range if you just drive it around."

Barbara chuckled.

"So you've managed to make the world's longest-range electric vehicle. Nice."

Bach smiled. Now, after two children, Barbara was more beautiful than ever, and she was as sharp as she had ever been. Then, once again, she proved it.

"Steven, I was thinking. I know we're concentrating on building an interstellar space ship, but is there any reason this device wouldn't replace airliners?"

Bach opened his mouth, then shut it. He tried again.

"I don't think it would be worth it, Barbara. Four hours from here to Los Angeles, roughly. Probably couldn't more than cut that in half."

"That may be enough, Steven. And don't forget – no aviation fuel required. But I was thinking more of the long-haul flights. It's over ten hours to Europe. More than twenty to Sydney. How much would it be if we built a big multi-deck seating box and ran it with a graviton device?"

"If you get to orbit, it's probably three hours to just about anywhere, Barbara. Getting to orbit and back is the big deal. A full low-Earth orbit is only ninety minutes for a whole revolution."

Bach thought about it.

"How much does an airliner weigh, Barbara? Do you know?"

"A 747 is a bit over four hundred tons. Well within our range. Without the wings and stabilizers, and without all the fuel, it's much less."

Bach nodded. Shit. That would work.

"You still have the issue of running around in commercial aviation with nuclear reactors aboard. You'd have to have redundant reactors and redundant devices. The whole nuclear thing may be a show-stopper."

Barbara nodded.

"We'll just have to see, Steven. But I know who could handle the job."

"Who's that?"

"George Fuller. I predict that, in a couple of years, he's gonna get bored. That's what happened last time. They didn't actually let him go. He left."

"Wow. So we've got that covered, at least. You know. When we get there. Premature, I think."

"Oh, sure. Couple years, like I said. So who's gonna take the truck out for a spin? First manned testing?"

"Not you or me, that's for sure. We have young kids, and it's not fair to them. Fred Durham volunteered."

"Fred?"

"Yeah. He's semi-retired, the kids are out of the house, and Ms. Durham's gone. He said it'll make his teenage grandkids think he's super cool, assuming it works out."

"Well, it probably will. Can't deny that. Man in space? It's a big deal."

"Yeah. First though is an unmanned orbital test. That's the big one."

"All computer-controlled?"

"Yeah, and with help from NASA."

"Oops. Didn't they have the Mission Control moniker first?"

"Yeah, but we worked it out. They're gonna be Mission Support for this one. We're Mission Control, because we will actually have control of the spacecraft."

"That works."

"Yeah, it's actually come up before, so they were pretty chill about it."

"Well, that's good. I guess the president gave them their marching orders."

"I think so. It sure seems like it."

Prior to the first orbital test, NASA sent them a couple of devices for inclusion on the truck. One was a transponder that would make it easier for NASA to track the vehicle while in orbit. The second was a bidirectional telemetry link compatible with NASA systems for downloading data from the truck and sending commands to it.

The Graviton Dynamics people had been communicating with the truck using local radio, but that would not work at long distances or when the spacecraft was around the other side of the planet. The NASA link would work in those circumstances.

NASA also gave them a dedicated virtual landline to connect to the NASA Mission Support Center. They ran multiple links over it, including the telemetry link and voice and text contact from Mission Control at Graviton Dynamics to Mission Support at NASA.

The first orbital test of the truck was conducted on a Saturday, as there would be fewer commercial flights in the air. With a new spacecraft, it was a sensible precaution.

NASA gave them a half-hour as a launch window, and they agreed that Graviton Dynamics would launch five minutes into the launch window. The flight profile would be locked into the Graviton Dynamics machines as well as the truck's, to ensure it carried on through any loss of the data link.

NASA would also check the tracking against the flight profile.

As the time approached, people in Mission Control were

getting nervous. Bach came in, joking around and getting people to settle down. Then Barbara came in and took an observer's seat. She was cool as a cucumber, as always, and that also helped people calm down.

"This is Mission Support. Launch window is now open."

"This is Mission Control," Rick Vermat said. "Acknowledge launch window open. Launch in two-nine-zero seconds, mark."

"All systems show green, Rick."

"This is Mission Control. We show all systems green. Launch is a go."

"This is Mission Support. Acknowledged. All systems green. Launch is a go."

It was all on automatic now, and they all watched the seconds tick down.

"This is Mission Control. Five, four, three, two, one, launch. The bird is aloft."

"This is Mission Support. Acknowledged. Bird is aloft."

The truck shot out of the pad at zero countdown. It accelerated to three hundred miles an hour in the first two seconds, and held that velocity as it ascended. On-board cameras showed the land falling away.

NASA had been a little skeptical of the flight profile, in that the truck would maintain three hundred miles an hour for the first sixty miles, then accelerate to orbital speed. This was decidedly not the flight profile of a rocket-based spacecraft.

After several minutes, several more monitors started showing data.

"This is Mission Support. We have tracking. We have telemetry."

"This is Mission Control. Acknowledge tracking and telemetry."

As the twelve-minute mark approached, Vermat gave

warning.

"This is Mission Control. Lift phase coming to an end. Acceleration phase will begin in four, three, two, one, now."

The truck went back to eight gravities of acceleration. In addition, the field was being shaped so that the truck started curving to the east, pushing for both orbital altitude and orbital velocity.

"This is Mission Support. Acknowledge acceleration phase. Bird is on profile."

"We're getting a torque from the field, Rick. The truck is starting to rotate on its vertical axis."

"Keep an eye on it."

"Why would that happen?" Barbara asked Bach quietly.

Bach shrugged.

"Could be something to do with the geometry of dark matter so close to the Earth. This is the first time we've sent the truck other than straight up or straight down."

"Ah."

After two minutes of acceleration, the truck was going a bit faster than the orbital velocity needed, while still rising slowly to the orbital altitude.

"This is Mission Control. Acceleration phase ending now."

"This is Mission Support. Acknowledge acceleration phase ended. Bird is on profile."

They waited another couple of minutes.

"This is Mission Support. We now show orbital altitude achieved. Stable orbit at three hundred miles."

There were cheers in Mission Control, and Bach and Barbara high-fived. Vermat keyed the mike for several seconds so Mission Support could hear.

"This is Mission Support. Acknowledge cheering."

That got a laugh out of everyone.

"The rotation is now up to two revolutions per minute, Rick. Should we correct it with thrusters?"

Vermat looked to Bach, and Bach shook his head. He also held up his hand, pointing down. Vermat nodded and turned back to the speaker.

"No. We're going to see if it unwinds itself when we bring it down, or if it speeds up."

Four hours and almost three orbits later, it was time to bring the truck down. Unlike the reentry of normal spacecraft, this one would be a mirror-image of the flight profile on the way up.

The truck itself did not change position. It remained roof in the orbital direction, tires trailing. They would have to flip it eventually, but first up was to see if the deceleration slowed the rotation or sped it up. To do otherwise was to risk tumbling.

"This is Mission Control. First deceleration phase beginning in five, four, three, two, one, zero."

"This is Mission Support. Acknowledge first deceleration phase beginning."

The truck went to eight gravities of deceleration from its orbital velocity. As it did so, and the velocity decreased, the orbit began to decay.

Soon the truck was plunging toward the atmosphere, roof first. As its descent steepened, more of the eight gravities was being applied against its downward speed.

"Rick, the rotation is decreasing. Down to one revolution per minute and falling."

"Roger that. Advise when rotation is zero."

The seconds ticked by.

"Rotation coming up on zero. Five, four, three, two, one, now."

Vermat halted the deceleration phase and used the attitude thrusters – two on the front and two on the back of the vehicle – to rotate the truck end for end and put the wheels down.

"This is Mission Control. First deceleration phase halted for inversion maneuver."

"This is Mission Support. Acknowledge inversion maneuver."

When the truck was right side up, Vermat discontinued the thrusters.

"This is Mission Control. Coasting phase begun."

"This is Mission Support. Acknowledge coasting phase."

The truck was now falling at several thousand miles an hour in an arc toward the planet, and, ultimately, Graviton Dynamics.

With the goal of being at three hundred miles an hour at sixty miles high, deceleration began again.

"This is Mission Control. Begin second deceleration phase."

"This is Mission Support. Acknowledge second deceleration phase. Bird is on profile."

This was a reentry like nothing NASA had ever seen. The spacecraft was down to three hundred miles an hour before ever hitting atmosphere.

Vermat used the computers to time the tipping of the truck to vertical very carefully, so as to bring it down on the pad sixty miles below. Then he *accelerated* the truck against the drag of the atmosphere to maintain three hundred miles per hour.

The truck came screaming down out of the sky at three hundred miles per hour, decelerated in the last five hundred feet, and touched down on the pad.

"This is Mission Control. Touchdown."

"This is Mission Support. Congratulations, Mission Control. Nice flight."

More Testing

When all the cake and ice cream and champagne had been served, Fred Durham came up to Bach.

"I guess I better go get the truck."

"You won't be able to open the door, Fred. Look at that barometer reading inside the truck."

"Half an atmosphere? It leaked then, didn't it?"

"It sure did. But right now it would take about five thousand pounds of pull to open that door. Just let it sit a couple hours and even out. What leaks out can leak back in."

"So the flight was unsuccessful then?"

"No, Fred. It was successful. It showed us what we have to fix."

"Ah. Got it."

NASA sent them a J-sized tank of a luminescent gas they could use to find the leaks on the truck. They put a fitting on the roof C-pillar – with a hand-operated spool valve inside – so they could pressurize the truck using the gas. Crawling all around the truck in the darkened work bay with ultraviolet LED flashlights, Gary Fram's people found two leaks within minutes.

The welders got busy, then they pressurized the truck again. It held pressure for three hours without the pressure moving at all, and Bach declared the problem fixed.

They also now had a pressure equalization valve inside the vehicle, so no one would be trapped inside without enough air and no way to get them out. They could open the valve any time they were below eight thousand feet.

The other problem – the rotation – was harder to deal with. Bach met with Colin Miller, the head of the experimentalists, to talk about it.

"The rotation could have been due to the air leaks we saw, except the leaks weren't in the proper orientation and the rotation reversed itself when we reversed the thrust, so it had to be due to the field."

"Right. I see that," Bach said.

"Now, we know the field can result in rotation. We tried to zero that effect out when we built the device, but clearly we were off by a bit. Not much, but it doesn't take much."

"Understood."

"What I propose doing is not fine-tuning the zeroing, but actually making the rotation adjustable. That way, when we apply the field, we can rotate the machine however we want. This will simplify getting the truck aligned for docking with the spaceship. No need to use the thrusters to do that, except for the fine adjustment."

"Nice. I like it, Collin."

"What that means, though, is disassembling the truck far enough to remove the device, disassembling that, putting in the mechanical means for that adjustment, and reassembling everything. We also need to add commands to the telemetry to control it."

"Right. Also, you probably want to make that part of the software on the spacecraft, so it corrects for rotational thrust as it flies."

"Right. Now, we can do all that, but we need your OK to proceed with it."

"No, all that sounds right to me," Bach said. "Proceed."

"We'll need to retest the device after all that."

"Understood, but that's easy when it's out of the truck. I

don't see a problem."

"All right, Steven. Just making sure we're on the same page."

It was after dinner, the quiet time in the evening when the kids were both in bed.

"Steven, I don't get something," Barbara said.

"Shoot."

"I was looking at the flight profile for the first manned flight, and you still have eight gravities of acceleration. You're gonna smoosh Fred."

"No, we won't, Barbara. Did you look at the gravitometer readings in the cabin? There's five of them. One below each seat, and one in the center of the cabin. They all read one gravity throughout the flight test."

"Yeah. I didn't get that."

"Simple. We run minus seven gravities through the cabin while we're generating eight gravities of acceleration. It's actually a bit easier to do that, because we have a graviton flux opposite the one we're imposing externally."

"OK, Steven, I get that. But that brings up another question. Why is it not nine gravities of thrust up, and seven gravities down, when you're fighting Earth's gravity in one direction and running with it in the other?"

"That's a variation on a theme. We block the graviton flux from the Earth when we're under graviton drive, so the Earth's gravity doesn't affect the acceleration. That's pretty easy compared to generating the external field."

"But it still orbits the Earth under Earth's gravitation."

"Yes, once we've shut off the drive. At that point, we're generating gravity in the cabin for passenger comfort, but we're not running the external field."

"OK, Steven. I guess I get all that. Amazing you can do that, though."

"It helped that you and I and Arthur had the experience of all that from the aliens' minivan. We knew it was all possible going in, so I made sure to challenge people to put all the pieces together the same way."

The static retest of the small device went without incident. So also did the retest of the unmanned orbital flight of the truck, and this time there was no rotation problem.

One difference for the retest of the unmanned orbital flight was that they turned over the truck as soon as it reached orbit. That got a reaction from Rick Vermat once the truck was back on the ground.

"Well, that went swimmingly. A lot less stressful than the first time."

"How so?" Bach asked.

"Flipping the truck over on the way down was a lot more stress, because the timing during the descent is so critical. Not a lot of spare seconds to play around with. This was easier."

He nodded.

"Much easier."

Next up was the manned orbital test, with Fred Durham in the seat. Durham was given training on some things, mostly safety things to ensure he could breathe throughout the test.

NASA had sent Graviton Dynamics a carbon dioxide scrubber. Of course, NASA's missions were much longer – and often in more cramped circumstances – than Graviton Dynamics', so they had more need of such scrubbers. Gary Fram's people mounted it in the console of the truck, where it could be turned on if Durham needed it.

Durham also had access to a compressed air bottle, which he could use to maintain air pressure and oxygen if the truck developed another slow leak.

Finally, Durham had access to the spool valve on the C pillar, which he could use to let air into the truck if he was below eight thousand feet.

As for the controls, there was no training on those. The vehicle's land controls wouldn't be useable in space anyway, they were standard and Durham already knew how to work them. As for the space controls, they weren't accessible to the occupants.

Not yet, anyway.

"I just got two questions."

"Sure, Fred. Go ahead."

"How's a fellow pee in this thing?"

"Umm. Good question. We'll add a couple of those bottles, like in the hospital."

"That works. And this test is on a Saturday, right?"

"Yes, that's right. Less air traffic to get in the way."

Durham nodded.

"Do I get time-and-a-half on Saturday?"

"Uh, sure."

"Great."

Durham came in early on Saturday, dressed as always in khaki slacks, a short-sleeve work shirt, and steel-toed shoes. He was also carrying a lunch pail.

"What's in the lunch pail, Fred?" Rick Vermat asked.

"My lunch. Like always."

"You want to get in the truck here or on the pad?"

"On the pad. No sense taking unnecessary risks."

For a guy who was going to get shot into space, that seemed weird to Gary Fram, but whatever.

"OK. We'll go down to the pad in the crane's elevator."

They moved the truck first with the crane, then Fram and Durham went down into the pad on what they called the elevator, a caged car on a separate winch.

When Durham got in the truck, he started belting himself in on the passenger side.

"You don't want to sit in the driver's seat?" Gary Fram asked.

"Why? All that climbing over the console, just to have the steering wheel in my lap? Can't steer it anyways. Might's well sit here and be comfortable."

"That's fair."

Durham got belted up, then closed and dogged the door. Fram made sure of the indicators on the outside that it was dogged, then went back up in the elevator car and headed for the company building.

"Five minutes to launch, Fred. Are you OK?" Vermat asked.

Vermat could see Durham on the cabin monitor, but he just wanted to be sure.

"Sure. It's real comfortable in here. Leather interior and all. It's pretty nice."

They watched the minutes tick by.

"All systems show green, Rick."

"This is Mission Control. We show all systems green. Launch is a go."

"This is Mission Support. Acknowledged. All systems green. Launch is a go."

It was all on automatic now, and they all watched the

seconds tick down.

"This is Mission Control. Five, four, three, two, one, launch. The bird is aloft."

"This is Mission Support. Acknowledged. Bird is aloft."

Vermat checked Durham in the cabin monitor. He wasn't smooshed, so that was good. He looked curiously out the porthole window.

"Boy, that's weird."

"What's weird, Fred?"

"I can see the ground falling back, but there's no sense of motion in here at all. You could be showing a movie on the porthole and I wouldn't know the difference. Kind of a subtle vibration, but that's it."

Vermat looked back to Bach, who just nodded.

"Yeah, the vibration is normal, Fred."

"Good. Getting a really nice view now."

After a couple more minutes, several monitors started showing data.

"This is Mission Support. We have tracking. We have telemetry."

"This is Mission Control. Acknowledge tracking and telemetry."

As the twelve-minute mark approached, Vermat gave warning.

"This is Mission Control. Lift phase coming to an end. Acceleration phase will begin in four, three, two, one, now."

Having maintained three hundred miles an hour in the atmosphere, the truck went back to eight gravities of acceleration. In addition, the field was being shaped so that the truck started curving to the east, pushing for both orbital altitude and orbital velocity.

"This is Mission Support. Acknowledge acceleration phase.

Bird is on profile."

As before, the truck was heading for orbit roof first, wheels behind. The hood was pointed up, so Durham was on his back from the Earth's point of view. The apparent gravity in the cabin stayed at one gravity, toward the floor.

After two minutes of acceleration, the truck was going a bit faster than the orbital velocity needed, while still rising slowly to the orbital altitude.

"This is Mission Control. Acceleration phase ending now."

"This is Mission Support. Acknowledge acceleration phase ended. Bird is on profile."

They waited another couple of minutes.

"This is Mission Support. We now show orbital altitude achieved. Stable orbit at three hundred miles."

"Fred, you OK up there?"

"Sure. The view is kinda boring now, though."

"We're gonna fix that now. Prepare for flipover."

"Sure. What do I do?"

"Nothing. Just sit there and see what happens."

"OK."

"This is Mission Control. Initiating inversion maneuver.

"This is Mission Support. Acknowledge inversion maneuver."

Vermat triggered the flipover routine in the truck. Thrusters fired for a short period, the truck flipped over, and the thrusters fired for a short period again to stop the rotation.

"This is Mission Control. Inversion maneuver completed.

"This is Mission Support. Acknowledge inversion maneuver completed."

"Hey, it's real pretty up here now. That's something else."

"You like that view, Fred?"

"Oh, yeah. It makes you realize just how small your troubles really are."

Four hours and almost three orbits later, it was time to bring the truck down. Vermat got in touch with Durham.

"You ready to come down, Fred?"

Durham was eating a sandwich, and had the cup from his Thermos bottle in a cupholder on the console. He held up a finger while he chewed and swallowed, then took a sip of coffee.

"Sorry. Just having a bite. Sure. Anytime is good. It's pretty up here, though. I been enjoying it."

Vermat chuckled.

"All right, Fred. We'll be starting the descent soon."

"Whenever. I'm good."

Vermat had the flight profile programmed in. The timing was critical.

"This is Mission Control. First deceleration phase beginning in five, four, three, two, one, zero."

"This is Mission Support. Acknowledge first deceleration phase beginning."

The truck went to eight gravities of deceleration from its orbital velocity. As it did so, and the velocity decreased, the orbit began to decay.

Soon the truck was plunging toward the atmosphere, wheels first. As its descent steepened, more of the eight gravities was being applied against its downward speed.

At the mark, Vermat halted the first deceleration phase.

"This is Mission Control. First deceleration phase halted for coasting phase."

"This is Mission Support. Acknowledge coasting phase."

The truck was now falling at several thousand miles an hour

in an arc toward the planet.

With the goal of being at three hundred miles an hour at sixty miles high, deceleration began again.

"This is Mission Control. Begin second deceleration phase."

"This is Mission Support. Acknowledge second deceleration phase. Bird is on profile."

The second deceleration phase was timed so that the truck was down to three hundred miles an hour before hitting atmosphere.

Vermat used the computers to time the tipping of the truck to vertical very carefully, so as to bring it down on the pad sixty miles below. Then he accelerated the truck against the drag of the atmosphere to maintain three hundred miles per hour.

The truck came screaming down out of the sky at three hundred miles per hour, decelerated in the last five hundred feet, and touched down on the pad.

"This is Mission Control. Touchdown."

"This is Mission Support. Congratulations, Mission Control. First manned flight. Well done."

There was cake and ice cream and champagne. A big cheer went up when Gary Fram brought Fred Durham back from the pad and Durham walked into the building. There were lots of congratulations for Durham.

"Nicely done, Fred," Bach said.

"I didn't do anything, Mr. Bach. Easiest day of work I ever had. Just went for a ride."

"In space."

"Yeah, but we knew it was all gonna work, Mr. Bach. You done all that testing and all. I was just along for the ride. For all that, it was real pretty up there. No doubt about that."

After half an hour or so, Durham looked at his watch.

"Well, I gotta be getting home, Mr. Bach, if that's OK."

"Sure, Fred. What's the hurry?"

"Well, we got a squall coming in tonight. I seen it from space. I really ought to get the patio furniture in before it hits."

Durham waved goodbye and headed home.

Bach chuckled.

Vermat came up to Bach.

"He seems awfully nonchalant about all this."

"Yes, but remember. He machined all those parts on the device himself. In some sense, he knows that device better than any of us do. He knows what tolerances we held. He never had a doubt about it."

For this occasion, Bach had arranged with the director of the NASA Johnson Space Center in Houston to have cake and ice cream delivered to Mission Support there. Alcoholic drinks weren't allowed in the facility, but he did have a non-alcoholic champagne delivered to Mission Support as well.

The first manned gravitonic flight was a very special occasion.

The Spacecraft

After all the hoopla had calmed down, it was a quiet evening at home that Saturday.

"Fred was a great choice. He was so cool and calm."

"He told me either he would join Marie in the hereafter or have something to impress his grandkids. And he would be the first gravitonic astronaut regardless. He won either way."

"And it's only fair. He was your first employee back when you were building it all yourself."

"Yup."

Steven chuckled.

"What?"

"Oh, just Fred, sitting there, eating his sandwich, with a cup of coffee in the console cup holder."

"An image I'll always treasure," Barbara said. "What's next."

Bach shrugged.

"Build the spaceship."

"Really?"

"Oh, yes. What else?"

"I don't know, Steven. It just seems such a big step. Will you do a press release on any of this?"

"I suppose at some point we should."

"People are going to notice. There will be UFO reports."

"There already are, Barbara."

"Really?"

"Oh, sure. One was pretty accurate. It described a pickup truck, going straight up, at hundreds of miles an hour."

Barbara laughed.

"What did the police make of that one?"

"Not much."

"I figured. Still, Steven, if you build the spaceship and run that sucker up, people are gonna notice."

"Yeah, especially because we can't go three hundred miles an hour in that one. More like thirty miles an hour."

"So slow?"

"Yeah, Barbara. Air resistance for an object that big would tear it apart."

"Well, start thinking about what you say and when. It's going to come up. Didn't NASA already have to tell other nations we were launching something?"

"Yes. International cooperative agreement thing. We let them know so they know it isn't a missile launch or something."

"I imagine if you're launching something with nukes in it, Steven, it's even more of a thing."

"Yeah. There's that. All right. I'll think about it. One of the issues is that, when we go public, the other agents of the hive queens will see it."

Barbara's eyes grew wide.

"You think that's an issue, Steven?"

"Of course. But they won't be able to find Arthur. That's one big advantage we have."

Bach met with Rick Vermat the next week.

"How's the spaceship design going?"

"We're doing well, considering we don't yet know how big the nuclear power plants will be."

"I can fix that for you."

"Oh, good. You've got dimensions, then?"

"Yes. Each is a forty-foot-long high-cube container."

"So eight foot by nine foot six by forty feet. Are those exact dimensions?"

"I don't know, but you can check them when they get here next week."

"Next week?"

"Yes. I just heard."

"How much do they weigh?"

"Nominal shipping weight is twenty tons."

"Each, I assume."

"Yes."

"That's not too bad. OK, Steven. We're on it."

The two trucks showed up one after the other. The gantry crane unloaded them out by the pad with a container grapple. The trucks left, leaving Bach and Vermat staring at the nuclear power plants. They had radiation markings on them, and stenciling in French.

"Wow. Oh, boy. This is great," Vermat said.

"Yeah. Isn't that something?" Bach asked.

"Why are the markings in French?"

"These got, um, diverted from another purpose. For, um, national security reasons."

"What does this one say?" Vermat asked, pointing to a legend by two up arrows.

"This side up for shipping. Didn't you take the Lingua Zinga French class?"

"No, haven't needed it yet. And this one?"

Vermat pointed to a legend by two horizontal arrows, pointing to one end of the container.

"This side up for operation. We specified vertical orientation for operation. They can build them either way."

"And what does this one say?"

Vermat pointed to a legend by the power connections, contained in a recess on the side.

"No user-serviceable parts inside."

"Ha! Don't want us to take it apart, do they?"

"No. Actually, that would probably be a really bad idea."

After that, Vermat laughed at that inscription every time he saw it.

Hamish MacGregor was Bach's new construction manager. The new spaceship was his baby. He had memorized every drawing, drawn up the schedule, and paced every item.

Barbara was trying to keep up with all that was going on by talking to Steven, but she needed this type of thing explained to her while she was looking at it.

So she walked over to the construction site one morning, and grabbed MacGregor.

"Mr. MacGregor, do you have any time this morning for showing me what's going on?"

"Aye, Ms. Bach. I can do that."

"All right, then, Mr. MacGregor. Have at it."

"Aye, ma'am. You'll see we have the whole bottom exterior surface laid down and welded together."

"I thought that was to be welded on both sides."

"Aye. We laid it out and welded the outside, then flipped the whole thing over and welded the inside."

"I see."

"Now, the bottom surface is set on three foot piles – those wooden blocks there – so we can get under it to look for leaks and repair them once we have the shell complete."

"I see that."

"Those great boxes standing up, the blue ones, those are the nuclear power reactors. They are standing up because it is the preferred direction. Otherwise, they would take up too much floor space. They're held vertical by those cables. They are also up on the same sort of blocks, in case we ever have to land the thing in some flat space like a parking lot or something. We canna have them sticking down, you see."

"I see. Mr. MacGregor, are you including feet on the device – some one-foot projections on the bottom or something like that – to allow the device to be landed on an almost flat surface that nevertheless has some projections that could puncture the floor?"

"No, ma'am, but I like it, so we will now.

"Looking at the center of the spacecraft, the walls around the reactors have been built as a tube, so we could weld the back side before we put them up and weld the front side. We don't want to do no welding by those things, that's sure. That's why we're using cables to hold them upright. We don't want to weld nothing to them.

"The reactors will be held to the ship with explosive bolts, so if we need to dump one, we can. It will just slide out of the hole we've built around it."

"Where did you get the explosive bolts, Mr. MacGregor?"

"From NASA, ma'am. NASA loves explosive bolts. They had the good ones in stock."

Barbara nodded.

"Now, those three rooms there. The ones between the two reactors. Three stories tall they are. The bottom room has the primary graviton device, and the top room has the secondary graviton device. Both the same. Both static tested the same. We're hooking those up now.

"That middle room is the electrical room, ma'am. We have electrical switches there for connecting either reactor to either device, so we could have a failure of one of each and still patch things together."

"Those reactors are working now, Mr. MacGregor?"

"Aye, ma'am. That's what all the welders and such are running on, tied into ship's power. Lot of electricity to have to pipe it over here from the shop when we've already got it here for free."

"And how are the graviton devices not powered on?"

"The switches that connect the devices are all turned off, ma'am."

"I want keyed padlocks on all those turned-off switches, Mr. MacGregor."

"Everybody knows better than to turn one of *them* on, ma'am."

Barbara set her face to a carefully neutral expression and swiveled her head to look at him. He hesitated.

"Aye, ma'am. I'll have all those boxes locked up first thing tomorrow."

"Thank you, Mr. MacGregor."

"From the center of the ship out, we're building up walls, floors, and bulkheads as we can, ma'am. Control room is first, so the electrical and computer people can get in there. The garage for the truck will be over on that side there.

"Cabins are on the first floor, as is the sick bay. Control room, captain's day cabin, galley and mess will all be on the second floor. The top floor will be all supplies storage, plus the garage.

"The nuclear reactors will stick out the top of the device another floor, ma'am, but the ship itself stops at three floors."

Barbara looked around as he talked. It was a massive project, eighty feet on a side and thirty feet tall. Forty feet where the reactors stood. There was barely ten feet of space all around it within the hundred-foot-square pad.

Still, it was completely enclosed by the fifty-foot-deep pad. Onlookers need not apply.

"Very well, Mr. MacGregor. Thank you. I'll let you know if I think of anything else."

"Aye, ma'am. Thank you, ma'am."

Hamish MacGregor, after all, knew who the president of the company was.

And he wasn't stupid.

Several weeks later, Bach was reviewing progress with MacGregor.

"We've finished the envelope, and are now fitting out."

"Did you pass the leak test, Hamish?"

"Eventually, yes. We had one leak from the leak test. It was on a weld seam."

"And your response?"

"We closed the leak, Steven. Then we had our best welder review all the welds performed by the welder who made the bad weld."

"You kept track of which welders did which seams?"

"Of course. How else could one assure quality? Anyway, our best welder went around and checked all his work, and she patched up anything she didn't like."

"She?"

"Aye. A lot of the best welders are women, Steven. Women like things pretty, and a pretty weld is a good weld."

"And now you've passed pressure test?"

"Aye."

"With fitting out, how long are we looking at to completion?"

"Three months, if we stay on schedule."

When the envelope was completed, Barbara made an appointment to meet with George Fuller. She asked him to come out to the company from the nearby state capital.

Fuller had done very well from Lingua Zinga. The company now offered two dozen languages, had retail outlets in fifty countries, and had revenues exceeding a quarter *trillion* dollars a year, even as pricing had been reduced to two thousand dollars a language. The market capitalization exceeded two trillion dollars.

George Fuller's stock in the company was worth forty billion dollars.

Fuller rode down to the university town in a chauffeured car, of course, so he could work on the way.

"George, good to see you again."

"You, too, Barbara. It's been too long."

"Well, we've been busy."

"Funny, though," Fuller said. "Even though I keep track, I never see you in the papers. Other than the celebrity stuff, I mean. And that's pretty sparse."

"We work to keep it that way."

Fuller nodded. Most people who were truly wealthy did. And Steven and Barbara Bach were truly wealthy. Graviton Dynamics' shares in Lingua Zinga were worth almost a trillion dollars.

She waved to a chair in her office and they both sat.

"Thanks for coming down today, George. I have two questions for you."

"Go ahead."

"One is, Are you bored yet? And the other is, Do you have a competent second to take over Lingua Zinga?"

"On the second question, of course. You never know what's

going to happen, and you owe it to shareholders not to leave the company in the lurch if something should happen to you.

"The first question is harder. There's certainly plenty to do with Lingua Zinga. That said, it's settling in for the long haul now, erasing the communication barrier.

"Why do you ask? You got something in mind?"

"Yes. Which is why I needed you to come down. Let's go for a walk. I want to show you something."

"Sure. Lead on."

They got up, walked out of her office, then out of doors. They headed up a rise to where a gantry crane was working on the edge of some concrete construction.

"I hope it goes without saying that this is all highly confidential, George."

"Of course."

As he came up to the lip of the concrete, Fuller had a sudden sense of vertigo. What had looked like a hundred-foot-square pavement was a hundred-foot-square pit fifty feet deep, inside of which sat the weirdest thing.

"Barbara, why have you built a windowless steel office building inside a concrete pit?"

"Because it's not an office building, George. It's a spaceship. It flies."

Fuller opened his mouth and closed it. He had learned years ago, after his first dismissal of Lingua Zinga, not to doubt Barbara Bach.

"That is an, um, interesting assertion."

"But it does, George. It does fly. Those two big projections on the top are container-sized nuclear power plants. It flies by manipulating gravity. We've already put a man in space by flying a pickup truck full of batteries into orbit and back."

"I didn't hear anything about that."

"We've kept it all quiet. NASA kept it quiet under orders from the president. Waiting for this. Because this isn't just a spacecraft, George. It's an *interstellar* spacecraft."

"My word."

"Indeed. Now, there's another part of all this. If we can make, as you say, a building fly into space, we can certainly do it with a fuselage. In fact, a fuselage is all you need to take hundreds of people into space, halfway around the world in an hour or so, then land wherever you want.

"You don't even need aviation fuel. Just a nuclear reactor, which will last as long as the airframe.

"That means the long-haul commercial aviation industry as we know it is dead. Probably short-haul, too. Once you get up sixty miles, there's no air and no drag, so you just shoot around wherever you want to go and come back down. No runways. No refueling. No changing tires after every ten landings. No engine rebuilds. None of that. You can just put an airport wherever you want. Right downtown. And fly the things with basically no maintenance."

"I see that. The implications are staggering. You've gotten rid of communications barriers. Now you're getting rid of transportation barriers."

"Right. So we're going to spin off a company. Graviton Aviation. But I don't think we want to get in the airliner business. All those passenger accommodation issues. Dealing with a hundred different airlines. The whole thing is a pain in the ass.

"However, I think there are a couple of companies that might be interested in purchasing the graviton drive."

"I would think. Boeing. Airbus. Bombardier. All of them. They already deal with all those issues."

"Right. I need somebody to head up that new company."

"Nice."

"It won't be easy. There's the whole nuclear problem. There's a redundancy issue. Acceptance issues by the public, because there's apparently nothing holding the thing up. All kinds of issues."

Fuller nodded, looking down at the spacecraft.

"Sure. I see all that."

He turned to Barbara and smiled.

"Sounds like fun. When do I start?"

"Today."

It was all over the business news, which was the head start George Fuller needed to make inroads in talking to people.

"What do you make of the news, Kevin?"

"John, George Fuller leaving Lingua Zinga, the company he built from a startup to a giant Fortune 50 firm in a few short years, is huge news. Then again, in some sense, he's not leaving the company. Lingua Zinga is a spin-off of Graviton Dynamics, Steven and Barbara Bach's company, and George is staying with Graviton Dynamics."

"That's Steven and Barbara Bach, the mysterious billionaires who hold the bulk of Lingua Zinga stock."

"Well, they own Graviton Dynamics, which owns the bulk of Lingua Zinga stock. More or less the same thing, I guess. Which makes them more like trillionaires. The point is, George Fuller is staying with Graviton Dynamics, and spinning off from it a new company, Graviton Aviation."

"So what is Graviton Aviation going to be doing, Kevin?"

"We don't know yet, John. But I'll tell you this. If George Fuller is involved, it's going to be making money. A lot of money. Shares in Boeing, Airbus, and other aviation stocks are down in early trading on the news."

"Well, there you have it everyone. We don't know what George Fuller is up to yet, but we know it's big."

George Fuller pulled some of his team out of Lingua Zinga, and their seconds all moved up into the top spots. They set up shop in the Bachs' university town, not in the state capital, to be closer to the action for now. Most of them had made a lot of money off of Lingua Zinga, and bought additional houses in town for the start-up period. They would move back to their homes in the state capital when the company got off the ground.

Fuller had less trouble getting in contact with the chief executive officers of the various airliner firms than he might have, given the news coverage. His opening line was simple: 'We don't want to compete with you. We want to sell to you. You already buy engines from somebody else, right?'

Fuller had his team looking for a manufacturing site in the nearby state capital. For something this advanced, they wouldn't take over an empty building, they would build new. Taking over an existing building assuming they would tear it down and start over was OK, though.

There was plenty of money available.

Testing The Spacecraft

With the spacecraft nearing completion, Bach's attention turned to testing. One of the problems was that the spacecraft would be a lot harder to hide.

The first reason was obvious. Its size. The ship was the size of a small office building, and four stories tall. Having it rise up out of the surrounding countryside would certainly gain some attention.

The second reason was less obvious. The truck had been much smaller, and it was also, at least somewhat, streamlined. They had been able to have it rise at three hundred miles an hour. They couldn't do that with the spacecraft. The aerodynamic drag was enough to cause problems for the structure.

As aerodynamic drag went as the square of the velocity, they were planning on having the spaceship lift at a rather sedate thirty miles an hour. This meant it would be in sight for a long time.

Various solutions were discussed. The easiest one was pretty simple. Test it at night.

Even that wasn't as simple as it might have been. The FAA wanted running lights on the thing, which negated the whole advantage of lifting at night.

While the FAA and NASA wrangled with that, Bach decided to test it by simply lifting it out of the pad and putting it back down.

That might not be able to be seen by anyone, because the massive grey toroid of dust the large graviton device might raise could obscure the ship from view.

The other piece of the puzzle was that Bach and Barbara had, in the past couple of years, bought up the other properties nearby. Altogether, they owned nine hundred sixty acres, the section across the county road from them and the half-section the company was located on that wasn't forest preserve property.

It was not possible to see anything from closer than a mile away without trespassing, except for along the county road itself.

For now, it would just have to do.

"All right. Let's do it," Bach said.

"We're set, Steven," Vermat called back from the control computer of Mission Control in the company building.

"Let's take it to zero gravity and just hold it there."

"Graviton device now at zero gravity. The spacecraft is just floating there."

"Bring it up a hundred feet or so, Rick, and hover it there."

Vermat brought the gravity up a couple hundredths, and the building slowly rose out of the pad. Vermat backed it down to one gravity as it approached fifty feet clear of the pad.

It just hovered there. At these power levels, there was no toroidal dust cloud, so they might get noticed, or not. The craft was below the tree line, but visible from the road.

"Get some power readings and such," Bach said. "How are our temperatures doing, Rick?"

"We're good, Steven. At this power level, we have hardly any elevation at all."

"Good. Excellent. Let's put it back on the pad."

"Reducing gravity by two hundredths."

The spacecraft slowly settled back into the pad. Its pilings creaked as they took up the load again.

Vermat shut down the graviton device.

"That's it. We're down."

Barbara took the problem to the one person who could probably solve it.

"The problem is, Mr. President, we just don't see how we can test it. It's the size of a small office building, and it's going to go up into space at thirty miles an hour or so."

"I see, Ms. Bach. Hard to miss that."

"Yes, sir."

"One solution for not wanting a little publicity, Ms. Bach, is to instead foster a great deal of publicity. We could try that, if you were of a mind."

"How would that work, Mr. President?"

"I attend. We invite the press, carefully roped off. Probably close the county road and then bring them out in shuttle buses. I say how tremendous of an achievement this is. That it will change the way we think about space and space travel. And then you launch your office building into space."

Barbara looked aghast at Bach, who was monitoring the call.

Surprisingly, he gave her a thumbs up.

"Yes, I think we can make that work, Mr. President."

"Splendid, Ms. Bach. And this plan has an additional plus."

"What's that, sir?"

"I get to watch."

When Barbara got off the phone, she had an immediate question for Bach.

"OK, Steven. What are you thinking?"

"Several things at once. One is that the president certainly knows more about the political background of all this sort of thing than me. I trust his judgment.

"Second is that we need to do something like this soon anyway.

"Third is that it will be a big help to George Fuller's efforts if the President of the United States is in on the deal, at least insofar as being a booster of it.

"Fourth is that this may finally be what we need to get the county to close off this section of road. We own the land on both sides of the road already, and it's not one of their major roads. We need to seriously upgrade the security around here after this, and closing off the road is part of that.

"Finally, we need to expand across the road soon, and this will help with selling that to county zoning."

"How are you going to ask them to zone it?"

"As a spaceport."

Barbara goggled at him.

"You know. Terminals, landing pads, hotels, restaurants. The whole nine yards."

"Yes, I know what a spaceport is. How are the space passengers going to get here, Steven?"

"On George's new airliners, of course."

First was to coordinate a date and a launch window between the president, Graviton Dynamics, and NASA. On a Saturday, once again. It was a month out, and Bach had some things he wanted to do in that month.

First thing was that he fenced off the entire one-and-a-half square miles of their property with a twelve-foot-tall chain-link fence. It turns out that you could get that done quickly if you didn't care what it cost, and Bach didn't. They ran a bulldozer around the inside of the fence to clear a trail for SUVs.

The property across the road was a square mile of corn fields, while the property on their side of the road was the edge of wooded hill country. The fence enclosed three sides of the square mile across, plus their property on this side of the road. The fence ran right across the edge of the state forest behind their property.

The second thing was to build a big square of pavement with four helipads across the road from their facility. They could definitely use them, but it also would make things much easier for the president's visit.

Bach also had a guardhouse built at the electric gates that were installed at either end of that mile of the county road. These would be staffed for the president's visit. When he got approval to close the road, they would be staffed twenty-four-seven. In the meantime, the gates stood open.

The county closed off the county road the night before the launch. The Secret Service helped with that. As this was an announced presidential visit, they were much more fastidious about this one. They liked the fence and the SUV trail a lot.

The president flew into the nearby state capital airport on Air Force One, then three Marine helicopters brought him, his science advisor, and his Secret Service detail to the helipads.

The press pool and other media arrived in shuttle buses later, either from the state capital airport or from campus in town. There was a press tent with various refreshments and food, and it had plenty of chairs. The president's podium was nearby, so they were happy.

"Hello again, Mr. President."

"Hello, Ms. Bach. Mr. Bach. I assume all the little Bachs are with Arthur?"

"Yes, sir."

"He's not involved in any of this, is he?"

"No, sir. Not without talking to you about it first."

"Good. I think that's too early. One thing at a time is best."

"I think you're right, Mr. President."

"So where is this thing? Can I see it first?"

He looked back and forth between Bach and Barbara.

"Of course, sir," Bach said. "Come this way."

They went outside and walked up the side of the hill that enclosed the pad. When they got to the top and looked down into the pit, the president gaped.

"Let me get this straight, Mr. Bach. You are going to send that steel box into orbit, and then bring it back down and land it right here."

"That is correct, Mr. President. We know it will work. We've already taken it a hundred feet high."

"Which was all you could do because people would see it."

"That is correct, sir."

The president looked to his science adviser, who just shook his head, pursed his lips, and shrugged. He had no clue.

"If you think about it, sir, this was the inherent outcome of the demonstration you saw the last time you were here, sir. That proved we *could* do it. Now we *have* done it."

"How much does that building weigh, Mr. Bach?"

"Two hundred and fifty tons fully loaded with people and supplies, Mr. President. About a hundred and fifty right now."

"And your current device has how many tons of thrust?"

"Fifteen hundred tons, sir."

"So you can accelerate that, that office building, at ten gravities?"

"Yes, sir."

"Oh, this is gonna be fun."

As NASA's launch window approached, the president spoke

to the press.

"Thank you for coming today, everybody. I promise you it will be worth it. We are about to see the most astonishing thing any of us has ever seen.

"That is not hyperbole. What you are about to see will change the way we think about space and space travel forever. Steven and Barbara Bach are opening a new door for mankind. A door that has never existed before.

"You will be able, in the decades to come, to tell your admiring grandchildren that you were here, today, and saw it happen.

"I won't take questions until after today's demonstration."

With that, the president sat down in the front row of the seats. The seats were all arranged to face some concrete construction with a gantry crane a few hundred yards away.

The members of the press, most of whom had been present for a NASA launch at some point or another, wondered what it could possibly be. There was only one thing they knew for sure.

They were awfully damn close for a space launch, so it couldn't be that.

There was a big television mounted where people could see it without it spoiling the view. It was a commercial outdoor unit, and had large speakers with it. They started to hear announcements after the president sat down.

"This is Mission Support. Launch window is now open."

"This is Mission Control," Rick Vermat said. "Acknowledge launch window open. Launch in two-nine-zero seconds, mark."

"This is Mission Control. We show all systems green. Launch is a go."

"This is Mission Support. Acknowledged. All systems green.

Launch is a go."

At that point several more people came out and joined the president in the reserved front-row seats. Members of the press recognized Steven Bach and his wife, Barbara Bach. They also had two children with them, a boy of about five, who sat in his own chair and was acting very grown up, and a girl, maybe two, who sat in her mother's lap.

Steven Bach sat next to the president, on the other side from his science advisor, then Barbara Bach, then the little boy.

What was going on? It couldn't be a launch.

The cameras were rolling, though, and that's all that mattered at this point.

"This is Mission Control. Launch in five, four, three, two, one, zero."

The damnedest thing happened. A large – we're talking dozens of feet on a side – metal box rose out of the concrete structure on the hillside and rose straight up into the air at thirty miles an hour.

It just went straight up. There was no noise, no big cloud of flame and smoke. Just this big metal box, going straight up.

The members of the press watched speechless as it ascended, then all started talking at once.

"This is Mission Support. We have tracking. We have telemetry."

"This is Mission Control. Acknowledge tracking and telemetry."

The president stood up and went to the podium. Members of the press shouted out questions, but the president held up his hands for silence.

"I can't answer many questions about what you've just seen,

ladies and gentlemen, but Barbara Bach can. She's the president of Graviton Dynamics. So I'll turn this over to her."

Barbara gave Daphne to Bach, then stood up and walked behind the podium. The president stood to one side.

Barbara couldn't have imagined this scene eight years ago, when she met Steven Bach. The White House press corps was largely made up of people she had seen on television. But she was thirty years old now, had started one of the world's largest companies, had headed up the company that would open space – once and for all – to humanity.

"What you have just seen, ladies and gentlemen, is the first unmanned test launch of the starship *Vegan Dreams*. It operates on a new principle, graviton flux. The launch you've seen uses no large burning of fossil fuels. No chemical rockets. It operates purely on electricity, supplied by two small nuclear power plants carried on-board.

"I will now take your questions."

There were a lot of shouts, and Barbara was at something of a loss. The president stepped up.

"Allow me, Ms. Bach."

The president pointed to a reporter in the front row.

"Sam, go ahead."

Everybody else quieted down. They were used to this game.

"Thank you, Mr. President. Ms. Bach, is *Vegan Dreams* a new space station?"

"No, sir. It is an interstellar spacecraft. That's why I called it a starship."

"Interstellar?"

"Yes."

"And why *Vegan Dreams* as a name?"

"Because Vega is only twenty-five light-years distant. *Vegan Dreams* should be able to get there in a couple of weeks.

Two follow-ups was the most anybody ever got, and there were shouted questions again. The president leaned into the mike and pointed.

"Charlotte, go ahead."

"Thank you, Mr. President. Ms. Bach, you said this was the first unmanned test launch. What happens now?"

"The starship will orbit the Earth three times, then come back down to Earth. We will evaluate all our data, and decide whether another unmanned test is necessary. Once we are satisfied, we will send *Vegan Dreams* up in a manned launch. At that point, we will be in a position to test the interstellar drive."

"Where will it land, Ms. Bach. Will it be a splashdown somewhere?"

"No, ma'am. It's going to land right over there. On those helipads. You're welcome to have your camera crews present for the landing."

"And when does that happen, Ms. Bach?"

"In about ten hours. Two and a half hours up, two and a half hours down, and four and a half hours for three orbits."

More shouted questions.

"Bill, I think you're up."

"Thank you, Mr. President. Ms. Bach, is this a government project or a private project?"

"It's largely a private project, sir, with some support from NASA. That voice you heard as Mission Support is actually NASA's Mission Control Center in Houston. We had help from NASA in determining safe launch windows, as well as using their tracking and telemetry facilities. The bulk of the project was funded by Steven and myself, and the work was done right here."

"So you own this technology?"

"Yes, sir."

"Where did the technology come from, Ms. Bach?"

"We stole it from aliens."

There was general laughter in the White House press corps. Stupid questions often got sassy answers.

Where did any technology come from? From the people who invented it, of course.

The president stepped in.

"I think that's about it for right now, everybody. You've all got some things to chew on there. I hope you all think it was worth your time to come out today.

"Thank you very much."

With that, the president, his science adviser, and the Bachs went back into the Graviton Dynamics building.

The president, ever the retail politician, shook hands with and congratulated every single person at Graviton Dynamics.

He also went back to the house – he, his science advisor, and the two select members of his Secret Service detail – and shook hands with Arthur.

"Thank you, Mr. Vegan. You have done more for your new country than most people who've lived here all their lives."

"Thank you, Mr. President. I… I don't know what to say."

"That's OK, Mr. Vegan. You don't need to say anything. You just keep doing what you're doing."

RICHARD F. WEYAND

Operational

Vermat and his crew stuck the landing, and *Vegan Dreams* ended up within inches of the exact center of the paved square across the road. While most of the White House press corps had left with the president – who was their main job, after all – the pool cameramen stayed to film the descent.

It was in the dark, but the helipad pavement had lights embedded in it at the corners of each helipad, so they did get some great footage.

All the publicity of the event moved the county board, and the county road was closed for this one mile.

The spaceport was a thing.

Bach's company meeting Monday morning was held in the big work bay. Also present was George Fuller and his team.

"All right, everybody. Big shift now.

"Mechanical engineers, your current assignment is to check out *Vegan Dreams* to spec. Everything. Pressure test especially. We need to make sure it came back like it left. We're not sending anyone up in that ship until we're sure it's flight-ready. Then we're going to paint it up all pretty and declare it operational.

"Design engineers. We need two new spacecraft. One is a survey ship, to go out looking at prospective planets for colonization. We need a spacecraft about the size of *Vegan Dreams*. It needs a parasite about the size of an airport shuttle bus, for surveyors to go down to the planet. All that stuff. There are new, denser batteries becoming available, so plan on that.

A GENT OF VEGA

"The other thing we need is a colony ship. Much bigger than *Vegan Dreams*. Something that can carry several thousand colonists in something like steerage, and hundreds of tons of supplies. Oh, and let's put the airlock and the supplies on the bottom floor of this one, as it's going down to the planet and we have to be able to unload it without infrastructure.

"Graviton device people. We need a device with much more thrust. Four or five thousand tons. Something like that. Enough thrust to space the colony ships. Aim high.

"George, what we need from your people is a new office facility and a new manufacturing facility. Both will be built across the road. We have an entire square mile to start with, so don't cramp us.

"We're pretty cramped in here now, and we'll move all of design across the road into the new office space. Two manufacturing facilities are probably desired, one to build the devices and one for the spacecraft hulls. Your initial aviation devices will come out of that shop, so do a nice job.

"All right, everybody. You all know what we're about. Let's get at it."

Bach had left the exterior of *Vegan Dreams* bare metal, as it would be easier to rework weld seams without the paint in the way. Once the ship had been pressure tested, and had passed all other structural tests, they painted it with heat-tolerant epoxy paint. The paint had to be something that would take the thermal abuse of a space application.

They painted *Vegan Dreams* baby blue, with 'Vegan Dreams' in a large navy-blue script on all four sides. The navy blue was the same blue they used for the star field of the U.S. flag they also painted on the ship.

Bach had some concerns about painting the bottom of the

ship. How did one even do that? One of the painters had said, 'Can't you just hover the ship? I can paint it from underneath then.' He would actually be within the one-gravity field of the ship, so that's what they had done.

He had stood right alongside the ship as Rick Vermat lifted it eight feet in the air, then walked under it and spray-painted the entire underside of the ship as it hovered there. He then stepped out from under the ship. Vermat set it back down and shut down the field before the painter walked away from it.

Bach set a hazard premium on his pay for that day.

Crewing the ship was the next hurdle to overcome. Where did you find crew for a spaceship? And one of an entirely new technology at that?

The merchant marine was one obvious choice for spacers who didn't interface with the new technology. But they were not suitable for the tech-adjacent crew positions. A better choice would be U.S. Navy personnel, but how did one do that without ceding control of the ship to the Navy?

Barbara took it up with the president.

"While we expect that the Navy or Space Force will ultimately purchase Graviton Dynamics ships for their own use, Mr. President, we don't want to cede control of our current ship to the government."

"Understood, Ms. Bach. But we have military personnel on temporary duty assignments under civilian control all over the place."

"We do, sir?"

"Yes, Ms. Bach. The simplest example is an officer in university classes. The fact that his class assignments don't come through his chain of command doesn't mean he doesn't have to do his homework."

Barbara chuckled.

"Let me have the Secretary of the Navy get in touch with you, Ms. Bach. He should have a bunch of tech-savvy people over there who want to transition to Space Force. The Air Force has been dominating Space Force for some time now, and I know the Navy wants to get an edge there."

"Thank you, Mr. President."

The President had been right. Rather than the Navy secretary sending them the officer he most wanted to be rid of, the Navy secretary sent them the officer he most wanted to be their guy in Space Force. A very competent and highly tech-savvy commander soon presented himself to Barbara Bach.

"Commander Hugh Kesson reporting for duty, ma'am."

"Have a seat, Commander."

"Yes, ma'am."

"Have they told you anything about your new assignment, Commander?"

"No, ma'am. Just that I was to report here and put myself under your orders."

"Very well. Did you see the structure across the road when you came in, Commander?"

"The baby-blue building, ma'am? It's a warehouse, isn't it?"

"No, Commander. That baby-blue building is a spacecraft. It has the capability of going from port, which is to say here on the ground, to orbit in less than three hours from general quarters."

"Wait. This is the spacecraft for which the president was here to watch the first launch, ma'am?"

"Yes, Commander. We've painted it since the test launch, so you wouldn't have recognized it. But here's the really unbelievable part. It is an *interstellar* spacecraft. It has the capability of going from here to any of the neighboring star systems in less than two weeks."

Kesson tipped his head and squinted his eyes.

"Truly, ma'am?"

"Oh, yes, Commander. And here's the good part. You are her first captain."

"Hot damn! Er, ma'am."

Barbara chuckled.

"Indeed, Captain. As far as being under my orders, I've never served in the military, but my father was Navy. I'll try not to disappoint you.

"Yes, ma'am. Thank you, ma'am."

"Your first job, Captain, is to rustle yourself up a crew. The Secretary of the Navy told me he would give you carte blanche, so go for the people you really want and I'll submit the transfer requests directly to him."

"Yes, ma'am."

Bach was really pleased with Commander Kesson. He was good. Very good. Having submitted his initial crew requests, he studied the ship.

The first thing Kesson did was go over every inch of the ship. Not knowing what he was looking at, in the case of the electrical room and the graviton devices, perhaps, but going over every inch of *Vegan Dreams* as she stood right now.

Kesson reviewed all the videotape of her unmanned test flight. The videos from the press pool. The videos from Mission Control. The videos from the ship's own internal and external cameras.

Kesson also asked for all the documentation they had on the ship, all of it created for internal use. He studied that documentation until he could quote it.

Finally, he went back over every inch of the ship again, with measuring eyes.

Only then did he submit his second crew requests.

Kesson submitted requests for furniture and other interior fittings that had not yet been installed.

He also submitted a request for a building to quarter support personnel and the crew when they weren't aboard the ship. They were currently billeted in a hotel in town, coming in by shuttle bus. As it turned out, the Navy had a shake-the-box kit for such a building, and Barbara requested one be installed by the Navy department.

That building went up Kesson's third week aboard. The Secretary of the Navy was breaking all records in meeting their needs.

As Kesson's crew came aboard, they repeated his actions. They also advised him on the third round of crew requests. These were mostly the enlisted crew. Kesson had waited until his choice of senior chief petty officer came aboard in the first round to make any enlisted requests. The petty officers of the second round selected the enlisted spacers of the third round.

As *Vegan Dreams* would be a training platform for the Navy toward future spacecraft, Kesson filled the cabin spaces with crew, leaving the two VIP suites and an extra officer's cabin for visitors. The total crew would be thirty-five, with five officers and thirty enlisted.

Soon, furniture, tools, supplies, spares, mess equipment and more was arriving for *Vegan Dreams*. They were all lifted to the third-story garage door by an elevator built for the purpose, as the garage door was the only entry to the hull of *Vegan Dreams*.

There were no emergency exits on *Vegan Dreams*. Where would one go?

The Navy had their own way of bringing new ships to operational status, and Barbara deferred to Kesson. The next launch of *Vegan Dreams* would thus be a shakedown cruise, to test all the ship's systems and then come back to port to work through any issues. As *Vegan Dreams* was over-crewed for a routine cruise, they would take one half of the crew on the shakedown cruise.

As the shakedown cruise approached, Kesson had a question.

"What do we do about leaks, sir?" he asked Bach.

"Um. What do you mean, Captain?"

"Well, in the Navy, we always had a protocol for patching leaks. More than one, actually, depending on the size of the leak. But don't we have the same sort of issue here, sir?"

As a result, leak patching stations were provided in multiple places on each floor, now called decks. For small leaks, hard rubber thin disks were provided, which would suck up to the hole. For larger leaks, a metal plate with a built-in aerosol sealant would be used.

Hopefully, they were a simple case of being well prepared.

The FAA had now listed 'Starport USA' on its sectional charts, and noted flight restrictions in the area of the spaceport. It was only for a one-mile radius, and even that was more than they needed. The big issue there is that the flight restrictions extended to sixty thousand feet, the ceiling of aviation operations.

NASA had a launch window for *Vegan Dreams* that was a little different this time. As a shakedown cruise, she was not simply going to orbit.

They would instead circumnavigate the Moon.

A GENT OF VEGA

With flight restrictions in place, they were no longer more or less locked into weekend operations. It was a Tuesday morning, after a busy Monday, when they were ready to depart.

Kesson called general quarters, and all *Vegan Dreams* crew members took up their positions. He gave the all-clear to Mission Control, and Mission Control took control of the spacecraft.

NASA Mission Support announced the launch window, and, five minutes into the launch window, Mission Control gave the final launch countdown. *Vegan Dreams* rose into the sky.

Commander Hugh Kesson sat back in his command chair and watched the ship's cameras on the multiple monitors of the control room, which he called the bridge. The aft camera showed the Earth falling away at thirty miles an hour.

There was nothing felt in the control room that was any different than sitting on the ground. There was no felt acceleration.

Kesson didn't mind Mission Control controlling the launch. That was no different in many respects from having a port pilot bring a ship into or take it out of port. His helmsman was locked out for the moment, but that would change.

Two hours later, his helmsman spoke up.

"We are at sixty miles, Sir. Going to six gravities of acceleration."

They were still under Mission Control, to get out of NASA's space protection volume, and would be until they cleared the synchronous orbit distance. After that, space was pretty clear.

The instrumentation changed, however. The acceleration went abruptly to six gravities, though Kesson felt no difference.

The Earth falling away beneath him, however, started to speed up.

The sky in the side cameras was now black, despite it having been morning when they left Starport USA.

Twenty seconds later, the helmsman spoke up again.

"Velocity increasing rapidly, Sir. We are now at twenty-six hundred miles an hour."

"Faster than an F-15," Kesson said. "Those Air Force boys don't know what they're missing."

There were chuckles around the bridge at that. Inter-service rivalry was a thing.

"Five thousand miles an hour now, Sir. Still going straight up. Speed continues to increase at one hundred thirty miles an hour every second."

They weren't slowing down. That was a hard concept to get used to. The velocity just kept increasing.

"We will pass through synchronous orbit at twenty-two thousand miles above the Earth in about fifteen more minutes, Sir. Our velocity at that time will be one hundred forty three thousand miles an hour."

"Helm, stand by for control transfer in fifteen minutes."

"Aye, Sir. Flight plan programmed into local computers."

Kesson waited as the velocity kept increasing. It was truly remarkable how fast they were going. Faster than any other human-created massive object. That is, anything other than a subatomic particle.

"Through the synchronous satellite belt, Sir. Coming up on control transfer."

"Roger that," Kesson said.

"Control transfer complete, Sir. Ship is under local control."

There had been no change in acceleration. No felt change within the ship. But now the Earth started moving off-center in the aft view.

"Local control is making direction change, Sir. On flight path."

Vegan Dreams swung out in a huge swooping path, aiming for a pass of the moon at nearly two hundred seventy thousand miles from the Earth. It was still accelerating.

Kesson watched the side cameras as the *Vegan Dreams* swung past the back side of the Moon. As it passed the Moon, the helmsman had an update.

"Acceleration now zero, Sir. The ship is reorienting. Flipping over on thrusters."

Kesson watched the Moon flip over in the side view.

"Acceleration back to six gravities now, Sir. We are decelerating."

The ship was now going over four hundred thousand miles an hour, decelerating over a long swooping arc that would take it back to Earth. It shot past the Moon and reemerged on the other side, aiming for a landing, hours hence, on the helipads outside Graviton Dynamics headquarters.

Once they were past the Moon, the galley served lunch to the crew in two shifts. No sense not shaking down the mess as well. Galley crew brought Kesson and the bridge crew lunch at their stations, standing watch as *Vegan Dreams* continued on her pre-programmed flight path. Hot grilled Monte Cristo sandwiches.

One thing to clean up when they got back to Earth, though.

The bridge crew needed cup holders for their coffee.

Vegan Dreams raced back to Earth in a great arc, decelerating all the way. Kesson hoped their calculations for the arrival speed were right. They were coming in awfully fast.

Then again, the computers showed the ship right on her flight profile. He ate lunch and kept an eye on things as the velocity display was rapidly counting down.

At twenty four thousand miles from Earth and a hundred and fifty thousand miles an hour, the helmsman spoke up.

"Coming up on synchronous satellite orbit, Sir. Transition to local control upcoming."

"Roger that."

"Transition to local control has occurred, Sir. We are now vertically descending. Spaceport USA is directly below. Continuing to decelerate."

Which was a good thing in Kesson's mind. They would otherwise leave a pretty big crater. Ever the military man, he considered again how potent a weapon the graviton drive was. If a graviton drive missile came in at several hundred thousand miles an hour, it didn't need a warhead.

Which also meant no radiation.

Survivors would likely have to deal with a volcano instead.

Vegan Dreams hit sixty miles altitude at thirty miles an hour and took two hours to settle to Earth, landing softly on the helipads across from the current Graviton Dynamics headquarters.

"Whaddaya know. Run around the Moon, and still be back in time for supper," Kesson said.

The whole staff of Graviton Dynamics turned out to watch the return of *Vegan Dreams*.

Five officers and fifteen enlisted crew was the most people anyone had ever put into space at once.

A GENT OF VEGA

For a circumnavigation of the Moon, it was extraordinary.

Going Interstellar

"What did you think of the flight, Captain?" Bach asked.

"It was exciting, if a little boring, sir. Not much to do but watch as the computers did the work."

"Yes, well, we're changing that soon, Captain. The next flight will be a circumnavigation of Mars. After that, we're sending you to Barnard's Star."

"Barnard's Star, sir?"

"Yes, Captain. A red dwarf about six light-years away. That will be more like a two-week trip."

"Anything interesting about Barnard's Star, sir?"

"The one thing most interesting is that we're pretty sure there's no intelligent life there. We don't want people – alien people – to get all excited about us before we're ready."

"Understood, sir."

"Also, we know the locations of its planets, which means we can send you there without you worrying about running into anything."

"Always a good thing, sir."

The ship was pressure tested again, as it would be after every flight. Stores were topped up, especially for water and the carbon dioxide scrubbers.

This time the whole crew would be going. It would be much like the circumnavigation of the Moon, but it would take much longer. Days, not hours. This would require the galley to serve three meals a day, rotations on the watch schedules, and other shipboard routines necessary to certify the ship as ready for service.

A GENT OF VEGA

There were cup holders on the bridge now. Also a new item: a virtual-reality headset system that allowed the wearer access to the ship's cameras in a spherical view. Wherever you looked, you saw what you would see from outside the ship, as if you floated in space wherever the ship was.

The Mars mission went without a hitch. Shipboard life settled into the routine of an ocean voyage. Meals, shift changes, watch changes. The routine of a ship on deployment in peacetime.

The virtual display headsets were popular. It was really something to be floating in space, looking around. Some people couldn't handle it, but the others thought it was terrific.

Then it was time for the big trip.

Barbara had one last request for Kesson before they went off to Barnard's Star.

"It's important that you keep transmitting your status, Captain. Even if *Vegan Dreams* was lost with all hands – which we do not expect – you'll only be six light-years away at most. Over the next six years, all your transmissions will arrive back here, and we can make some sense of what happened."

"I understand, ma'am."

The preparations, the launch, lift out of atmosphere, even the acceleration to synchronous satellite orbit, all went as before. It was only when they were out from Mission Control that this mission was different.

Barnard's Star lay along the celestial equator, visible at night in the summer time. Departure was thus set for ten in the evening, so they would be nearly on a bearing to Barnard's Star from the time they left Earth's rotation behind.

There was a minor course correction performed by the on-board computers, then *Vegan Dreams* was outward bound. It continued to accelerate at six gravities, hour after hour, day after day.

At the end of the first day, the helmsman had an update.

"Twenty-four hours from launch, Sir, including the two hours of lift. We are now at ten point three million miles an hour. Still accelerating."

At the end of the second day, a similar message.

"Forty-eight hours from launch, Sir. We are now at twenty-one and a half million miles an hour. Still accelerating."

The end of the third day.

"Seventy-two hours from launch, Sir. Now traveling at thirty-two point eight million miles an hour. Still accelerating."

The end of the fourth day.

"Ninety-six hours from launch, Sir. Current velocity is forty-four million miles per hour. Still accelerating."

They had passed the orbits of Jupiter, Saturn, and Uranus, though none of those planets was currently along their course. They had not yet passed the orbit of Neptune.

They were over two billion miles from home.

Aboard ship, it was the routine of any long voyage. Members of the crew of *Vegan Dreams* were all shipboard types. There were no desk sailors aboard.

One fellow got a little upset about the situation. They had expected some troubles. The senior chief petty officer was sympathetic, but not on the same page.

"Hey, Smitty. So whaddaya think happens if a ship sinks mid-ocean? Same shit. Everybody dies. At least there ain't no sharks."

"No sharks? Chief, there's no *air*."

"Quicker'n sharks, ain't it? Relax, Smitty. It's just the same old shit. Less, actually. Seen anybody watchin' the weather?"

"No."

"See? No bad weather. Easy voyage."

Kesson had been expecting something called the crease to form at fifty million miles an hour or so. A mysterious phenomenon, it was the key to going interstellar.

Steven and Barbara Bach had been a bit cagy about how they knew such a thing would happen, so Kesson guessed they knew things they weren't saying. That was OK. No different than any other posting, for that matter.

But he had his suspicions. After all, how else could they know?

It was early afternoon their fifth day under way when it happened.

They were approaching fifty-two million miles an hour.

"Crease forming, Sir," the helmsman said.

Kesson could see a black circle forming ahead of them. He was glad he knew what it was, because it didn't look good. It expanded as he watched, as if a tube was extending toward them.

It passed over the ship, and extended past them until all of space was black, except for the small outlet of the tube at either end, a long ways forward and a long ways aft.

"Now accelerating at thirty-two thousand gravities, Sir."

It was what Kesson had expected, but it was still staggering. He had felt nothing as the crease passed over them.

Even at such a staggering acceleration as that, it would take them days to reach Barnard's Star, one of the Sun's nearest neighbors.

Space was just that big.

It was two days later that the helmsman announced they were approaching the halfway point on their voyage to Barnard's Star.

"Computers say we're coming up on halfway, Sir. Preparing to reverse thrust and start slowing down. Current velocity is one hundred twenty-three billion miles an hour."

The helmsman turned to look at Kesson.

"Can that possibly be right, Sir? A hundred *billion* miles, in an *hour*?"

"I think it has to be, Fergy, if we're ever going to get there. Six light-years is a ways."

"Aye, Sir."

She turned back to her displays.

"Halfway, Sir. Thrust reversal completed."

No flipping the ship. The inverted gravitonic field was now pushing against their tremendous velocity.

Slowing down would take just as long.

Being in the crease was a bit disturbing for people using the virtual reality headsets. Everything other than the tiny inlet and outlet of the tube fore and aft was the black of space. There was nothing – absolutely nothing – there.

When people found out you could ask the computer to display as if you were at stop in every point along your route, with all the stars displayed, it was much better.

Even at their velocity, stars did not go streaming past, like in some science-fiction movie, but the star field did change a bit over time, as nearer stars moved against the apparent background of more distant suns.

A GENT OF VEGA

People enjoyed that view more than the unnerving reality of the crease.

The flight-velocity curve was symmetric with acceleration and deceleration, so, two days after thrust reversal and four days after entering the crease, *Vegan Dreams* exited the crease. They exited the end of the tube and it fell away behind them.

It would take *Vegan Dreams* a bit over four and a half days to slow down to zero velocity relative to Barnard's Star, and four and a half more days to accelerate back up to the crease velocity.

The system of Barnard's Star lay before them. The star itself was a dim red speck at this distance, while its four close-in planets – all smaller than Earth – were not yet visible at all.

The Sun was visible to the naked eye, as a bright star aft.

The mood in the ship lightened a bit for being out of the crease. As everything was new, there had been no guarantees in their minds that they would exit the crease, and it had begun to wear on everybody.

The trip back would be much easier. It would have a 'been there, done that' feel to it.

Four and a half days of deceleration, and they were at their closest approach to Barnard's Star. They did see one of the planets as something more than a distant spot, though they did not get closer than several million miles away.

Vegan Dreams came to a stop relative to the star, and kept accelerating at six gravities. She started to pick up velocity in the other direction, back toward Earth.

She was on the way home.

Kesson addressed the crew on the occasion. It was near a watch change, and everyone was awake.

"All right, everybody.

"We're halfway through our mission. We got here. Now we do it all again, in the opposite direction. We're heading home.

"Know this, though. We have already made history. We are the first humans to ever go to another star system. Ever. That will always be true, whatever happens at this point.

"It turns out we packed cake and ice cream when we left Earth, and we're going to party a bit now. No champagne, though. You'll just have to wait until we get home for that.

"So we're headed in the other direction, and, in another two weeks, we'll be back on Earth.

"Now let's party."

Four and a half days later, *Vegan Dreams* entered the crease.

This time, people didn't get upset about it. This was just how space worked. You did it going out, you had to do it going home. No big deal.

Future starship trips would always have people aboard who had done it before. Initially from *Vegan Dreams*, later from other ships. But there would always be experienced people aboard, people who could say, 'Yeah. Like always. Nothing to it.'

Only this first trip, on the way out, had been new.

It made a big difference.

Two days later, it was time to reverse acceleration.

"Computers say we're coming up on halfway, Sir. Preparing to reverse thrust and start slowing down. Current velocity is one hundred twenty-three billion miles an hour."

It was the same message as on the way out, but it had a ho-hum, same-old-same-old feel about it.

A GENT OF VEGA

Two more days, of deceleration, and *Vegan Dreams* emerged from the crease. A star, dimmed by distance lay ahead of them.

The difference was that it was the yellow Sun of home.

Bach and Barbara had been getting nervous. They had no idea what the alien ship's acceleration had been on their trip to Vega. They knew it had taken nine days to Vega, and the duration of a trip was not linear with distance, due to the extension of the very high-speed portion of the trip.

Beginning at fourteen days, they were watching for some communication from *Vegan Dreams*. It would have taken the alien ship no more than fifteen days to make the same trip, then emerge at this end of the crease.

They had seen *Vegan Dreams* disappear into the crease when its communications had abruptly ceased. Any communications from the Barnard's Star end of the trip wouldn't arrive for six years. But they should see the ship emerge from the crease at this end on the way back.

They waited, and they worried.

More than twenty-one days had passed since launch when *Vegan Dreams* finally emerged from the crease on the way back from Barnard's Star.

Kesson reported that all was well.

They breathed a sigh of relief for the men and women aboard.

More than that, they had done it. The first human interstellar flight.

Four more days of shipboard routine – meals and crew rotations, watch changes and housekeeping chores – and they were approaching Earth. The longest trip a human ship had ever made was coming, after nearly four weeks, to an end.

Kesson was in his command chair on the bridge as he watched the preparations for turning control back over to Mission Control.

"*Vegan Dreams*, this is Mission Control. Welcome home."
"Thank you, Mission Control. It's good to be home."

They were twenty-four thousand miles out, approaching the synchronous satellite orbit distance, when Mission Control got in touch again.
"This is Mission Control. Prepare for control transfer."
"This is *Vegan Dreams*. Control transfer enabled."
"This is Mission Control. Roger that, *Vegan Dreams*. Control transfer in progress. Control transfer complete. All right, you guys, sit back and enjoy the ride."

Vegan Dreams hit sixty miles altitude at thirty miles an hour and settled to Earth at that reduced speed. She touched down gently on the helipads.
"Kesson to crew. Shore leave for everyone."
The party was great.

Vegan Dreams, in twenty-seven days in space, had traveled over seventy trillion miles, and achieved a top speed in the crease of over a hundred and twenty-three billion miles an hour.

Expansion

Things happened fast after *Vegan Dreams* returned from Barnard's Star.

The president feted the crew at the White House. The president insisted it was a civilian flight, though all of the crew appeared in their Navy uniforms.

The announcement that the United States had interstellar capability, and that an era of colonization was opening, caused some consternation internationally. Some countries insisted that the U.S. share the technology.

How the president handled it was typified by his interaction with the chairman of the Chinese Communist Party. Conducted in Mandarin Chinese, of course.

"Look, Mr. Chairman. I think you should look on this as an opportunity. Think about it. You've got a bunch of people causing trouble, right? Democracy activists and all that. Ornery sorts. Just the kind of people who are good at colonization.

"Send them off to a colony. You can have a Chinese colony, and get rid of your troublemakers at the same time. It's just not that expensive. You've got to do something with all the dollars you make in foreign trade anyway. Pay us to get rid of all your troublemakers for you. It's an easy solution."

Variations on the theme were used for other countries, depending on their government and relations with the U.S.

Bach and Barbara bought three more square miles of farmland, making Spaceport USA four square miles, two miles on a side. It was all fenced in, and the county closed the roads through the facility. The county also upgraded the road to the center of the facility from town, on the opposite side of the facility from the Bachs' house.

George Fuller's team had the office building completed, and Graviton Dynamics staff moved across the road into the new building. The mammoth manufacturing facility was nearing completion, though it looked like it would have to be expanded almost immediately.

A subdivision was being built toward town from the facility, to house all the people they would be hiring. George Fuller's team built in plans for a people mover with multiple branches: from the subdivision to the Graviton Dynamics facility, from the parking lots to the spaceport terminals, and from the Graviton Dynamics facility to the terminals.

The president also came out to Graviton Dynamics for a visit, ostensibly for the opening of the new building and to see *Vegan Dreams* for himself. They met privately in the house, and Vegan was present, as was the president's science advisor.

"That ship is amazing. That's the same one I saw go up on its first flight, Ms. Bach?"

"Yes, sir. We painted it, and of course, it's been back and forth to Barnard's Star since then, but it's the same ship. The only one at the moment."

"Amazing. Well, there's some things we need to talk about now. Military things, among others. Am I right in thinking you could put a graviton device on a missile, and just accelerate it at somebody? Like from the Moon or something?"

"Or from a graviton ship. Yes, Mr. President. You need to have it far enough out it could build up a head of steam coming in, but you could make a pretty big bang with that, no doubt about it."

"And no warhead. No radiation."

"Well, there would be radiation from the power plant, sir. We still need to power the device."

"What about a big brick of batteries, Ms. Bach? Could you do it that way, instead? Batteries keep getting better, don't they?"

"Yes, sir. We'd have to look at the energy budget, but that sounds possible."

"Please look at it and let me know, Ms. Bach. Another question. Could you make a fighter platform with one of these devices? By putting the graviton device on some sort of pivot?"

He turned to his science advisor.

"What did you call it, Matt?"

"A gimbal, Mr. President."

The science advisor turned to Barbara.

"Could the graviton device be mounted on a gimbal, Ms. Bach, and thus accelerate a weapons platform in any direction?"

"Yes, sir. But the cabin gravity would change axis with it."

"My understanding is that you set the cabin gravity. Could you set the cabin gravity to a lower value, say one-half gravity, and solve the problem that way?"

Barbara looked to Bach, and he answered.

"Yes, sir. We can do that. For atmospheric use, you still have air resistance to worry about. And sonic booms. That sort of thing."

"But you can change the shape, right, Mr. Bach?" the president asked. "Make it sharp edged, like a flying saucer or something?"

"Yes, sir. We can do that."

"OK. Good. Because we have these laser guns now. They need a nuclear power plant to run them, but you already have two of those aboard. What we would end up with is an attack plane that could exceed the velocity of anything else out there, and then shoot them at with a laser cannon."

"That certainly sounds doable, sir."

The president turned back to Barbara.

"All right, Ms. Bach. DARPA has a hidden budget. I'm going to have them get in touch about doing some prototypes. Charge them what it costs. Don't lose money on the deal. We need you guys around."

"Yes, Mr. President."

"Another thing we need to talk about is colonization. Have you given any thought to that?"

"Yes, sir. We have planet survey ships and colony ships on the drawing boards right now."

"Good. I keep thinking about the hive queen, Ms. Bach. We need to get colonization under way, because she's the biggest national security threat we have at the moment."

"I agree, sir."

"You may not have seen it if you don't pay attention to the scandal rags, but I heard that two college kids in town here were supposedly visited by buglike aliens, looking for another of their kind."

"Oh, my."

"Yes. They were living in your former apartment, Mr. Bach."

Bach nodded.

"Arthur had an implanted transmitter when he came to Earth, Mr. President. So they could always find him. Before we moved out here, he took it out and we hid it behind one of the baseboards in the apartment."

"Well, they came looking for him, Mr. Bach, so I'd say the hive queen is probably a little annoyed with somebody."

"Agreed, sir."

"So we need to get the colony effort under way. I'm prepared to buy those survey ships and colony ships as fast as you can make them, Ms. Bach."

"Yes, sir."

"One last thing before I go. We have another election coming up. I can't run again, but my vice president is going to run. I think he'll likely win. The other side can't seem to get their direction together, and they don't know what to make of the space stuff, which has been very popular."

Bach and Barbara both nodded, and the president continued.

"Depending on which way the election goes, it could make a big difference in the situation you guys find yourselves in. We can talk about that in November, after the election. I can tell you, though, that the VP is a good man, and he's been kept up on things."

The president looked at Vegan and back at Barbara.

"Most things, anyway."

Barbara smiled.

"I understand, Mr. President."

"All right. I've got to go. Get those things going for me, will you, Ms. Bach? We've got to keep this all moving. Our only mistake now would be to slow down."

After the president left, Arthur was upset.

"She's after me, Steven. The hive queen."

"Calm down, Arthur. She can't find you here."

"But she knows I was with you, Steven."

"He's got a point," Barbara said.

"Yes, but that was years ago, and with the security around here, they can't get at you anyway."

That security increased markedly when DARPA got involved. Graviton Dynamics was now a defense contractor, and the rules were different.

Among other things, the FBI now went through the process of getting their employees security clearances. Six of them were found to have hidden pasts that were problematic. They were let go. All of them were more recent hires, not the people Barbara had brought on initially and who had been with them so long.

The Bachs did not have to go through any investigations. The president unilaterally gave Top Secret clearances to Steven Bach, Barbara Bach, Arthur Vegan, and George Fuller.

"Nothing else makes any sense," he said. "I need them working on their project, and not wasting time on nonsense."

Mindful of the previous run-in the IRS had had with this president with regard to the Bachs – and the mysterious character Arthur Vegan, whoever he was – over the initial gold bullion investment in Graviton Dynamics and Lingua Zinga, the FBI did not object.

Todd died that year, of old age, and the children were very sad about it. Bach bought two more guard dogs from the same outfit, one for each of the kids. Of course, Arthur normally took care of walkies, but two such highly trained dogs were better by his lights than one anyway.

Bach also bought Vegan a handgun that fit his hand, and the alien carried it in a pouch he wore on a shoulder strap. Once he had the feel for it, he was an excellent shot. The aliens were stronger than humans, and Vegan was the only person Bach had ever seen who was able to double-tap with a ten-millimeter semi-automatic pistol.

Two more designs were laid down in the Graviton Dynamics design department. A gravitonic attack ship, and a gravitonic space-to-surface missile. These were on the DARPA side of the house, and security was tight. They were just getting started.

The designs for the survey ship and the colony ship were proceeding apace, however. Survey ships would be built first, because the colony ships would have nowhere to go until the planet surveys came in.

Battery technology improved to the point that the truck could be run mostly with the batteries under the hood, with just a few in the back. This opened up some of the bed of the truck – and all the volume of the topper on the back and over the cab – for supplies transfer to a ship in orbit.

Airport shuttle buses would also be fitted with a graviton device and batteries. Some of them were electric already, so it was a quick conversion. These vehicles were required for the survey ships to carry engineers and scientists down to candidate planets that were still candidates after orbital survey.

The survey ships themselves would be modeled on the *Vegan Dreams*. A bigger garage, for the shuttle bus, was the big change. As *Vegan Dreams* was over-crewed on the trip to Barnard's Star, that meant the survey ships would have more room for single cabins for the scientists and engineers doing the surveys.

The colony ship design was massive in comparison. Eight decks, a hundred and sixty feet on a side, it was over ten times bigger than the *Vegan Dreams* in volume. Its garage door would be on the lower deck, as the colony ships would make landfall.

These ships – and Fuller's aviation applications – required different sizes of graviton device. As they worked on the devices, they became smaller for a given thrust. The concrete pad by the old building was used a lot in proofing out these designs.

When the new three-thousand-ton device came out, it was small enough to be retrofit into *Vegan Dreams*. Commander Kesson supervised the upgrade.

From the time it took *Vegan Dreams* to complete the Barnard's Star mission, Bach had concluded that the alien ship they had taken to Vega and back was making more like ten gravities. *Vegan Dreams*, with its original fifteen-hundred-ton devices, was making six gravities.

Now with three-thousand tons of thrust, *Vegan Dreams* would be able to make twelve gravities, and outperform the alien ship.

The vice president won the election. With a friendly transition under way, he found time on a trip home to stop in at Graviton Dynamics. The eight-thousand-foot runway at Spaceport USA was a help.

"The president said I should stop in and say 'Hi,' Ms. Bach. That there were things he could not tell me, but that you could."

"Yes, sir. But your Secret Service detail will have to leave. Everybody but the head of detail."

There was pushback on that, but the new president-elect was made of the same stuff as his predecessor.

"Do you see anything here that one of you couldn't handle? I thought you guys were good at your jobs."

The others left, then Bach cautioned the remaining agent.

"There is no danger here. Do not get trigger-happy."

He simply nodded, and Barbara turned back to the president-elect.

"When I said at the press conference that we stole the technology from aliens, sir, I was not kidding. Arthur, come in, please."

Vegan walked into the room. The Secret Service agent twitched, but Barbara held up a finger to him.

"Hello, sir," Vegan said. "My name is Arthur Vegan. I'm pleased to meet you."

Vegan held out his upper right hand. The president-elect, quick to recover, jumped to his feet and shook Vegan's hand.

"It's good to meet you as well, Mr. Vegan."

They were both seated.

"Arthur, you need to tell the vice president your story."

Vegan told the president-elect about his friendship with Steven Bach, his being recalled to the hive queen, Bach and Barbara both going along. About the hive queen's sentence of death for all three, and Bach's threat, as well as the queen's threat in return. About them stealing the alien technology, and using it to create Lingua Zinga and Graviton Dynamics. About the current president making him a citizen of the United States of America, and how proud he was of that status.

When Vegan wound down, Barbara said simply, "And that's how we got where we are, sir."

"What a remarkable story, Mr. Vegan. But it also points out a terrible danger."

"That's correct, sir," Bach said. "The hive queen and her cronies are still out there. They know what we're up to. And they can destroy the Earth anytime they want. We desperately need to go interstellar, to forestall their possible actions."

"They know what we're up to, Mr. Bach?"

"They've been trying to find Arthur."

"Vegan agents here on Earth?"

"Yes, sir. There's a reason the Secret Service never has a problem with our security here. We keep it very tight. To protect Arthur."

"Well, now I know the rest of the story. The president has played this very close to his chest, but he thought there were things I needed to know before taking over in January, and you were a big part of that."

"Yes, sir. They're a huge national security hazard. The alien queens. That said, the first survey ships will come out of manufacturing in February. It's up to you what we do then."

"Oh, we're going to buy them from you, Mr. Bach, staff them, and go find some colonies. I can commit that to you right now."

"They're not cheap, sir," Barbara said. "Just so you know. There's a lot of high-precision machinery in there."

"Oh, it'll come out of the defense budget, Ms. Bach. We have the funds."

"Very good, sir. We'll be in touch."

Five survey ships rolled out of manufacturing in February and into March, one a week. Their crews included one officer and five crew each from the *Vegan Dreams*. They would not be totally green crews.

The Defense Department bought them all and the Navy staffed them. The Secretary of the Navy was as careful of his captain choices as he had been with Commander Kesson.

Then one ship took off, every week, to go and survey planets that astronomers had discovered around the nearby stars.

They concentrated on the southern hemisphere of stars, the northern hemisphere being strictly off-limits.

For they did not know which stars in Vega's direction the hive queens inhabited.

The First Colony

The first colony ship came off the line over three months after the survey ships. It was massive.

The bottom three decks – A Deck, B Deck, and C Deck – were each twenty feet tall, to accommodate double-stacked containers of colony supplies. The next deck, D Deck, was the command deck, which combined all the control and mechanical spaces, as well as cabins for the crew. The next deck, E Deck, was the supplies for the trip.

The next three decks were steerage decks, for the colonists themselves. It was crammed, no two ways about it. Cabins were six by nine feet, with three-high bunk beds on either side, each three feet wide. Six folding chairs hung on the end wall between them.

The three-foot-wide doors were placed slightly off center. If three couples wanted to push the bunk beds together, they could do that and still get in and out. The doors opened out into the three-foot-wide corridor, there being no swing for the door in the room. The doors could be latched back against the wall of the corridor.

There was a galley on each of F, G, and H Decks, but they would eat in shifts, all day long. Each deck held fourteen hundred colonists, and there was no way to have them all eat in one sitting.

Bathrooms were segregated male and female. These were cramped as well, stalls being a luxury they could not afford for showers, urinals, and stools.

It was spartan living, to be sure, but they would only have to put up with it for two or three weeks.

Crew cabins, by contrast, seemed luxurious. Only one cabin mate for enlisted, and separate cabins for officers. Then again, the crew would space the ship in both directions, and then, after being serviced and reloaded, they would do it again.

The gravitonic devices used in the colony ships were the new, massive, twenty-five-thousand-ton-thrust units. They were the only thing that could get the four-thousand-ton loaded colony ships to six gravities.

The reasons for containerizing the colony supplies were simple. The colony ship would not make just one run per colony. Each colony ship was dedicated to a colony. The faster they could empty the colony ship the sooner they could get the next load of supplies and colonists.

The other reason was that the empty containers themselves constituted permanent shelter. It would be tents for quite a while at each colony, as it had been in the American Old West. But as containers kept coming in, and were emptied, they could be used for more permanent shelter.

The military threw up two dozen more quarters buildings on Spaceport USA, to collect colonists preparing for departure. There was some training involved, and they needed them gathered together before departure.

The decision was made to have the first load of colonists for each colony be military people and their dependents. This was all wives and husbands, as no children would go in the first load to any colony. Military people nearing retirement or end of enlistment were given the option of signing up for colony deployment to finish out their active service.

The initial colony efforts would be in primitive conditions, but it wouldn't be any more difficult than some of the deployments they had been on.

And nobody would be shooting at them.

There were two garage doors on the colony ships. One was a massive fifty-foot drop-down door on A Deck. This would allow forty-foot containers to be unloaded sideways, which made the container grapple much safer and smaller for loading and unloading. Containers were loaded from C Deck on down. When A Deck and B Deck were loaded, the elevator between A, B, and C decks was itself loaded as well. Not one square inch was wasted.

The second garage door was on E Deck, the supplies deck. Seventy feet off the ground, this normal-sized roll-up garage door allowed entry and exit for personnel and supplies was on the supply deck, to make loading supplies easier. It was reached by an elevator built into the ship for the purpose.

The colony ships were also different from Vegan Dreams and the survey ships in another way. A, B, and C decks were isolated from the other decks. They were air-tight, and sealed off from the others. This would become important when livestock was transported.

Also, and little talked about, the command deck or crew deck, Deck D, could be locked from the colonist decks. There was no way four thousand colonists could take over the ship, as the ship's crew could isolate themselves from the colonists.

There was a cache of emergency supplies on Deck D – enough to get home, though meals would not be fancy – in case, somehow, things got out of hand.

When the first colony ship came off the line, it was floated on its own graviton devices, then shoved to its takeoff location.

It was taken into orbit and back as a shakedown run, then pressure tested on its return to Spaceport USA.

Loading started immediately upon its return. Containers of barracks tents, mess tents, and hospital tents, a nuclear power plant, containers of tools and equipment, containers of MREs. The list was endless, and hundreds of containers gradually took their places on the bottom three decks of the ship.

Colonists, too, were being assembled. Over four thousand people for the first colony ship alone. Training on some items was conducted, in separate tracks, for the various groups coming in.

One nice thing was that training on other items – like setting up barracks tents, galley tents, and hospital tents – was not required. The incoming colonists already had people who knew these tasks. So, too, for some specialty skills, like handling a container grapple. The military people selected from the colonization volunteers included necessary specialties for each of the colony ships.

The colonist galleys on the colony ships would be manned by the colonists themselves. No sense taking galley cooks along only to deadhead them back to Earth. They would run the galleys on board the colony ship, then move directly to the mess tents as the colony got set up.

In the meantime, it would be MREs for everyone.

They were sitting around after dinner. The kids were playing quietly on the floor. Mostly quietly, anyway. Some game or other involving dolls and toy trucks.

"Well, the first colony ship is ready to go," Barbara said.

"And the second one is off the line and being loaded," Bach said. "All we need now is a planet."

"At least the new president is keeping his word."

Bach nodded. As each survey or colony ship came off the line and was turned over to Department of Defense, they had submitted invoices for them, which had been paid.

Like Lingua Zinga, Graviton Dynamics was now making money. A lot of money. The stock price had gone crazy. Graviton Aviation, meanwhile, had passed its airworthiness trials with the FAA, and Boeing, Airbus, Bombardier and other manufacturers were starting to roll out new airliners with graviton devices as their engines.

"So, Ms. Trillionaire. Do you want to build a new house? A pretty castle of some kind?"

"No, Steven. After all the craziness of the day, I just like to walk across the road to our pretty little house in the woods. Watch the children play. Have our quiet evenings. And a big house requires staff. Just more work to do, in my mind. Dealing with all that."

"I guess I'm not surprised."

"Well, you shouldn't be. We know a lot of wealthy people now, and most of them are utterly miserable. Driven by their work. Driven by their stock price. Driven by their desire for a big, fancy house. Who needs it? Not me."

"I love you, Barbara."

"I love you, too, Steven."

They sat and watched the kids, then Vegan spoke.

"Steven, I have a question."

"Yes, Arthur?"

"I am surprised the survey ships are taking so long. I would have expected a four- to eight-week round trip. Yet it has been several months."

"Yes, Arthur, but it's more than just spacing out there and back. First, they have to approach the planet and do things like spectrometric tests on the atmosphere and such.

"Then they have to send the shuttle down and do many more tests before even leaving the shuttle. More tests upon leaving the shuttle.

"Then they have to find a good spot. You can't have a colony ship, with four thousand people crammed in close quarters for two, three, four weeks blundering around looking for a good spot. They need to find a nice hospitable place, like San Diego, or Costa Rica or something – as opposed to Minneapolis or Chicago, say – and then place a homing beacon for the colony ship.

"Finally, once they're out that far, they might as well check more than one system. Maybe the first planet is good and maybe it's not, but, either way, you're better off checking two or three or four systems once you're out there."

"I see, Steven. That makes sense. I was thinking just in terms of the transit time to a single system."

"That's actually the smallest part of it, Arthur. I don't expect anybody back for a while yet."

The first survey ship returned a month later. It had checked planets in four systems. It found one excellent colony planet, a marginal one, and the rest were all unacceptable for one reason or another. This despite checking only those planets that astronomical planet surveys from Earth thought might be suitable.

The marginal planet was so declared because its apex predator bore an uncanny resemblance to Tyrannosaurus Rex. One had chased after the shuttle bus when it landed, and it had taken an anti-armor rocket to bring it down.

On reflection, they decided that planet was a pass as well.

One excellent planet was one excellent planet, however, and

that's all the first colony ship needed. The site the survey crew had marked was also excellent. Semi-tropical, just miles from the ocean, on a bluff above a river. The bluff kept it above the flood plain, while the river was a source of fresh water. There was also a flat surface on the bluff for the colony ship to land. What more could you want?

The lift of the first colony ship, CS-1, was set for a week hence. They started loading refrigerated perishables aboard the ship preparatory to launch.

On launch day, forty-two hundred colonists gathered on the tarmac around the gigantic ship. It took fifty buses just to transport them to the launch pad. A hundred feet tall and a hundred and sixty feet on a side, the ship towered over the people and buses on the ground.

Barbara was asked to make a speech. She got up on a small podium and simply said, "Good luck, everyone. All our best wishes go with you."

Even with a hundred and fifty people at a time, it took twenty-eight trips to get everyone up to the E Deck garage door using the elevator. Everyone had their cabin assignments on an ID card on a lanyard, and knew the location of their cabin, so there was no confusion there.

With the colonists up and in the ship, the crew went aboard. All the VIPs and well-wishers were bused away from the ship.

It was still an hour to the launch window.

"This is Mission Support. Launch window is now open."

"This is Mission Control. Acknowledge launch window. Launch in two hundred and ninety seconds, mark."

The minutes ticked down, then Mission Control gave the countdown.

"Ten seconds to launch. Five, four, three, two, one, zero."

The great behemoth of CS-1 lifted off the ground and moved vertically at thirty miles an hour into the sky. There was no noise, no thunder of rockets, no giant plume of smoke. The insane bulk of the ship simply left.

Two hours later, free of the atmosphere, CS-1 went to six gravities of acceleration away from Earth.

Arriving at the first colony planet, as yet unnamed, CS-1 descended to within a few feet of the ground on the location the survey ship had chosen, and hovered there.

A team of Navy SeaBees came down in the elevator from E Deck as the A Deck drop-down door opened. Chained to the inside of the A Deck door was a small, electric bulldozer and several boxes of supplies.

When the A Deck door hit the ground and formed a ramp, the SeaBees took the supplies boxes and moved them away from the ship. They also unchained the bulldozer. One of them got up on the bulldozer and drove it off the ramp.

The A-Deck door them closed, and CS-1 rose to a hundred yards above the ground.

Four SeaBees took laser measuring markers out of one of the boxes, and set them to a precise one-hundred-eighty-foot square, just bigger than the ship by ten feet in each direction.

The SeaBee on the bulldozer began working the square. It was pretty flat, he had to give the survey crew that, but it wasn't landing-pad flat.

He had trouble with two small rock outcroppings that the bulldozer could not handle. The other SeaBees set charges, then dynamited the rocks. The SeaBee on the bulldozer came back then and worked them.

He looked up to the massive grid of girders that formed the

landing footprint of the ship and nodded. Good enough.

The SeaBees moved out of the way, and CS-1 slowly settled all the way to the ground.

The first colony had arrived.

Colony Expansion

"Well, they should be there by now," Barbara said. "I guess we'll find out how they did in another three weeks.

"Another five weeks, you mean. It'll take them two weeks just to unload everything."

"Oh. Right. Then three weeks back."

"Right."

"So do we send out other colony ships in the meantime?"

"Of course," Bach said.

"Not wait to see how it went?"

"No. We need to keep things moving along. I worry about the hive queens."

"Over four thousand people, though, Steven. On every ship."

"And there are eight billion on Earth. Do we put them at risk?"

"No. You're right. I just worry."

"I know. So do I, Barbara. But we have to keep playing the odds. One failed colony isn't a statistical sample anyway. It could be a fluke."

"Well, I guess we'll find out how it went in five weeks."

"Here's hoping."

The survey ships were being operated on a dual-crew model. Gold Crew went on the first mission. When the first survey ship came back, it was serviced and loaded for another trip. Meanwhile, Gold Crew briefed Blue Crew on what they had learned, and then Blue Crew departed on the second mission for the first survey ship, SS-1.

A GENT OF VEGA

In the meantime, other survey ships were coming back from their first trip. As they came in, they were serviced and reloaded and sent back out with the alternate crew.

Every month, another colony ship came off the line. It was sent on a shakedown orbital cruise, then loaded with all the colony supplies. As the survey ships came in with new planet data, those colony ships were loaded with perishables, populated with colonists and crews, and sent out.

CS-2 and CS-3 had left before CS-1 returned.

Bach and Barbara were relieved when CS-1 returned, though they acted ho-hum about it in front of their employees. The trip had been routine, nothing had gone wrong. They got all the colonists and supplies unloaded in two weeks and returned to Earth.

As the barracks tents and mess tents had been the first things unloaded, CS-1 had left a tent city behind. The crew of CS-1 took shore leave on the planet, enjoying hot meals, while the colonists unloaded the ship.

One additional thing they had unloaded, besides the contents of Decks A, B, and C. They had stripped all the bunk beds out of the colonist spaces, as well as all the folding chairs. The bunk beds came apart to set on the ground individually, so every colonist had a bed and a chair of his own when CS-1 left.

That had been the plan from the start. No sense deadheading all that stuff back when it was useful on the colony.

The servicing of CS-1 thus included refurnishing all the colonist spaces for the next load. Forty-two hundred new beds and forty-two hundred new folding chairs were waiting.

When a colony needed something that had not been anticipated, and requested it, that had to happen on a delayed basis. There was no radio contact with the colonies over light-years of distance. They would have to build up a list of their desires, and send them back on the next arrival of their colony ship. They wouldn't receive those items until the second arrival of their colony ship.

The exception to this rule was things they realized they needed while the colony ship was still there, unloading. There were a few such requests that came back with CS-1 from the first trip, and Graviton Dynamics and the Department of Defense filled them on the second trip.

They were by and large simple things.

How did they forget to send oregano?

The colony ships were also being run on the dual-crew model. When CS-1 arrived, Gold Crew stood down and Blue Crew took over. Some transfers between crews on different ships were made so that no ship left with a totally green crew.

Whenever some green crew member got upset about being in the crease for days at a time, there were always crew members present who could say, 'Yeah, same old shit. No worries.'

With a new survey ship rolling out every week, a new colony ship rolling out every month, and returning survey ships and colony ships being turned, Spaceport USA was starting to live up to its name. It soon got to the point where there was a ship arriving or departing just about every weekday.

In addition to the colonists, each of those ships had a Blue Crew and a Gold Crew, at least one of which was always in residence.

Department of Defense built another two dozen barracks

buildings at the spaceport, then another two dozen.

When volunteers for colonization from within the service branches started to drop off, they opened up the process to veterans and military people with children. When that started to drop off, they opened up the process to civilians.

It startled some people just how many U.S. civilians were willing to pack up and head off to a colony. Then again, the U.S. had been settled, originally and since, by people who had done just that. A nation of immigrants found that the urge to move on, seek something better, still lived among its people.

Language was never an issue. Part of the package, for anyone leaving as a colonist, was a Lingua Zinga course in English from whatever language was their native tongue. Everyone on every colony would be fluent in English, regardless of where they were born or the language they grew up with.

Given that, there were people from other countries who applied for entry to the U.S. with the goal of going out to the colonies. Given that there would be no language problem, after a background check the U.S. pretty much took all comers. They were transported directly to Spaceport USA for language training and colony placement.

The president stopped by for a visit late in his first term. He was not enthusiastic about his ability to win the upcoming election.

"What does that mean for us, sir?" Barbara asked.

"Nothing, I think. One of the things my opposition has done is endorse the whole colony project. If he didn't, he wouldn't have a chance. People like the idea of things happening, of new horizons, even if they don't actually want to go."

"I wonder, though, how honest his support is," Bach said. "If he'll try to subvert us somehow, while pledging support."

"I do, too, to be frank, Mr. Bach. One thing I'm doing is seeing to it you get paid through the contract period, which we've just extended for two years. I don't think he can mess with that. The two years after that, well, I just don't know."

"For two years, we can self-fund," Barbara said. "We certainly have the funds for that. What I worry about is that he can tie us up with rules. Regulations, litigation, the whole nine yards."

"You can probably take that to the courts, Ms. Bach. After twelve years of appointments, the federal courts are pretty much ours now. You should be able to tie anything new up for years."

"Why would people change, though?" Bach asked. "If the colony effort is so popular, and you own that issue, why is there even a contest?"

"The American people like a change once in a while, Mr. Bach. Twelve years is about the limit for one party in the White House now. It wasn't always that way, but it has been for a long time now. Since five terms for FDR and Truman. There hasn't been a fourth term by the same party since."

"So we carry on, regardless," Barbara said.

"Yes. And if they give you too much trouble, they put their potential second term in jeopardy. People really like the whole colony project. So it will probably be OK."

The president did lose his quest for a second term. The new president did not come out to visit. One thing the new president did is to cut off the survey trips, and to stop construction of any new colony ships. Without a visit or speaking to the Bachs.

But there were twenty-eight human colonies now, and the president did not cut off the continuing trips to the existing colonies by the existing colony ships. That would have caused him serious political problems.

So Spaceport USA continued in operation even as the colony ships production line was closed. The survey ship production line had long been turned over to production of the new graviton attack ship and the graviton missiles. Also, the Graviton Aviation segment was going great guns, and always needed more skilled people.

Some production people were turned over to colony ship support, which had been starting to be a little short-handed. Also, vacancies due to retirements were not filled.

In these ways, Graviton Dynamics avoided layoffs under the new administration.

Several things began to happen in this four-year period. Some of the colonies were getting pretty big. With a round-trip of a colony ship every eight to ten weeks, some of the colonies had received twenty or twenty-five trips. And the young couples going to the colonies were having children.

That amounted to, round numbers, a hundred thousand people on the colony, and growing steadily.

Those people discovered things on their new planets. Spices. Vegetables. Animals. Things the Earth did not have. The colony ships started coming back with return cargo, packed in the containers that had originally gone the other way.

Humpback deer from New Maryland provided a superior form of venison and was popular, if stupidly expensive, on Earth. The two-week trip back was not an issue because that was how long the meat had to hang anyway.

Several new spices – easy to pack in bulk – from Biarritz and

Stanhope were popular, and began to appear in recipe books and on-line recipes.

The silk of the monkey spider – so called because it only had four legs – on Direggio proved strong and resistant to stains. In fact, special dyes had to be used even to color it. That product took off when it was discovered to be a superior filament for plastic surgeries.

Gradually to be sure, but steadily, an import market developed from the colony worlds.

Four years on, the then-president failed in his own re-election bid. While he had, for the most part, kept the colony effort going, his other policies, so hopeful in promise, proved unpopular and unworkable in practice.

A protégé of the two presidents under which the Bachs had grown their business into a mega-corporation won the presidency.

That prompted Bach to consider some things.

"I think it's time, Barbara."

"To do what, Steven?"

"To visit the hive queen."

Barbara didn't know what to say, but she thought about it. Steven was probably right.

They brought it up with the new president when he came to visit. They had actually met him before, when he was a senator, during Congressional testimony before the Senate Subcommittee on Space and Science. They met privately in the house. Without prompting, he had limited his Secret Service to the head of his detail.

"Ms. Bach. Mr. Bach. It's good to see you again."

"And you, sir," Barbara said.

"My predecessors – not the last one, but the two before – told me I should meet with you early in my term, and they told me why. Can Mr. Vegan join us?"

Barbara cast a glance at the Secret Service man, and he simply nodded. So he'd been briefed. Good.

"Come on in, Arthur."

Vegan walked in and walked up to the president, who stood.

"It's good to meet you, Mr. President."

"And you, Mr. Vegan."

They shook hands, and everybody sat.

"How much of the story do you know, Mr. President?"

"All of it, I think, Ms. Bach. The hive queen's threat, in particular. They thought I should know."

"Excellent. Then you know that her threat is real, sir."

"Yes, though I don't know what to do about it."

"We think we need to go back and talk to her, sir," Bach said. "While your party has the White House. We need to 'head her off at the pass,' as it were. Before she does anything unilaterally, without the other hive queens."

The president nodded.

"I've been thinking the same thing, Mr. Bach. Will she take action against you individually, however? She almost did so once."

"I don't think so, sir."

Bach didn't sound sure, however.

"I think I can make that less likely, Mr. Bach. I can make you an ambassador of the United States."

"Doesn't that take Senate approval, Mr. President?"

"For established positions, yes, Ms. Bach. But not for special cases. Ambassador to the Middle East, for instance. Presidential envoys is another example.

"That's probably a good idea, sir," Bach said. "But make Barbara your envoy."

The president raised an eyebrow.

"It's the opposite of the Middle East case, sir. She is the hive *queen*. A female. In their society, females automatically – and biologically – have special status."

"Very well, Mr. Bach. Let's do that."

He looked around.

"I forgot to ask. Where are your children today?"

"At school, sir."

A private school, in town, that the Bachs largely funded. It was associated with the university. An experimental school. Now age fourteen, Jared was already taking university classes in some subjects.

"Ah. As for when we go to the hive queen, I think we should wait a year or so. Maybe two. Let me soften the ground. Mention the possibility of aliens. That sort of thing."

"That makes sense to me, Mr. President," Bach said. "Just don't wait too long."

One thing the new president did was reinstate the colony project to its full extent. It would take a while to get colony ship production under way again, but there would be more colonies starting soon.

When he restarted colony ship production, the president held a news conference. One question gave him his opening.

"One question that keeps coming up, Mr. President. Do you think we will ever discover other intelligent life?"

"I think it's a certainty, Bill. It's a big universe. Anything that can happen once probably happens thousands or millions of times. Sooner or later, we're going to run into them out there.

We need to make sure it's a peaceful interaction from the very start. No mistakes, no accidents. We don't need an interstellar war on our hands."

Another thing the new president did was order a new pair of airplanes to serve as Air Force One. He specified that they both be graviton-device aircraft.

The Hive Queen

It was two more years before the president was ready. Bach fretted, but the president was probably right. It was the summer of his third year in office that the president gave them the go-ahead.

In the meantime, the president had mentioned the likelihood of encountering aliens a number of times, treating it as merely a matter of time. The press picked up on it, and there was a lot of speculation, both in the media and by the public.

What would they be like? Would they be very much like us? The concept of parallel evolution suggested it. Would they be giant hairy beasts, like some modern science fiction suggested?

Or would they be giant insects, like some 1940s science-fiction trope?

The president had put it out there, and the media and the public ran with it.

It was time.

When Bach and Barbara were getting ready for the trip, they ran across the outfits they had worn when they had confronted the hive queen the first time, nineteen years ago.

"Can you imagine wearing these now?" Barbara asked.

Bach held up the stretch dance-leotard top he had worn.

"I can't imagine we wore them then."

Jared and Daphne, now sixteen and just fourteen, were hanging around watching them.

"I bet they'd fit us," Jared said.

"Oh, yes," Daphne said. "Let us try them on."

"Um," Bach said, and looked to Barbara.

She shrugged.

"All right," he said.

"Here. Don't forget the shoes," Barbara said.

The kids took the stretch outfits and shoes and ran to their rooms. The reappeared minutes later.

Jared was just coming into his masculine bulk. The limited athletics facilities at the experimental school had made weight lifting the bulk of his physical education classes. He filled out the costume pretty impressively for his age.

Daphne was another issue. Early to full breasts at just fourteen, in that outfit she was an incitement to riot. It was just as painted on as it had been for Barbara back in the day, and, like her mother, she had the legs for it. Lolita and change.

"Oh, my. That brings back memories," Barbara said.

"Indeed. Did we ever really wear those?"

Jared looked to Daphne, and she nodded back. He turned to his parents.

"That tears it. We're going with you."

"No, you're not," Bach instantly said.

"Yes, we are. Think about it. The hive queen is female. The only female in the hive. What gives her such exalted status is having children. Without children, Mom has no status there. She might as well be a worker. If she introduces us to the hive queen as two of her children, she has instant status."

"But I only have two children," Barbara said.

"She doesn't know that."

"On another issue, if it comes to war, it puts the president in a better position," Daphne said. "If the Vegans kill women *and children*, it'll be a Pearl Harbor moment. How dare you!"

"But this is going to be very dangerous. You could be killed," Bach said.

"If it comes to that, it will be war," Jared said. "We will be in terrible danger anyway. Do you think Spaceport USA won't be a primary target?"

"He's got you there," Barbara said.

"I can't believe you're in favor of this?" Bach asked.

"It makes some sense, Steven. I have to think about it. We should talk to Arthur about it."

"On another issue," Jared said, "what if you have to make a run for it?"

Jared produced a nine-millimeter semi-automatic pistol from a pocket holster in his bulge, while Daphne produced one from an inside-the-belt holster in the small of her back. Both kids were proficient in their use, having been taught, usually by Vegan, from the time they were six years old. And of course they had heard the whole story of the original confrontation with the hive queen.

"Between us and Arthur, with that cannon of his, you've actually got a chance to make it back to the ship," Daphne said.

"Yeah," Jared said. "You're getting too old for that kind of stuff."

The forty-five-year-old Bach looked at the forty-two-year-old Barbara. She raised an eyebrow in return.

"And you can't take other guards," Daphne said. "That would be impolite."

They discussed it with Vegan. He considered before answering.

"I understand your hesitance to expose the children to danger. Their arguments do have merit, however. Particularly Barbara's increased status with the hive queen for having had children."

"But the danger, Arthur," Bach said.

"If it comes to that, Steven, they will not be safe here."

A GENT OF VEGA

And so the decision was made.

Jared and Daphne would go along.

They would be taking *Vegan Dreams*. The fifteen-year-old airframe had been updated again, with the next-generation five-thousand-ton-thrust graviton devices, and had a cruise acceleration of twenty gravities.

Vegan Dreams was now fitted as a luxury yacht. Graviton Dynamics had been leasing the yacht, with crew and services provided, to wealthy people who wanted to experience space travel. Some wanted to visit the colonies as sightseers. Some wanted to go hunting the humpback deer. Some even wanted to go hunting the Tyrannosaurus Rex they had found.

Such people weren't put off by the tens of millions of dollars it cost to lease the yacht.

Bach and Barbara themselves had not been into space since their trip to Vega twenty years ago.

They were always so busy.

"Arthur, I have a question."

"Of course, Barbara."

"How long was the trip to Earth from Vega when you first came here seventy years ago?"

"Nine days."

"And it was nine days when we went to Vega to see the hive queen twenty years ago."

"That's right, Barbara. Still nine days."

"Hmm."

The trip to Vega took them a bit over five days aboard the newly upgraded *Vegan Dreams*. It was five days of study and preparations, with all four of the Bachs and Vegan discussing options and possibilities. They felt ready when they boarded the newly upgraded truck for descent to the planet's surface. Vegan and the two kids sat in the back seat while Bach and Barbara sat up front.

The descent to the hive queen's palace was without incident. They landed on the landing pad where they had landed before, in the Vegans' minivan-like shuttle.

They all got out of the truck. A Vegan – a worker – came out to greet them.

<We are here to meet with the hive queen. You will announce us to her drones,> Vegan said, in Vegan.

Unlike before, all four of the Bachs understood what he said.

<Very well. Follow me.>

They were shown, as before, to a suite and told to wait there.

"How long do we wait this time, Arthur? Days, again?"

"I wouldn't think so, Barbara. She is bound to be curious. Hours, I would think."

"We're going to change," Jared said.

While Bach and Barbara both wore pants suits, the kids were currently in jeans and T-shirts. The two kids went into side rooms of the suite, together with the backpack Jared had brought down with them. They reemerged in the outfits Bach and Barbara had worn to the meeting with the hive queen twenty years ago.

"I just had a feeling of déjà vu," Arthur said. "I never understood the term before."

<You will come with me,> a Vegan said two hours later.

<Of course,> Arthur said.

They followed him through the passages of the palace, heading generally up to the peak of the tower.

<Wait here.>

They didn't wait long before a drone came into the vestibule.
<Come with me.>

The drone led them into the presence of the hive queen. As before, eight-foot-tall drones awaited her needs.

<Stand here.>

They stood before the hive queen as before. She stirred on her couch, awakened from her nap, and assessed them.

<Monkeymen.>

"Yes, Your Majesty," Barbara said.

<You understand my language. Who are you?>

"I am Barbara Bach, Your Majesty. I met you twenty years ago, when you considered the infraction of Arthur here, in revealing himself to the monkeymen."

<Yes, I recall.>

"I also brought my drone, Steven Bach, and two of my children, a drone and a nascent queen."

<Impressive. And yet you are still a primitive race.>

"We are now an interstellar race, Your Majesty. We occupy twenty-nine planets."

<Technology which you stole from us.>

"Yes, as you stole Wi-Fi from us. As the <bug-people> stole the graviton technology in the first place. If we are nevertheless still a primitive race, then so are the <bug-people>."

Barbara used the Vegan word they used to describe their own species, one of the words of Vegan she could pronounce. It sounded like an impact wrench working a particularly stubborn fastener.

She was counting on a hunch. The Vegans were not an industrial society. And the trip Arthur Vegan had taken to Earth had been nine days, both seventy years ago and twenty years ago. They had not further developed the technology. No progress meant they had stolen the technology and used it as it was. They didn't understand it enough to enhance it, although Bach and his physics people now did.

<That is neither here nor there. Why are you here?>

So they *had* stolen it.

"To propose peace between our species, Your Majesty. I am here on a diplomatic mission, as the ambassador of our most powerful hive queen, to seek peace. I have brought from her a snack, a delicacy, as a token of her esteem for you."

Barbara took a three-pound chunk of raw filet mignon out of the pouch she wore on a strap over her shoulder. She unwrapped the plastic and held it out in front of her.

The queen made a gesture and a drone took the meat from Barbara, leaving the plastic. He snipped perhaps a quarter-pound from it with his mandibles.

<It is delicious, Your Majesty. Wonderful, in fact.>

He took it to the queen, who munched on a piece of it. She let out a low thrumming sound indicating her pleasure. She sounded like a poorly tuned Volkswagen Beetle at idle.

<A magnanimous gift.>

"We have millions of such animals, raised for their protein, Your Majesty. Interstellar trade in such, in return for such items as you may have of interest to us, is one of the benefits of peace. Another benefit would be to cut your travel time to your convocation of queens in half, as we have enhanced the technology we stole from you."

The queen considered that. Not a minor matter.

<And what if I were to kill you instead, for your effrontery.>

"Then there would be war, Your Majesty. If you were to kill a hive queen sent as ambassador, two drones, and a nascent hive queen, there would be war.

"Instead of the two advanced races we both pretend to be, our two primitive races would use our stolen technology to attempt to destroy each other.

"I am sure your majesty appreciates the destruction that would result from the impact of a graviton-drive missile at half a million miles an hour on this palace. The destruction of you, your eggs, and your genetic line.

"The hive of which I am descended, Your Majesty, has a history of reprisal to premeditated attacks. You may wish to consult the results to Hiroshima and Nagasaki, which you should have in your memories.

"As ambassador of our most powerful hive queen, I beg you not to go there."

The hive queen munched on the filet mignon as she considered. Damn, but it was wonderful.

<How would such a peace work?>

"We would guarantee each other's planets, Your Majesty. Expand only to such planets as the other species has not settled. We would commit no violence against each other. We would trade with each other. We would hold our own people to account for following these rules.

"The point is, Your Majesty, that we would work out any problems between ourselves by talking about them, by coming to agreement about them, not by fighting over them."

<Very well, monkey-queen. You can have your peace. With my hive at least. I will communicate with the other hive queens as to what I have done, and we will consider the matter further at our next Convocation.>

"Thank you, Your Majesty. I think it is a wise decision."

<What of this one, monkey-queen? Is he not one of ours?>

The hive queen indicated Vegan with a gesture.

"Not any longer, Your Majesty. He has petitioned to join our hive, and our hive queen has granted his request. He is now of us."

<Yet he is not of your species.>

"No, Your Majesty, but our hive is especially accepting of others. We find it contributes to our abilities to accept all kinds of people. Even such as he.

"He is further a demonstration that we can, after all, be friends, Your Majesty. Our two peoples. We have been friends with him now for twenty years, and it has been good for us all."

<Very well, monkey-queen. Extend my regards to your other hive queens.>

The hive queen made a shooing gesture, and a drone led them out of her chamber.

Once back in the truck, Vegan had some feedback.

"The most important thing was the last thing she said to you."

"'Extend my regards to your other hive queens'?"

"Yes. It is important. She was treating you as an equal."

It was billed as an important announcement, in the East Room of the White House, the largest room in the executive residence. Hundreds of chairs were set up, for the press, for dignitaries, for members of Congress, for cabinet officials.

No one present had any clue what it was about. The absolute silence out of the White House on the topic ensured top attendance.

Even White House officials had no clue what it was about.

Equipment crates, food crates, any number of items were brought in to the White House every day, often through tunnels from the Eisenhower Executive Office Building next door, which was part of the White House complex and within its security cordon.

One such crate was checked by a senior Secret Service man, one of the heads of the president's detail, and passed on through. He accompanied that crate as it was delivered.

In that crate was Arthur Vegan.

No one recognized Jared and Daphne Bach, the children having been scrupulously kept out of the press by their protective parents. They did wonder about the teenagers seated in the front row, but couldn't make heads or tails of it.

"Good evening, ladies and gentlemen.

"I am here tonight to share with you something of tremendous importance, not just for the United States, but for the world.

"We have been, for some time, in contact with an alien race."

The president waited for a while for the hubbub over that to die down.

"What I can announce today is that we have concluded negotiations for peace between our species. There will be no War of the Worlds, no high-tech destruction from space on our part or theirs, delivered against them or us. We instead have constructed a peace with the hive queens of Vega, which will result in friendly relations and trade between our species."

There was applause for that. One of the speculations that had come up when discussing the possibility of an intelligent alien species, is whether they would be peaceful or not. The odds were not considered good.

"Three U.S. citizens have been instrumental in carrying out these negotiations. They have just returned from Vega with the news of their success. Steven Bach, Barbara Bach, and Arthur Vegan."

Bach, Barbara, and Vegan walked in from the side door to

applause that faltered after Vegan became visible. He waved at everyone with both right hands.

When they got to the podium, the president shook hands with each in turn as the audience sat stunned. Then Jared and Daphne started clapping again, and others took it up.

"Arthur Vegan, as you can see, is one of the aliens. He has petitioned and received United States' citizenship. So he's one of ours now."

The president turned to Vegan and applauded, and the audience, still stunned, followed suit.

"These three have surprised us with the success of these negotiations. As you can imagine, humans and aliens have different points of view, different values, different ways of looking at things. It was not a sure thing, by any means, and they have surprised us with their success.

"Now I am going to surprise them. They know nothing about this part.

"Steven Bach, Barbara Bach, and Arthur Vegan, I am pleased to award all three of you the Presidential Medal of Freedom for your services to the United States."

Aides came out carrying presentation cases for the medals, and the president hung the medal on each of them in turn.

Arthur Vegan looked like he was going to cry.

Please review this book on Amazon

A GENT OF VEGA

Author's Afterword

Let's talk about the title, "A Gent of Vega." Yes, it's something of a rip of James H. Schmitz' 1949 story, "Agent of Vega" and the 1960 anthology of the same name. First, book titles aren't copyrighted or trademarked, so that's the legalities.

The title of this book, though, is an homage to Schmitz, the first science fiction author to include strong, independent women in his stories, a characteristic of my own work – and that of many others – these seventy-five years later. Prior to Schmitz, women in science fiction were largely damsel-in-distress characters, or sexy partners along for the titillation, which I refer to not-so-obliquely on the cover.

So here's to James H. Schmitz! He was a huge influence on us all.

On to the book. This book started as something of a farce. A 1940s-trope insectoid alien visits our hero, who promptly faints. They trade his gold bars for cash, which gold bars are a waste material on his planet. They spend their time developing the womanizing skills of the main character. The main character and one of those women dress up like typical 1940s science fiction cover characters for a science fiction convention to sell his first novel, at which convention the alien himself appears, as though in cosplay.

Then it turns deadly serious, as the alien's hive queen is not pleased with the alien. Or with humans, for that matter. Our heroes are now on a mission to save humanity by going interplanetary before the collected hive queens can destroy the human race.

Barbara Nowak is there through it all. It is she who thinks to grab extra clothes when they are going to be taken by the aliens. It is she who thinks to take the pistol. It is she who sees the commercial possibilities of the translation device, which gives them the resources to take on space. It is she who sees the application of the graviton engine to the commercial aviation industry.

Which is not to say our hero isn't resourceful as well. It is his idea to steal all the alien technology. It is he who credibly threatens the hive queen, forestalling her actions. It is he who drives the project forward, first by getting to the bottom of the alien gravitonic technology, then by driving it forward at breakneck speed.

And then there is Arthur. What can I say about Arthur?

Throughout the book, my four civilizational motivations are there – love, honor, duty, and loyalty. When Arthur helps out Steven with his various issues. When Steven and Barbara stand by Arthur before the hive queen, at great personal risk. When they all work to forestall the hive queens' potential for destruction, even though none of them will live to see it,

In writing this book right now, I am at the beginning of building the spaceship, *Vegan Dreams*. How will this book end? I have no clue as I write this, even though you, by now, do know how it ends.

I hope you enjoyed this book. I had fun writing it.

Richard F. Weyand
Bloomington, IN
May 29, 2025

A GENT OF VEGA

www.ingramcontent.com/pod-product-compliance
Lightning Source LLC
Chambersburg PA
CBHW061324170626
46817CB00001B/300